JOPPA ROCKS

BY

BILL FLOCKHART

Edinburgh - 2020

JOPPA ROCKS

November 15, 2010

'Morning' said the passer-by sheltering his face from the cold East wind blowing in from the Firth of Forth which Eric Henderson was having to endure as his Labrador King relieved himself against a lamppost. It was eight o'clock on a November morning and Eric was thinking of better things he had to do that day. Scouring the grey stormy sea featuring surf decorated with white horses, he was drawn to the commotion on the rocks below. It was caused by an unprecedented number of seagulls dive-bombing a large object just under the surface. They were all competing to be first to enjoy the prey. Initially Eric thought it was possibly the carcass of a large fish, which on occasions, beached itself on Joppa Rocks to end its life. On closer examination he realised it was a body. Letting King off the lead Eric clambered down over the rocks for a closer view aided by his dog barking to scare off the gulls.

The body, which was just becoming visible when the waves retreated, was a female, devoid of any clothing, lying downward in the clear salty water. Her back and legs were covered in blood from the seagull pecking. Eric had enough sense not to touch the deceased and instead reached into his pocket for his mobile phone and dialled 999.

'What services do you require?' a recorded message answered

'Police please.' replied Eric with urgency in his voice

Two seconds later a live voice asked, 'How can we help Sir?'

Eric excitedly replied, 'My name is Eric Henderson and I have just found the naked body of a young woman on Joppa Rocks.'

Calmly the operator asked. 'Mr Henderson, can you tell me your exact location so that I can get assistance immediately.'

'Yes, I'm at Joppa Rocks, on the beach just off Joppa Road at the far end of Portobello promenade. I live nearby and my postcode is EH15 2JE if that helps.'

The operator responded. 'Remain where you are Sir, assistance is on its way.'

Five minutes later Eric could hear the sirens of police cars arriving in the shape of three patrol cars whose occupants quickly traversed from the grass banking above down to the jagged rocks. The first officers to arrive shouted back to a colleague to have the area taped off and bring down with them a cover to create a temporary shelter for the unfortunate corpse.

A local sergeant took control shaking hands as he spoke to Eric, 'Morning Sir, Sergeant Aitken. I understand you were unfortunate enough to come across the body. For our records can you please give me an account of how and when you discovered this corpse. I will start though by taking your personal details'

Twenty minutes later the constabulary were joined by Detective Chief Inspector Grant McKirdy, Detective Sergeant Ian Lomax and completing the murder squad Detective Constable Avril Luxton. McKirdy wasted no time in approaching Sergeant Aitken who briefed him by reading out Eric Henderson's statement.

Turning around McKirdy looked at the body for the first time, 'A young girl, probably early twenties whose face we cannot see at present. As this looks like a murder scene, nothing can be disturbed until after forensics arrive and carry out their initial investigations.' Raising his voice, he continued, 'Do not on any circumstances speak about this incident to anyone until such times as my office gives you permission to do so. The last thing we want at this stage is the press giving their slant and creating speculation as to how this young lady came to be washed ashore. Is that understood everyone?' His words were met with a nodding of heads from the assembled company.

D.C.I. McKirdy approached Eric Henderson, a slightly built man in his forties with black curly hair greying at the sides, dressed in outerwear for early morning dog walking. Putting out his hand to shake Eric's gloved mit the detective began, 'Morning Mr. Henderson, sorry to have to meet under these circumstances. You will appreciate that the instructions I have just given to my force apply to yourself as well, until we can deliver more information regarding this incident.'

'Understood Chief Inspector. Call me Eric.'

'Eric do you regularly bring your dog along this route?'

'Yes, I live up the hill in Coillesdene Grove, so I bring King down every morning for exercise along Portobello Beach.'

'Have you noticed any unusual activity out in the Forth recently?'

Henderson scratched his chin for a few seconds then answered, 'Not really. You get the usual cargo ships heading to and fro from Leith or Grangemouth, the odd fishing boat searching for shellfish and the rowing club are often out for some early morning exercise.'

'Thanks for that. I will have your observations followed up. That's all for now but here's my card should anything further spring to mind.'

'Thank you, I better be off home. My wife will be wondering where I have got to.'

After Henderson's departure McKirdy signalled his D.S. to join him, 'Ian get Avril to go through the usual procedures checking missing persons register, any unsolved domestic complaints and also look at the tidal movements for today as forensics will have to move quickly before the tide turns and washes away any important evidence. Also see if the Rockville Hotel along there is still doing breakfast and get me a coffee and a bacon roll.'

'Yes Sir, only one bacon roll?'

'No get one for yourself and Avril. We may be here for a while.'

The murder squad had finished their make-shift breakfast by the time the forensics van with four scientists on board arrived led by Dr John Mason. McKirdy quickly got out his car to greet Mason who he had worked with for years. Dr Mason was in his forensic overalls complete with welling-ton boots and a woolly hat, which hid a thatch of ginger hair and the mask he donned made his blue eyes more pro-nounced. With a hobby of fell running Mason had a lean figure for a man nearing fifty.

'Morning John, I hope you have your thermals on, it's bloody cold down here and these rocks are pretty slippy.'

'You're spot-on Grant, this is where our lined waterproof suits come into their own. Lead me to the body and we'll do a quick survey before removing it back to the lab for a full post-mortem.'

'Follow me John.'

The tide had receded enabling Mason to kneel over the body on the seaweed clad rocks covered in small shells while his team searched the surrounding area for any sign of clothes or jewellery. 'Well, looking at her hands she was not dumped here overnight - let us turn her over and see what else we can conclude.'

'Miss X' as the forensics classified her was an extremely attractive girl who had exercised on a regular basis judging by her well-toned body. Her face was severely bruised, and pressure had been inflicted on her neck possibly until she died. She also had a large bruise on her right arm which looked as though it had led to her shoulder being dislocated. Her body had been in the water a sufficient length of time for it to have been nibble by the sea's occupants and scratched by the movements of the tide as it pushed her back and forward over the shell covered rocks.

'A bit of a mess', was the pathologist's first verdict, 'Judging by the angle of the blows that were delivered to her face, she's been beaten about the head by more than one person but not necessarily all at the same time looking at the different shades of bruising. I will know more when we have carried out a full examination. Time to move her to the mortuary up at the Cowgate. I will leave a couple of my assistants here to search for any clues we may have missed, although I think that may be clutching at straws as she has arrived here on the tide.'

'Thanks John, I will carry out a search of the area but bearing in mind what you have just opinionated that the body has been in the water for a considerable length of time it may not be the best use of police manpower. Let me know when you have completed the P.M. and I will come into the Cowgate Mortuary with my team to hear your verdict.

Three days later the murder team gathered around the aluminium slab covered by Miss X's body to listen to the pathology report.

John Mason began: 'We have some doubt about the cause of death being strangulation as the pressure points in the neck are not deep enough to cause choking. The victim had been subjected to a considerable amount of sexual activity judging by the internal bruising we discovered so she may have been 'A lady of the night' but a classy one, judging by the condition of her hair and nails. The nails are interesting in that we did not find any blood under the nails which is normally the case when a victim is being heavily

7

assaulted at close range. Instead they were full of fish flesh but curiously from more than one type of fish. What we suspect is a mixture of skate, halibut or possibly perhaps tuna. This makes us think Miss X had been thrown alive into a ship's hold of freshly caught fish causing death from hypothermia and exhaustion in her attempt to get out of the freezing hold. A somewhat horrible death. The time of death was probably ten days ago, but you will require to get the coastguards to assist you in working out which way the tide would move a body during that time bearing in mind the changes in weather patterns.

Our DNA records have not revealed any identification of the victim which makes us suspect she was East European or possibly Icelandic as they do not keep the same level of DNA information you find in the U.K.'

Silence filled the mortuary before D.C.I. McKirdy spoke, 'Thanks John, as you said a horrible end to a young life, but from a policing perspective it narrows down our suspects to those involved in the fishing trade. Avril get on to the Sea Fishing Authority and get the movements of all fishing vessels in the Forth and Tay estuaries in the last two weeks.'

'Sir Pearson Arbuthnott speaking. How can I be of assistance to Police Scotland?' Sir Pearson, a former admiral in the Royal Navy, had taken on the role of Chairman of the Sea Fishing Authority who were responsible for monitoring the fishing industry in Scotland.

DC Luxton replied, 'Morning Sir, DC Avril Luxton here. I am phoning to say there has been the body of a young woman found on Joppa Rocks at the East end of Edinburgh. After forensic examination, we believe the victim may have come into contact with a fishing vessel, the purpose of my call is to ask you to provide records you may have of all fishing boat movements in the last twenty days.

'Good Morning to you DC Luxton. We do have that information, but it is classified, however I am all for co-operating with the police so can I suggest you and anyone else you want to bring with you come up to the office. I will be able introduce you to our data processing people who keep tabs on British fishing boats as they move about in Scottish waters.'

'That would be extremely helpful, Sir Pearson. Can we arrange an appointment for Thursday November 18 at say 10 o'clock?', suggested Avril.

There was a shuffling of papers on the phone before Sir Pearson answered, 'Could we make it slightly later, say 11.30 as I have a meeting earlier that morning.'

'Certainly, Sir, I look forward to meeting you.', replied DC Luxton punching the air in acknowledgement of her investigational progress.

Miss X's face, along with the circumstances of her death was circulated to police forces throughout the U.K. but there had been no positive responses by the time the murder squad entered the Georgian offices of the Sea Fishing Authority in Leith. The middle-aged receptionist behind the shiny oak desk, with her computer and telephone at hand, greeted the police and showed them into the boardroom. The room had a nautical décor with a large table, highly polished, surrounded by seats with brass backs to them. On the walls were paintings of fishing boats being buffeted about on the high seas and even the windows were rounded to give the feeling of portholes.

One of the double doors opened and in strode the elderly figure of Sir Pearson Arbuthnott, white hair closely cropped as was his beard. He was dressed in a navy-blue blazer under which was a light blue sea-island cotton shirt and a Royal Navy tie, grey slacks and black brogues completed the look. He was accompanied with a bespectacled younger premature balding gentleman who he introduced as Andrew Turner, his computer systems manager. Sir Pearson pointed his visitor in the direction of a tray of coffee and biscuits which they all helped themselves to before sitting down at the table.

'Welcome to our premises the SFA offices. Perhaps it best that you start the proceedings and young Andrew here can probably come up with some useful information for you.'

Grant McKirdy replied, 'Thanks for seeing us. What we are about to discuss is confidential and I would seek your assurances it stays that way.'

The two fishing executives opposite nodded in approval.

D.C.I. McKirdy continued, 'Last Monday morning the body of a young lady completely naked was washed up on Joppa Rocks without any form of identification. On closer examination by our forensic team they reversed their original verdict that death was caused by strangulation. The reason for this turnabout was they discovered fish flesh under her nails and no signs of blood despite her being beaten around the head, she had not apparently made any attempt to defend herself. Their conclusion is she was thrown into a hold of freshly caught fish - dying shortly afterwards of exhaustion and hypothermia.'

'Good God! What evil so and so would do that to anyone!', exclaimed the admiral restraining from using his usual more colourful language in front of a lady.

'Well sir, that's what we were hoping you can help us with. Mr Turner, I understand you keep constant surveillance over all fishing boat movements in Scotland so presumably you can tell us which boats were out catching in Scottish waters over the last twenty days.'

Turner took a sip of coffee before responding, 'Everything you ask is on our systems daily. We track the boats while watching the weather so if there are any emergencies the coastguards can be alerted immediately. Unfortunately, Our systems do not apply to any foreign vessels which are entitled to plunder our fishing stocks and they could be anywhere.'

McKirdy asked, 'Am I not correct in saying that they usually operate in the North-West of Scotland off Ullapool or Shetland.'

'You're well informed D.C.I. McKirdy.'

Grant smiled at the compliment before continuing, 'I would like you to supply us with a complete index of all the boats registered in the Forth Estuary who were out at sea during the last twenty days. I am right in assuming that it is probably impossible for a body to be carried downstream to Joppa Rocks from anywhere out with the Forth Estuary?'

Sir Pearson spoke up, 'Your assumption is possibly correct although if the body were to be despatched overboard just outside the Tay Estuary on a stormy day there are strong currents which could push it towards the Forth. It's not the first time that yachtsman have got into difficulties having set off from Dundee and found themselves with a choice of heading for Aberdeen or Leith.'

Andrew Turner intervened, 'The recent weather we have had in the period you are monitoring would not suggest that argument is relevant. If you give me a few minutes I can run off the data you are seeking, or would you rather I emailed it to your office?'

'Both if you don't mind Mr. Turner.'

'Okay I'll leave you all to chat while I set the wheels in motion. You will appreciate that the Forth Fishing Fleet is quite extensive as the area covers everything from North Berwick on this side of the estuary to Crail on the Fife coast so this will take a little while. There must be in the region of five hundred ships going out to land a catch every week but a good proportion of them will be chasing shellfish which does not fall into the category of evidence revealed by your forensic team. Nevertheless, you are welcome to look at all the records and I will make them available to you.'

Andrew Turner's words were met with some disappointment by the Police Murder Squad, so they changed their mind about waiting for the physical report and instead thanked their hosts for helping their enquiries and returned to their car. On the way back to police headquarters at Fettes D.C.I. McKirdy discussed his strategy for attempting to solve 'Miss X's' murder.

'Ian', said McKirdy addressing his detective sergeant, 'I'll leave you to co-ordinate the surveillance of the Forth Fishing Fleet. Set up a team in the office to make initial contact establishing which boats are involved in shellfish or white fish. I think following the coroner's report we only send interviewing teams to visit those catching the latter species. Don't expect to get results immediately as we have to appreciate a lot of ships will be currently out at sea.'

The dutiful sergeant smiled before replying, 'Fine sir, I'll see to it but I'm a little disappointed not be getting a few days cruising in the North Sea!'

Grant McKirdy laughed, 'Try the coastguards Ian, they're always looking for volunteers,'

'Avril can you arrange for our technical staff to go to the morgue and build an identity face for Miss X as we can't put her on television in her present state. Once they have completed it, we shall wait a few days before putting it out on the media.'

'Certainly, Sir, what level of cover do you think we should get from the media?'

Grant McKirdy sighed then replied, 'At this stage it looks like all the press and television coverage we can get and if that fails a reminder on 'Crimewatch' in a couple of months' time.'

Back in Leith Admiral Arbuthnott was deep in conversation with Andrew Turner, 'Andrew, remove the Caledonian

Princess from the information you are sending to D.C.I. McKirdy. Our paymasters will be landing a large consignment of drugs this week at Eyemouth which may or may not be connected to the body on Joppa Rocks.'

A distressed Turner re-acted, 'Christ this gets worse Admiral. We should never have got involved in assisting the drug traffickers. The money's good, but I want to terminate any future activities immediately.'

The Admiral fixed his stare at the computer genius, 'Turner you're in, whether you like it or not so just bloody well get on with it! We have been getting 'Royalties' from drug dealers in a number of ports around the country by warning them of the location of coastguard and Customs & Excise vessels in their area. This has given them time to find safe hiding places for the drugs, or if that was not possible, ditch them at sea. I have no intention to reduce my lifestyle for some P.C. Plods trying to solve a homicide which at this point in time has no connection to our activities.'

Turner scowled at his superior before leaving the room. Pearson Arbuthnott remained seated looking out his window at the activity of Leith Docks where ships of all sizes, decked out in flags representing a host of nations, were offloading their cargo whilst others filled the holds of ships with Scottish exports.

Pearson reflected how his gambling addiction had led to him running up large debts with local bookmakers and more worryingly the Royal Casino. It was in the Royal Casino, situated not far from his office, when he was having a bad night on the roulette wheel that he introduced himself to the man sitting next to him who was Geordie McNab a local drug dealer.

'Not my bloody night! Lost again – I am beginning to think it is time I got home to the wife if she had not left me for someone else! Otherwise I'd be in for another bollocking!'

Just as he was about to get off his seat the casino manager, kitted out in a smart dinner suit and bow tie, approached the roulette table, 'Admiral I would like to see you in my office regarding your account which is getting a little too high for comfort.'

McNab overheard the manger's opening gambit and intervened, 'Mr Sneddon, this gentleman has been unlucky tonight and I would be willing to be good for any money he owes the R.C.'

'If you insist Mr McNab but we are talking about a five-figure sum.'

'Okay get me the details.' Instructed McNab before turning to the retired admiral, 'Let me buy you a drink Admiral and I'll explain to you how we can mutually benefit each other. I have a scrap metal company which is a front for my main business. We consider ourselves to be in the leisure industry, as we supply drugs.'

The last few words startled the sailor who protested, 'I want nothing to do with drugs and the misery they inflict on the population!'

'Hold on Pearson it is members of your industry who supply me with a range of drugs which they pick up out at sea and land it at a variety of harbours around Scotland. How you can be of use to us is that your organisation monitors not only all the fishing boats out at sea but the whereabouts of the maritime security fleet. If we had access to that information, it would make our task far simpler.'

The Admiral held his ground, 'No I refuse to get involved with the likes of you!'

The smooth talking McNab changed his tactics by taking out the slip of paper that casino manager Sneddon had handed him and sneered at Arbuthnott before continuing, 'Fifty thousand pounds! That is, one would say a hell of lot of bad luck Admiral. How are you going to repay me? I normally deal on seven-day terms, but only after I have added interest of twenty per cent. I have taken control of the outstanding debt, so it's me you owe the balance to. If the money is not forthcoming, I will send one of my security staff to extract it from you and believe me you will not enjoy his presentation.' The naval pensioner winced at the thought of physical violence as McNab went on to say, 'However, if you come on board with my company not only will you clear your slate with the casino, you would in future be on my payroll and earn considerable 'royalties' paid into an account in Bermuda. The Choice is yours.'

A long silence proceeded until Pearson Arbuthnott took a swig of his drink and answered, 'You've got me McNab, but I need a week to think about it. I do not have the computer skills to produce the information you require – a member of staff is responsible for trailing all shipping movements. He's a young man with three kids and a wife who doesn't work so he is constantly strapped for cash so I may be able to persuade him to join us.'

McNab re-acted positively, 'I'll leave that to you Pearson but under no circumstances bring my name into your discussions.'

'Of course not, Geordie.', responded the worried admiral.

'Right, we'll leave it at that for now. Goodnight.' McNab departed but only after he had signalled his two bodyguards, who had been camouflaging themselves at the Blackjack table, that he was leaving.

Next morning it was a very pensive Admiral Arbuthnott who phoned Andrew Turner and asked him to come up to his office, 'Morning Andrew, did you have a good weekend?'

A glum Turner answered, 'Not really Sir, one of the kids has got the measles and our washing machine broke down, so more expense when we can't afford it.'

Andrew's last comment gave the Admiral his opportunity to talk about McNab's proposition, 'How tough are things for you Andrew?'

'Well Sir, I have three kids, although the last one wasn't planned. My wife Patsy does not work and there is the mortgage to pay. Getting about is not easy as I don't have a car and both our parents live miles away, so we have no access to babysitters and nursery charges are too expensive.'

Pearson sat back in his swivel chair before beginning his plea to the computer manager, 'Last night I was at the Royal Casino, where I had a bad night, but I met a man who was prepared to offer money in exchange for information on the movements of all boats at sea around Scotland. If we agreed to pass the data his only contact here would be me, but to comply with his wishes, I need you on board. He indicated the rewards would substantial and paid into a bank overseas so no one would know about it.'

Turner was shocked by what he just heard but curiosity forced him into finding out more, 'Why does he want to know about marine movements at sea and what is he going to do with the data? Do you think it is anything to do with the Russians who are always sniffing about our waters?'

'No Andrew, its more domestic than political. This gentleman is already dealing with a number of fishing boats around Scotland who deliver merchandise to him which, how would you say, is not legal.'

Turner exclaimed, 'By that I take it you mean contraband of some sort, probably drugs but possibly refugees or weapons!'

'Look Andrew, I have no idea about the level of business this organisation produces, but I thought his offer was an opportunity for you to make some money on the side without your identity being revealed.'

It was Andrew's turn to go silent, 'Admiral Arbuthnott, let me think about it and I will give you my answer tomorrow.'

That night Andrew returned to his two-bedroom flat in Granton Road, 'Hello, I'm home!', he called but was met with silence. He proceeded to the kitchen where he found Patsy sitting with Rory aged eighteen months in her arms and tears in her eyes. 'What's wrong?'

'What's wrong! What is bloody wrong!!', she screamed. 'This one's cried all day with the measles and the other two have argued with each other since they came in from school. I have sent them to their bedroom. This house is useless, and it is only going to get worse as they get older and space is tighter. Andy there's time when I could go out of here and not come back!'

Andrew put his arm round his wife, 'Well dear, I may have some good news. Admiral Arbuthnott told me today there could be the possibility of a promotion which may make things easier for us.'

The couple looked at each other before Patsy kissed him on the cheek and murmured, 'Let us hope so.'

During the next week, the Police Scotland investigation machine got into drive quickly, eliminating a large amount of the shellfish boats on their lists, then going out to visit the white fish crews. McKirdy knew this would take time as some of the fishing boat captains were still out at sea. The technicians produced Miss X's facial profile, so the Murder Squad decided to release it to the public. Unsurprisingly, her face produced very few sightings – even from the usual time wasters who had a habit of phoning in, hoping to enjoy as Andy Warhol would have said 'Their thirty minutes of fame.'

Chapter 2

One month earlier

Moonlight shone over the docks in Parnu, the centre of the Estonian fishing industry, as a van drew up next to the 'Koidutaht' a large fish processing ship about to sail west through the Baltic Sea heading for the North-west Atlantic Ocean. The driver, wearing a black balaclava, opened the doors of the van and six young women emerged carrying small suitcases. They were hurriedly escorted up the gangplank and disappeared down into the hold of the vessel where they were shown into Captain Igor Shertsov's office.

The girls stood nervously waiting for the ship's commander as he got up from behind his desk looking them up and down as he did so. Igor Shertsov stood over six -foot tall and was a handsome man with blonde hair, an earring in his right ear. He wore a black polo-neck sweater with holes in it caused by burns from his smoking habit. He towered over the girls, moving like a commander inspecting his troops as he moved into their intimate zone, his eyes surveying up and down their bodies and stroking their hair.

Returning to his desk without taking his green eyes off them he briefed them: 'This ship processes fish for trawlers who transfer their catch to the Koidutaht where it is processed by the thirty members of staff who package and freeze it ready for the market. My staff have not been told of your presence so you shall be kept in quarters separate from the rest of the crew. Do not stray into the processing area. Now, please introduce yourselves.

'You are first.', said Igor pointing at a red-haired attractive teenager.

The girl stuttered before commencing, 'I'm Greta Horschal from St. Petersburg a seamstress looking for work in England. Nineteen years of age.'

'Next.' Igor instructed

A plump blonde replied, 'I'm Sophia Baumen, twenty, a trained beautician from Riva.'

'Thank you, Sophia. You are next.'

The most attractive of the sextet, a blond girl with blue eyes and an excellent figure smiled and looked Igor in the eye. 'Svetlana Gorsky, twenty-three from Leipzig originally, but have lived in Gdansk for the last six months. I trained as a hotel receptionist so hope to get into the leisure industry in the U.K. My friends call me Lana.'

Igor smiled to himself, 'Oh you'll be getting plenty of leisure time, mostly lying on your back.'

'Next!'

'Heidi Lotheram, twenty-two from Berlin. I want to enrol for nursing in England.', answered the brown-haired beauty with the green eyes.

The next girl stepped forward before being asked to, 'Anna Berkovitch from Leningrad and like Heidi I am seeking a career in nursing.' The slim Blond with deep blue eyes joined her friend as Igor pointed a finger at the last girl.

Alena Karensky was younger than the rest and found it difficult in speaking to Igor but eventually managed to mumble she was seventeen, from St. Petersburg, and wanted to study economics at a college in the U.K.

'Okay you have all paid to be taken to Great Britain. In two days, you will be transferred to a fishing boat and taken to Eyemouth on the East coast of Scotland. From there transport will take you on to your ultimate destinations which will either be Glasgow or Bradford. Boris will show you to a cabin which you will only leave to have food or go to the toilet. Do not deviate from this area as we have work to do and anybody disobeying my rules will suffer the consequences. Boris, show them to their room.'

Boris Andropov was a fearsome figure of solid muscle standing over six foot three and weighing one hundred and ten kilos. His greasy thinning black hair gave way to a spotty coarse skin with a large scar running down his left cheek. He directed the women out of the captain's cabin and along the corridor downstairs to a dormitory. The room was pleasantly furnished with three bunk beds on the right, a wardrobe and positioned to the left was a wooden table surrounded by six dining chairs. The women decided amongst themselves who was sleeping at what level in the bunk beds.

The big sailor turned to exit the dormitory, but he was halted by Alena who asked, 'Boris where are the toilets?'

Andropov grunted back, 'Next on the right. Remember you go there and come straight back here.'

The girls nodded their heads in agreement. Two hours later the door was opened by two sailors carrying crockery and cutlery then returning with a large urn of vegetable soup, bread rolls plus six yogurts. The food was welcomed by the girls, who had not eaten for over eighteen hours, and wasted no time in serving it up. The meal was interrupted by the sound of the ship's engines starting up, coupled with the listing of the ship as the Koidutaht cast off. The sailors returned and offered their guests coffee and biscuits. Soon it was time for bed, and they all retired for the night.

Boris returned to his captain's quarters where Igor had poured out two large vodkas.

'Have a seat Boris. Now the girls are settled in, how is our other passenger?

'Not very well Captain. He has been sea-sick, and we haven't even left the dock!' Boris laughed.

'When the Caledonian Princess arrives, I want him to be transferred first well out of sight from the six girls.'

'Understood Sir.'

Three hours later at two a.m. Lana looked round the room to assure herself everyone was sleeping. She took a pen torch disguised in the handle of her suitcase and pulling the covers over her she opened a map of the 'Koidutaht' concealed in her bra and studied the lay-out of the ship. The Koidutaht was an excessively big ship sixty metres long and capable of storing seven thousand tons of fish, all gutted and ready for the supermarkets. Lana had acquired the map from a maritime museum in Tallinn by posing as a naval architecture student writing a thesis on fish processing vessels. Her real reason for boarding the Koidutaht could not have been further removed from what she told the museum attendant.

Slipping silently out of bed she opened the door and proceeded to commence touring the ship, which was not as quiet as she had hoped, since the nightshift were working gutting and filleting the latest haul of marine life. This catch came in all shapes and sizes everything from mackerel, herring, and tuna. Lana was not surprised at the size of the operation as she was aware this ship was capable of processing three hundred tons a day, As she looked along the production line a forklift truck sped by her, catching her by surprise but not noticing her hiding in the shadows.

Ten yards in front of her was a staircase leading down to the lower decks which she descended in her quest to find the evidence of the drug trafficking her masters were seeking. At the foot of the stairs she saw the ship's galley to her left where a cook was preparing breakfast and she headed right to what she presumed were stock rooms. This proved to be the case and she entered the first one and shone her torch quickly over the stock but failed to find anything she was looking for. The second storeroom proved to be the same and she left it only a minute later, closed the door and turned to return to her room only to be hit twice in the face by Boris Andropov's large fists, the second blow knocking her unconscious.

21

When the lights came back into her life Lana found herself in a spacious well-furnished bedroom and as she rubbed her aching chin, she realised she was lying in a bed with a cover over her. Standing at the foot of the bed was Captain Igor Shertsov and First Mate Boris Andropov. Igor was first to speak: 'Ah welcome back to our world Miss Gorsky there are a few questions we would like your answers on. What were you doing walking aimlessly round my ship when you were specifically told to remain in your cabin where you had access to a nearby toilet?'

Protesting her innocence Lana replied, 'I went to find the toilet and must have lost my way.'

'Nonsense!', shouted Boris, 'You knew precisely where the toilets were, but you decided to proceed down into the bowels of the ship searching for something. What was it you were looking for?'

'No Sir, you're mistaken I was only looking for the toilets.' Lana continued to claim.

'You really are a stupid bitch!, 'screamed the captain of the Koidutaht moving closer to the shaking girl, 'we have been watching you on our CCTV cameras and you seemed to know the lay-out of the ship very well and any unlit areas you illuminated with this torch pen which is not something readily available in stationery shops! So, stop wasting my time!!'

By now he was very close to Lana and grabbed her round the throat, as she struggled to fight him off, he pressed harder until she was gasping for air and collapsed to the floor. Igor had weakened his grip and Lana clasped her throat as Igor pulled her on to her feet and began punching her in the face several times causing her nose to bleed as she fell in a heap on the floor. Lana howled in pain as Igor continued with his assault, kicking her in the stomach before standing back and waiting for her to recover. Reaching down he picked her up and threw her back on the bed.

'Right, Svetlana, let us start again. Who sent you and what were you hoping to find?'

'Nothing' she murmured, tears streaming down her face, 'Nothing, believe me.'

'That's the problem, I don't. Boris have you got your knife? I think it's time we had a little fun with our prisoner.'

Boris produced a six-inch Bowie knife from the sheath attached to his belt and handed it to Igor who brandished it near to Lana's face whilst uttering, 'Now where shall we start? Don't scream young lady or I will terminate your life very quickly.'

Igor moved the blade further down Svetalana's body cutting away the front of her blouse and her front bra strap, exposing the upper half of her body before lowering the knife down to the button holding up her trousers. Igor plucked the button off before unzipping her trousers and signalling to Boris to help him remove them and her silk pants. Lana was now in a shocked state as she anticipated that both men were about to subject her to sexual mistreatment. She did not have long to wait as Igor removed his trousers, exposing his considerable manhood, and moved towards her.

Svetlana held up her hand in protest, 'Look, I have a great deal of experience in entertaining men so let's do this, so we all enjoy ourselves. All I ask is that you both use condoms.'

'Sorry lady, you're out of luck, we don't carry a family planning service on board but feel free to give it your best.'

For the next hour Lana entertained first Igor and then the massive ugly body of Boris Andropov whose bad breath was equally as vile as his sexual performance. Over the next few hours, the two sailors repeated their performance until Lana was physically exhausted. Thinking her co-operation had saved her she picked up what was left of her clothing and prepared herself for the short journey back to her cabin.

The naked sea captain arose from his bed, 'Where do you think you're going?'

'Now you boys have had your money's worth I was going back to join the girls. If you don't mind, I'll go to the bathroom.'

'Help yourself it is just through to the left.', informed Captain Shertsov, who began to pick up the tattered outfit he had decimated earlier. As he did so a scrap of paper fell to the floor which he picked up and began to read. It was the detailed map of the Koidutaht which made Igor realise Lana was spying on him and a definite threat to his narcotics business. He was now raging inside but without speaking he quickly showed the plan to Boris before their prisoner returned from the toilet.

Lana made to exit the room and Igor remarked, 'Just a minute and we'll come with you. Boris, remember and bring the tape to fix that broken window at the hold.'

Boris smiled, 'Will do.'

Igor turned to Lana smiled in a friendly way, 'You're some girl, sorry about being so rough. Look, leave these clothes which have been slashed to bits and put on my coat.'

Svetlana took up his offer and stood naked as he placed his coat over her shoulders which came down to her ankles.

The trio left the skipper's accommodation and headed towards the visitor's quarters. Igor whispered to Lana, 'Would you like to see in the hold where we keep the catch before processing it for the supermarkets?'

'Yes, that would be interesting,' she replied, happy to agree with anything that would keep her on good terms with her captors.

Up ahead Boris stopped and opened the large hatch exposing the most recent fishing catch amounting to thousands of fish alive and still fighting for survival.

Igor looked in and turned to Svetlana and pointing down at the marine life asked, 'What do you think of that Lana?'

Lana moved forward to get a better view and did not notice Boris cutting off a strip of sticky tape which he held over her head and placed it over her mouth, as Igor held her tight. Lana became hysterical as Igor removed her coat before bungling her unceremoniously into the hold full of frightened fish. Initially she disappeared but managed to claw back to the surface only to realise she was now in complete darkness and being subjected to the freezing waters of the hold. After ripping the tape from her mouth, she screamed for help but her efforts for survival lasted about twenty-five minutes when she succumbed to exhaustion and hyperthermia.

Boris returned to Lana's cabin to pick up her small suitcase. Heidi Lotheram was surprised to see him and asked, 'Where is Lana?'

'Oh, Captain Shertsov sent me to get her case. They are, shall we say, enjoying each other's company so much that she is going to stay on board for the duration of the voyage, but she said to say she wished you girls all the best.'

Heidi smiled to herself, 'Lucky girl, looks like she may have a good future for herself whilst I don't know what will become of the rest of us.'

An hour later Igor and Boris opened the hold's hatch and removed Lana's body by putting a hook round one of her arms and wrenching her body back on to the deck and placing it in a body-bag, Large ships carry body bags as part of their inventory in case they should have a sudden death on board which necessitated a burial at sea. They did not throw the body overboard as Igor did not want it discovered anywhere near the Koidutaht as that could arouse suspicion from the local authorities. Any interference from them could cause a halt to his lucrative trade in drugs and slave labour. Instead, the Caledonian Princess, which sailed out of Eyemouth on the Berwickshire coast in East Scotland, would be drawing up soon alongside to pick up a batch of hashish and Igor would transfer Lana to that boat with instructions to cast her into the sea nearer Scotland.

At first light Captain Igor Shertsov received a message from the bridge of the Koidutaht that the Caledonian Princess, a large fishing trawler had arrived alongside, and the skipper Peter Fraser was about to come aboard. Igor quickly dressed and made his way to the side of the ship where there was a gangplank for the use of visitors at sea. He looked over and saw two fishermen from the Caledonian Princess climbing up towards the ship. Peter Fraser at thirty-five was young for a skipper but he had been at sea since he was fifteen on his father's boat taking control when his dad prematurely died eight years ago. Solidly built with a head of thick blond hair accompanying his blue eyes Peter was joined by his cousin Martin Watson. Martin was much taller, older than his skipper with greasy black hair tied in a ponytail sticking out from his baseball cap. He had a lean lithe physique which had been honed from a lifetime at sea.

Igor greeted his guests, 'Morning Peter, morning Martin how are you guys doing?'

Peter replied, 'Good Igor, but probably a lot better once I see what you've got for us.'

Igor responded, 'Come on down to the boardroom for some breakfast and we can sort out the transactions for today. Boris, get the galley to cook up some breakfast for us all – is bacon rolls and coffee all round okay for everyone?'

The other three nodded their approval and they all headed for the Koidutaht's boardroom where the freshly cooked breakfast arrived twenty minutes later. Taking the last gulp of coffee from his mug Peter Fraser opened the conversation, 'What have you got for us this time Igor?'

Igor smiled at the two Scotsmen across the table, 'A bit of a mixed bag, half a ton of cannabis and five girls for the white slave trade plus our main drug supplier. He wants to slip into the U.K., undetected, for his own purposes and has arranged to pick up car which he will have pre-delivered to Eyemouth. Where he goes after that is up to him. There was a sixth girl who we found sniffing around below decks and we saw her as a threat to our operation, so we terminated the threat.'

Igor's last few words made the Eyemouth sailors sit up and Martin Watson gasped, 'You killed her! How?'

'By throwing her into the hold where there were tons of fish fighting for survival and she perished by drowning and possibly freezing to death.'

Silence filled the room until Igor continued, 'There is no way we can dispose of her body in any way that would connect her to the Koidutaht, so in return for a discount on your purchases I want you to take her body and dump it in British waters.'

'Igor, we'd have to see if McNab was in favour of your suggestion.'

'If you want Peter, but I'm certain five percent off a multi-million pounds cargo, will appeal to McNab and meet his approval.'

'Let me give him a call. While I'm doing that Martin do a sample check on the merchandise then round the girls up and tell them to be ready to transfer to the Caledonian princess.'

A still shocked Watson, at the thought of the horrible death Igor described, replied, 'Will do Peter.'

McNab was in his scrapyard's office when he got Peter's call which he reflected on before answering, 'Look we're in this for the money, so do what Igor is suggesting and I'll give you a bonus of twenty-five per cent of the value of the money you've saved me.'

'Sound good to me Geordie.'

Peter Fraser returned to the boardroom to tell Igor he had McNab's approval and proceeded with arrangements to transfer the drugs which were concealed within fish boxes, stored in flat sealed epoxy resin containers and held at the stern of the trawler away from the main catch. The girls were transferred to the Caledonian Princess where they would share more cramped accommodation for the next few days. Mohammed al-Baseri, casually dressed in warm clothing and sporting a black woollen beany hat was directed to Peter Fraser's cabin where he would stay for the duration of the journey. The girls, like the other three trawler crew on board, were totally unaware that the large package in the hold contained the body of Lana Gorsky.

Three days later the Caledonian Princess on its journey returning from the fishing grounds near Iceland passed the mouth of the Firth of Forth near Crail. Before preparing to head home to Eyemouth in Berwickshire Peter set the Caledonian Princess on a course a few miles inland. It was a stormy night with the high wind bringing heavy showers of rain which kept everyone except Peter Fraser and Martin Watson below decks. Peter took this opportunity to signal to Martin it was time to fetch Lana's body from the hold. Putting the trawler on automatic pilot, the two men brought the black parcel on deck. Looking around to see the other passengers were not watching he instructed Martin, 'Let's get this done quickly you unzip the bag and lift her out before anyone sees us. I'll nip downstairs and get something to weigh her down.'

Peter's last few words were lost on Martin, who didn't hear them for the howling wind and panicking, he unzipped the body bag causing him to screw up his face as he breathed in the smell of decaying flesh. Wasting no time, he picked up Lana with his gloved hands and dropped her overboard into the swelling waves. Seconds later Peter returned carrying a lead pipe and some rope as Martin was folding up the body-bag.

'Where's Lana?'

'Overboard.', replied the first mate.

'Overboard! You stupid bastard! We haven't weighed her down.'

'It's okay I made sure she submerged.', protested Watson.

'Oh, she'll have submerged alright, but the sea will return her to the surface in due course and she could wash up anywhere in this turbulence. Christ if that happens and the police can link it to us, we're dead men - if Geordie McNab doesn't see to us first!'

Eyemouth on the Berwickshire coast had been a fishing port since 1753 when a local merchant John Nisbet commissioned an architect, John Adam, to construct a harbour for the town. His reasons for doing so were not completely altruistic as Nisbet himself was a smuggler bringing in contraband of brandy, tobacco & tea which were all subject to large taxes imposed by the British government. Peter Fraser, the modern version of John Nisbet docked the Caledonian Princess into a berth at Eyemouth Harbour as the sun was setting. He immediately unloaded the fish he had caught at sea and despatched them in fish boxes up to the market where they were laid out in large freezers ready for sale the following morning.

Fraser had held back a consignment of fish boxes which only had a thin covering of fish to hide the drugs in the epoxy resin containers. His excuse if asked for not attaching this batch to the rest of the catch was that he was fulfilling a contract for a fish merchant in Billingsgate Market in London who wanted a supply of good quality lemon sole.

The five girls were told to stay below decks until after darkness and did not see al-Basiri slip ashore. He headed up the hill to his car which he opened after retrieving the keys from behind the rear passenger wheel. A refrigerated lorry bound for London arrived later to take the girls South – but in their case it would only be as far as Yorkshire. There they would be split up and sold over to Asian gangsters who would further sub-divide them by sending Heidi Lotheram and Alena Karesky to Scotland, whilst Greta Horschal, Sophia Neuman and Anna Berkovitch's new home would be in Bradford. Fraser and Watson warned their crew to say nothing about the girls or the drugs they had loaded into the lorry, which would do an about turn at Bradford and head for a warehouse in Shotts mid-way along the M8 between Edinburgh and Glasgow.

Chapter 3

December 3rd, 2010.

D.C.I. Grant McKirdy sat across the desk from Superintendent Stephen Law who had requested his presence. Law ushered McKirdy to sit down as he wanted to look down from his raised desk at the taller man as he commenced his interrogation.

'Grant good morning, how is the investigation into 'Miss X' going?' It's now over two weeks since her body was discovered on Joppa Rocks and we still don't know who she was.'

McKirdy shuffled uneasily in his seat before replying, 'Sir this case has proved to be a real mystery. Following the coroner's report, I thought we would have little difficulty in identifying Miss X with John Mason's opinion that she had come to an end with fish flesh under her nails. I received information on movements on shipping vessels in Scottish waters and sent my team off to interview the skippers of the boats. To date there has been no positive response from our investigations. I am beginning to think we should widen our search. The logistics of doing that are mind blowing, when you consider there are five hundred fishing boats out there at any one time including those from Europe.'

'Yes, I see your problem Grant, something on that scale would strain police resources all over the U.K. I was surprised when Dr Mason reported there was no DNA match, that is most unusual in the present day. Well look, keep investigating as you know something will turn up sooner or later. The local media are making the most of it at the moment. 'Miss X's' presence will fill many newspaper columns with all sort of conspiracy theories - from her being thrown off one of the cruise ships which dock at Hound's

Point to being a local gangster's moll who didn't keep her mouth shut in public when she was in a drunken stupor!'

Throwing his arms in the air McKirdy sympathised with his boss' comments, 'Yes, I have been getting my ear bent by some of the local scribes but there's nothing much I can feed them at the present time.'

Superintendent Law brought proceedings to a close. 'Okay Grant that's all I have time for this morning. Keep me informed of any developments.'

At MI6 headquarters in London Assistant Controller Richard Hartley was interrupted by a knock on the door, followed by the entrance of the short slim figure of his personal assistant Freddie Sharpe. A picture of sartorial eminence he was carrying a folder which he opened and laid out on Hartley's desk. 'Sir, this has just arrived in from Police Scotland.'

Hartley opened the folder and sighed, 'Good God, if I'm not mistaken the girl in the photo is Lana Gorsky or to give her a MI6 identity, Elke Kohl. Thanks for bringing this to my attention, I think I had better speak to Police Scotland.'

Later that afternoon he placed a call to the highest ranked officer available at Police Scotland and was connected to Superintendent Law.

Hartley began the conversation, 'Afternoon Superintendent, Richard Hartley MI6 here. How are things in your beautiful city? I must confess to be being biased having boarded at Loretto School in Musselburgh, just down the road from Edinburgh. I know Joppa Rocks where my schoolmates and I used to go crab hunting or investigating shells with the biology teacher.

This morning, your report on the body found on Joppa Rocks reached my desk, which to date has only been identified as 'Miss X.' I regret to say the girl in the photograph, we are certain is one of our agents. What I am about to say is highly confidential and naturally covered by the Official Secrets Act which we all operate under.'

'Understood' the police chief remarked.

Hartley continued, 'We believe the girl in question is known as Lana Gorsky or in MI6 as Elke Kohl. She was investigating the drug warlords who have been bringing their merchandise overland from Afghanistan to Estonia. Elke was trying to follow the Baltic Trail which had taken a new route from the traditional one coming out of India. Last we heard from her was a few weeks ago when she was in Estonia what used to be Northern Russia and we feared for her safety. We have suspected, for a while, that the new drug trail may have something to do with the fish process- ing vessels which leave from Parnu, a port near Tallinn. How she got from Parnu to Edinburgh is a mystery. Have your investigations unravelled any new clues?'

Superintendent Law replied, 'The post-mortem on Miss 'X's' body initially indicated the cause of death was stran- gulation as she had severe bruising on her neck coupled with marks on her face and body where she had been badly beaten by two different assailants. However, on closer ex- amination John Mason, the coroner, concluded that she'd been thrown into a hold of live fish. The cause of death in his opinion was drowning from a mixture exhaustion and hyperthermia.'

Hartley let out a gasp, 'Oh, what a fiendish death. She was one of our very promising officers.'

Law continued, 'Our crime search has been hampered by the victim not having any DNA record which is unusual nowadays.'

Hartley intervened, 'I know how that happened. At MI6 we remove all DNA records from the official listings for agents who are operating in sensitive areas so as not to sup- ply any intelligence to our enemies.'

'Good', replied the superintendent, 'at least that fills in a piece of the jigsaw. My crime team has been in touch with the Scottish Fisheries Board who have co-operated fully by giving us the movements of all fishing vessels operating around Scotland at the time. Unfortunately to date we have drawn a blank. This makes us think we shall have to broaden our search to the rest of Britain, and possibly beyond if EU boats from France, Spain or Ireland were in the vicinity.'

Hartley screwed up his face with disappointment, 'Yes, it is not going to easy for you. I will alert our field staff in the Estonian theatre about Elke's death and get them to put out a brief to their informers. I hope we can flush out some new leads to help us findi out who killed Elke Kohl. I think that is all we can do at this stage Superintendent - tell me who would be our contact if we have any new information to share with you?'

'Please refer everything to Detective Chief Inspector Grant McKirdy. Who will be McKirdy's contact at MI6?', asked Ian Law.

Richard Hartley thought for a moment then answered, 'Commander Hugh McFaul will act on our behalf. I think we should leave it at that for today, but I will get Hugh McFaul to phone D.C.I. McKirdy and introduce himself.'

'Thanks Assistant Controller Hartley, I will tell McKirdy to expect a call from Commander McFaul. Good afternoon.', the superintendent cut off the call before phoning and updating D.C.I. McKirdy.

Hugh McFaul was relaxing at home in his flat at Godalming in leafy Surrey with his wife Amy when he received a call from Richard Hartley. He had recently returned from Kenya having served a five-year consignment, monitoring the movements of al-Qaeda terrorist cells operating in East Africa. He recognised the phone number and answered assertively, 'McFaul speaking Sir, how are things with you?'

'Busy as usual Hugh, I have a new assignment for you. Could you please be in my office tomorrow morning at ten o'clock?'

'Certainly, Sir, are there any preparations I can make prior to the meeting?' Hugh enquired.

Hartley gave a tongue in cheek reply, 'How about tidal movements in the Firth of Forth. I'll explain tomorrow.'

Hugh McFaul arrived at MI6's London headquarters in Vauxhall. After security clearance he took the lift to the top floor where the Assistant Controller had his office. He was met at the lift by Elaine Bowie, Hartley's personal assistant, who shook hands as she greeted him, 'Nice to see you Hugh, have you settled in after your stint in Africa?'

'I have but I have a feeling I may not be here long.', replied Hugh.

'I'll pass on that one.', said Elaine, opening the door of Richard Hartley's office.

Hartley was on the phone but signalled for Hugh to make himself useful by pouring the coffee which had been delivered shortly before McFaul arrived. Richard terminated the call and sat down on one of two Chesterfield armchairs he had positioned at the fireplace with a small table between them.

'Sorry about that Hugh, trouble in the Middle East this morning but it can wait. It is good to see you again. Did you enjoy Kenya? I understand you met your wife out there.'

'Yes Sir, I was introduced to Amy by my friend John Johnston in South Africa when we went on that trip to Swaziland which led to the capture of Ephraim Mguto the Mogadishu terrorist. We got married eighteen months ago in Johannesburg and she is now adjusting to life in London. Amy is a neuro-surgeon, and she has managed to get a post at St. Thomas' Hospital.'

Hartley picked up a biscuit and had a sip of his coffee before continuing, 'I'm glad everything is going well for you Hugh. You did an excellent job in spotting Mguto who is now well out of harm's way. In recognition of the fine work you carried out in Africa the Service is promoting you to the rank of Commander. You will only use that title within the British security circles but will receive all the benefits that go with the title.'

McFaul could not resist a broad smile, 'Thank you very much Sir.'

'What I wanted to see you about today is not such a pleasant subject. We recently had an operative Elke Kohl investigating a new Baltic Trade route the drugs trade has been using in Eastern Europe to flood the U.K. with product, mostly hashish. We had recruited Elke when she was a student at Leipzig University, doing an exchange course at Durham. She was a very bright girl and we had high hopes for her.'

Hugh interrupted, 'You have used the past tense twice sir.'

'Yes, we had a notification from Police Scotland that a naked body had been found in the sea at Joppa Rocks on the east side of Edinburgh. It turned out to be Elke who was using the pseudonym Lana Gorsky. How she managed to turn up thousands of miles from where she was operating is a mystery? The Police Scotland coroner has given the cause of death as drowning, following substantial beatings by more than one person. It is not a normal drowning, as she had fish flesh under her nails, which indicated she had been thrown into an area full of freshly caught fish. Not nice.

She had not been in touch for a few weeks but her last report related to us she was making good progress and very hopeful of exposing the leading suppliers. I have spoken to Superintendent Law at Police Scotland who informed me that they are investigating all fishing boats movements in the two weeks to Elke's body being washed up. So far there has not been any positive response to their enquiries. I would like you to liaise with Police Scotland where your contact will be Detective Chief Inspector Grant McKirdy, to assess how the local search is progressing on an ongoing basis. Regarding '6's' involvement, here is Elke's movement file for the last twelve months which you can study before travelling to Eastern Europe to find out what her final movements were before she died.'

Hugh picked up the file from the coffee table and flicked through it as Richard Hartley continued, 'Hugh, you will be up against what is effectively the Russian Mafia and as you can see they don't take prisoners, so tread cautiously.'

'Will I be working solo sir?'

'You could, but I think you would benefit from a female accomplice as you will be prying into areas where data could become more relevant from a woman asking the questions but I will leave that up to you. The British Embassy in all the East European countries will be at your disposal should you require it.'

'When do you want me to start?', Hugh asked.

Hartley smiled at the younger man, 'As soon as possible, the Service has always had a policy of avenging assassinations of our agents with immediate effect.'

'I'll get on to it right away sir', concluded McFaul and exited the Assistant Controller's office.

Hugh was so curious to find out more about his new assignment he took the file on Elke Kohl back to his flat in Godalming where he and Amy had set up home. He had no sooner made himself comfortable in his armchair with a coffee and was about to open the file when he heard Amy open the front door. After laying down her laptop and hanging up her wet raincoat she joined Hugh in the lounge.

'Man, what bloody awful weather in this country! It will be a beautiful spring day in Johannesburg probably with temperatures in the mid-seventies.' she moaned.

'It could be worse', said Hugh cheerfully, 'We might have settled in Belfast where you inherit all the rainy weather America sends you over the Atlantic. Anyhow, what sort of day have you had? Tell me while I get you a glass of cold white wine from the fridge.'

Amy put her feet up on the couch opposite Hugh's chair and began, 'I was very fortunate not to be operating today as I was able to observe Sir Patrick Websdale removing a large tumour from a patient's brain which was lying in a very dangerous position. Sir Patrick is one of the world's top neuro-surgeons and it fascinating to see close-up his operating technique.'

Their wedding in Johannesburg, three years after being introduced to Amy by his best friend John Johnston. What had started as a blind date flourished into marriage. Amy and John are both doctors who worked together in the Neuro Surgical department, at Baragwanath hospital. John decided to play cupid for his boyhood friend he grew up with in Belfast. Shortly after the wedding the couple had set up home in Nairobi and then moved to Surrey which suited Amy who had got a registrar's role in the neuro- surgery department at St. Thomas' Hospital.

'Did you have a good meeting with Richard Hartley? What was the new project he wants you to do?' Amy enquired.

Hugh passed the wine to Amy and sat back in his armchair, 'Good and bad dear. The good is you are now looking at Commander Hugh McFaul.' Amy let out a scream of delight and crossed the room to embrace Hugh and plant a big kiss on his lips,

/ Hugh continued 'The bad news is Hartley has lost one of his agents, a female, in some very mysterious circumstances and he wants me to investigate how she died. I have also to take up where she left off and hopefully bring the bad guys to justice. It will mean that I could be travelling around periodically and staying away from home.'

'That is a pity Hugh, but you did warn me about the unusual nature of your job before we got married so I can live with it. Besides, it will leave me with more time to mix with my team at work and get involved with them socially. How soon do you leave?'

'Almost immediately, once I have digested what's in this file. My first trip will be a short one up to Edinburgh, to meet up with a local police, Detective Chief Inspector Grant McKirdy who is handling the police enquiry. I have never been to Edinburgh before so that will be interesting.'

Amy's eyes lit up, 'I wish it were me, it is supposed to be a beautiful city, known as the 'Athens of the North'.

'I know where this is leading Amy, no you can't come with me! Now what are we having to eat tonight?'

'Well if I can't get a romantic night in Scotland's Capital, I suggest you book a table 'Les Deux Amours' down the road for eight-thirty! I shall go and pamper myself in preparation for my night of passion.', Amy added mischievously before heading for the bathroom.

Chapter 4

Next morning Hugh was in the office early and told his personal assistant Moira Graham that he did want not to be disturbed as he was going analyse the Elke Kohl file.

The file was a complete account of Elke Kohl's activities written often in the present tense which made the reader feel they were in her company. Hugh reckoned she had written in that manner as it allowed her to have total recall, in detail, of her previous evening's activities.

Elke Kohl (23) had joined the Service when she was recruited by MI6 whilst on a secondment to Durham University. She was only nineteen at the time and was swayed by the offer from the British Secret Service who promised to pay for her education.

MI6 classed her as a low-profile agent whose role was to report on anything unusual happening in the Leipzig area which may be of interest to the British authorities. Elke had lived all her days in Saxony which had been in East Germany since 1945 when Germany was partitioned after the second world war until the Berlin Wall, erected in 1961, came down in August 1989.

During the forty-four years Germany was divided East Germany was under the control of the Stasi, the secret police. The Stasi believed in absolute domination of the state and recruited thousands of civilians to spy on their fellow citizens. The system they adopted was based on fear and they handed out torture regularly. Their policies, which included the removal of all political rivals, were copied by some African regimes with despotic rulers. The Stasi provided 'observers' to train their military leaders strategy, as a means of guaranteeing they achieved their goal of remaining in power.

Elke's father Heinz was originally an accountant at one of the major heavy engineering companies in Leipzig. Freedom brought with its problems for Leipzig industries, who found they could not compete with their high-tech competitors in West Germany and many businesses failed. Heinz was very resourceful and made a career switch, by re-educating himself in computer studies at night classes to prepare himself to get employment in the city's emerging financial services industry. Elke was named after the German film actress Elke Sommer who Heinz worshipped as a teenager.

The new career introduced a far higher standard of living for the Kohl family which consisted of Elke and her two younger brothers, Otto and Helmut, who were looked after by their mother Marlene. Leipzig has a history of great classical musicians such as Wagner, Bach, Mahler, and Mendelssohn who either had been born or lived in the city. It was little wonder that Mrs. Kohl enrolled the children at the Leipzig Academy of Music where Elke excelled as a violinist, Otto on the trumpet whilst Helmut concentrated on the drums.

The children provided the music at family gatherings where they were joined by their tone-deaf father, who fancied himself as Leipzig's answer to Tony Bennett. After one performance, a close friend sent him a CD featuring a recording of the previous evening's musical ensemble, minus his children's contribution, thus ending a not too promising vocalist career to the delight of all who had suffered in the past!

After finishing school Elke took some time off and went to Berlin, one hundred miles north-west of Leipzig where she got a temporary job in an advertising agency, Adenaur Hause. Elke loved her new surroundings and set her heart on moving to the German capital when she finished her studies. She shared an apartment with three other girls one of whom was Heidi Lotheram, a trainee nurse who took more drugs than she administered to her patients. This was a world completely alien to Elke who disciplined herself never to take any substances which would threaten her life. She tried in vain several times to woo Heidi away from drug dependency.

Returning to Leipzig she enrolled at the university to take a degree in economics and politics and was soon involved in several student clubs which included a considerable amount of socialising. In her second year she was sent on secondment to Durham University in the North of England which she found exciting but expensive for a girl from communist Eastern Europe. One of the elderly lecturers at Durham Dr Raymond Robertson recognised Elke found Britain expensive and took a close interest in her as she had all the qualities to be spy for MI6.

As a good-looking stunning blond, with a good physique honed regularly by her judo sessions, Elke was constantly stalked by men which she found difficult to resist. She constantly had a man in her life which satisfied her high libido and through time she found herself unable to curb her desires. She quickly came to realise that not many of the students at university shared her sexual motivation. Elke began satisfying her fix by attracting high power businessmen in the bars of the local luxury hotels. She just loved being around powerful men.

On her return from Durham, having been successfully 'tapped up' by MI6 she decided to put her pleasure activities to good use. Elke produced regular dossiers of information on many unsuspecting senior executives of leading businesses who attended seminars in Leipzig. Not all the men she entertained were trading legitimately and one client who was of great interest to her was Mohammed al Basari.

al-Basari was a tall attractive man in his mid-thirties who always dressed immaculately and stopped of regularly in Leipzig to break his journeys from Afghanistan to Estonia.

He was obviously wealthy and remunerated Lana generously for her services, enjoying both the physical and mental side of their relationship. Often, after concluding his sexual desires, he would talk to Elke about his business problems. At first, he was coy about disclosing the nature of his company apart from saying he had distribution problems to overcome to get it to market. Six visits later he was in an ebullient mood one night, ordering expensive champagne and caviar for his room. Elke was pleased for him and enquired the reason for his exuberance.

'Elke, I have finally knocked it off, after months of stopping off here to talk with former members of Stasi they have responded to my request to arrange for my exports to go from Estonia to the United Kingdom.'

Elke was curious, 'Why has it taken so long? Could you not have sent products from Afghanistan straight to the United Kingdom.

Mohammed smiled, 'No my dear, I deal in specialist products which are not subject to normal trading?'

Elke laughed, 'So I'm in bed with a smuggler! C'mon what is it you do? Gun-running, drugs or supplying precious jewels stolen from wealthy individuals.'

The Afghan moved his body on top of Elke, 'That's for me to know and you to use your expertise to prise the answer out of me.'

For the next hour Elke used all her talents giving him her full repertoire of sexual positions which left Mohammed gasping for air. 'That was excellent my dear', he exhaled, 'and all done without me giving you one of my free samples to get you going.'

'What sample do you have in mind Mohammed?'

Mohammed got off the bed and went to his suitcase, returning with a sachet of white powder. 'Here try this, it will make you feel high as a kite.'

'No thanks, not after all the champagne.''

'Well, I will.', said Mohammed emptying the contents on to the bedside table and snorting them up his nose. 'Oh, that's better, sure you won't try some, I have plenty with me.'

Elke saw her opportunity to continue her examination of Mohammed, gently stroking his skin to extend his good mood, 'How long have you been dealing in drugs Mohammed?'

Al-Basari lit a cigarette before answering, 'My family has been growing poppies for generations but our efforts to get our harvest to market has been hampered by war for the last twenty years. First it was the British who left, only to be replaced by the Russians who failed to control us and they also left, leaving it to the Americans assisted by the British and the French to sort it out. They are all wasting their time as the Taliban will always wage terror on the indigenous population and make it impossible to arrange a ceasefire never mind a peace agreement.'

'It must be difficult and dangerous to bring drugs out of Afghanistan to here. How do you manage it Mohammed?'

'Traditionally dealers used the Baltic Route moving consignments through Pakistan then on to India where they were shipped globally from Bombay. This worked well but has now become more closely scrutinised so now we use Tashkent and into Russia where the Russian mafia guarantee us a safe passage until Leningrad. The drugs are then taken to the Estonian border, where they are moved into grain tankers bound for Tallinn.'

'So, what has Leipzig got to do with this?' asked Elke.

'Plenty Elke, old habits die hard in Eastern Europe and none more so than in the brotherhood of the Stasi, who prior to the break-up of the Soviet Union, controlled the whole of Eastern Europe with an iron fist. They still have great influence in the region, we have found them easy to bribe - at rates far cheaper than say Pakistan who have more experience in bargaining.'

'Do you have enough product to keep the whole of Estonia supplied Mohammed?' asked Elke innocently.

al-Basiri laughed, 'Yes and no, Estonia is not a big enough market for us. We are looking to supply the whole of Britain! But enough of this, I will be moving on tomorrow but not without having the pleasure of your body once more.'

Elke lay on her back, 'C'mon lover, you're in charge and I want to give you something to bring you back again soon.'

Elke's next report was a couple of weeks later when Mohammed al-Basiri arrived back in Leipzig. She was feeling quite pleased with herself having reported on a possible Afghani drug ring and was anxious to find out more. Al-Basiri called her and they agreed to meet in the bar at the Lindtbaum Hotel in the centre of Leipzig. Elke arrived first and got a Bloody Mary which she put on Mohammed's account. She took a seat where she could observe all movements of the guests arriving, most of them businessmen attempting to keep the wheels of industry turning. People watching was one of her favourite pastimes, allowing her imagination to run riot on how she would entertain specific guests who came to her attention. They were not always young bucks as Elke had a strong interest in older powerful men who had reached their position of authority.

Elke knew how to attract men and tonight was no exception. Her hair and make-up had been applied to perfection, before she put on a tight black see-through blouse accompanied by a short gold satin pencil skirt above black stiletto heels to display her lovely legs. She had received more than a few glances before Mohammed arrived looking as though he just stepped off a luxury yacht. He was immaculately dressed - cream trousers, a light blue open-neck shirt which partially hid his gold chain and a Hugo Boss blazer.

'Elke, lovely to see you. I was going to ask what you wanted to drink but I see you have beaten me to it.' Mohammed sat down beside Elke as a waiter arrived to take his order, 'A large Johnnie Walker with ice please and could you let us see the menu. I have been travelling most of the day and I am starving.'

The waiter returned with Mohammed's drink and handed out the menus. Silence prevailed for the next couple of minutes while the pair made their selections which the waiter took on board after establishing Mohammed's wish to be served as soon as possible. Elke now turned her attention to her target for the evening.

'So how are developments for your business going Mo? Do you think your Stasi contacts will have paved the way for you to despatch your trade from Tallinn?'

'Elke you are looking beautiful tonight. I consider myself to be a lucky man, the envy of all the male diners in the restaurant. You will observe, most tables are occupied by single diners, all cautious not to reveal any trade secrets to someone who may be a competitor. They will probably drop their guard later in the evening when they have had a few drinks in the bar, but I prefer the company of a beautiful lady. To answer your question, I have had an excellent response from my contacts at Stasi and tomorrow I will sign an agreement with them which my family are delighted I have been able to secure.'

'So, does that mean we are on the champagne again tonight Mr Basiri?' asked Elke, sliding her shoe up the inside of Mo's leg to rest on his groin.

Looking down at her foot rubbing his manhood he replied, 'You can have as much as you want for as long as you want.'

Immediately after the meal the couple retired to Mohammed's accommodation which on this occasion was the best suite in the hotel, 'I told you I was celebrating tonight, nothing is too good for you Elke.'

Elke smiled then replied, 'I bet you say that to all your 'Girls'.'

Al-Basiri laughed, 'Yes I do - and they all love it!'

For the next few hours passionate activities filled the suite until Mo who was travel weary fell into a deep sleep. Elke slipped out of bed with the ready-made excuse rehearsed that she was going to the bathroom, but instead crossed the room through the double doors into the lounge where Mo's diary was on the bureau. She opened it at tomorrow's date hoping to get a clue as to who Mohammed was meeting in the morning, but all he had written down was the name 'TOGVOR SHIEL PANTURA'. Elke memorised the name and returned to bed.

Next morning Elke stayed long enough to share breakfast with Mohammed who was in a more sombre mood. He gathered his papers together for his meeting with Colonel Gert Schlosser who had previously controlled all Stasi activities in Saxony. After finalising his thoughts for his meeting Mohammed turned to Elke and gave her more than the agreed rate for her services.

Elke took the money and was slightly embarrassed as she counted it mentally, 'Oh Mohammed, that's far too much!'

Mohammed stared back at Elke and stammered, 'E...Elke it is in order. You will never see me again after today if all goes to plan. You more than earned what you have in your hand. Good luck and thanks.'

Elke was shocked, she thought to herself, 'He is leaving just when I thought I was getting close to his illegal practices'.

She returned home and wrote up the report Hugh McFaul had just finished reading. In her final paragraph she requested a new identity, including a passport in the name of Svletlana Gorsky. Her justification for this was she was getting closer on a regular basis to some dubious characters and preferred to work undercover. Her handler at MI6 sympathised with her request and planned for Elke to pick up her new identity from the British embassy in Berlin.

Looking down at Elke Kohl's file Hugh sighed, 'What does 'TOGVOR SHIEL PANTURA' mean?', he asked himself, 'some sort of anagram. I'll pass it through to coding and see if they can come up with anything.'

That was the end of Elke's reporting but not on how she ended up on the Koidutaht.

Chapter 5

Mohammed Al-Basiri tapped his fingers nervously on the glass coffee table in the Leipzig Garten Hotel as he waited for Gert Schlosser, a former colonel in the Stasi. He was already twenty minutes late and Mo was starting to panic that he would not show up or worse still that he had walked into a police trap and probable imprisonment. His fears were muted by the approach of an elderly, thin, wiry man with receding white hair and rimless glasses. Surprising for a man of his years he was casually dressed in blue denim jeans, a scarlet woollen polo-neck, which was partially covered by a black leather bomber jacket.

Holding out his hand he asked, 'Mohammed al-Basiri I presume? I am Gert Schlosser. Can I get you a drink?'

Schlosser attracted a waiter's attention and placed his order, 'A cafetiere for two please with some biscuits.'

Turning back to business to al-Basiri Schlosser asked, 'Did you have a good time at the Lindtbaum Hotel last night, in the company of an attractive young women?'

Mo was startled, 'How do you know where I was staying last night and who I was having dinner with?'

'Mr Basiri after thirty years of policing I make it my business to know everything about everyone who arrives in Saxony. Have no fear, we only take reprisals against those people who choose to outsmart us illegally. I am certain our transactions will be strictly above board. We have communicated by e-mail, but I would like you to outline our agreement verbally before I commit myself to any formal written agreements.'

Mo checked out who was within earshot before answering, 'My family have been involved in harvesting poppies for generations and we are seeking ways of delivering hashish by different routes. Our chosen route is to send our produce to the United Kingdom, which is potentially an excessively big market, via Russia and then on to Estonia. My sources tell me you have contacts in Estonia, and we are prepared to offer you ten thousand euros per consignment in return for arranging a safe passage for our products out of Parnu. We appreciate there will be further shipping charges involved as the boats will be involved in a mid- ship transfer to a Scottish fishing trawler who will take them to our dealer in Scotland.'

Gert Schlosser sat up at the mention of money, 'How often will you be sending consignments to the U.K.?'

'Weekly to start with, but this could increase subject to our satisfaction with the arrangements and of course the demand for good quality. Do these terms meet your approval Gert? From your perspective I would have thought it was easy money as there is limited risk to yourself. What do you think Gert?'

'Very attractive Mr Basiri. To give you a bit of background to my organisation – prior to the Berlin Wall coming down the Stasi had total control of Saxony and put the fear of God into anyone who disagreed with us. Executions of dissenters was not uncommon and long prison sentences with hard labour were the norm. From October 1990 everything changed, and I was replaced soon afterwards by someone from the West. Here in Saxony our standard of living was far lower and salaries in West Germany were much higher. However, when it came to our pensions we didn't get parity with the West and since 1990 there has been a substantial rise in the cost of living which has made it difficult for our families to maintain our standard of living. We've enhanced our pensions by offering services which were associated with the old Stasi under the banner of 'security services.' They include protection rackets and bodyguard services. We operate extensively across Eastern Europe which includes Parnu, so I can help you.'

Gert's last remarks made Mo sit up, 'So who would you recommend?'

Gert went into his pocket and pulled out a notelet, 'I have a name for you here, but before I give you it to you, here are my bank details. You must arrange for ten thousand euros to be transferred into Executive Security Services tomorrow morning. Failure to transfer the funds will be treated as a breach of contract which as I told you earlier is not recommended.' Handing Mohammed the notelet he added, 'Phone this man, Kurt Jansen, he will introduce you to Igor Shertsov, Captain of the Koidutaht a fish processing vessel which specialises in your market.'

Mo took the paper, put it in his pocket picked up his cup of coffee and toasted the German, 'Prost Herr Schlosser, hopefully this will be the first of many transactions!'

Chapter 6

A couple of weeks after she had parted from Mohammed al-Basari, Elke received an unexpected early morning call from Heidi Lotheram in Berlin.

'Elke, how are you? It's Heidi, I've got myself into a lot of trouble in Berlin.'

'What sort of trouble Heidi?'

'I went to collect drugs for a dealer but instead of delivering them I started selling them off at lower prices and have pocketed the money to help me make a new start. I have just received a call from the dealer Fritz Kahn asking where the money is, and why I was selling them when I had no authority to do so. He has given me until tomorrow lunchtime to return the money or expect a visit from one of his minders. I am scared Elke! These people are ruthless!'

'So, what are you going to do now Heidi?' asked Elke who was bewildered by what she had just heard.

'I'm getting out of Berlin tonight on a train to Leipzig before heading for Tallinn where I may be able to pick up a boat which I understand will deliver me into the United Kingdom.'

'How are they able to do that?'

'One of the girls I was sharing a flat with, Greta Horschal, told me about it before she left for Tallinn. There is a fish processing vessel, 'The Koidutaht' sailing in two days, whose captain will smuggle us into Scotland, via a fishing boat which will transfer to in the middle of the North Sea.'

'Slow down Heidi, what do you want me to do?'

'Elke, I need to go into hiding for the next forty- eight hours so I wondered if I could come and stay at your flat, then you could drive me to Tallinn. Don't worry, I'll pay for all the transport and accommodation costs. What do you think?'

Elke went silent before answering, 'Okay, on one condition - I come with you to Britain and you refer to me at all times as Lana Grotsky and tell everyone I have been working in St. Petersburg as a hotel receptionist for the last six months.' Since she had been recruited by MI6 Elke had conjured up a new identity as Svetlana Grotsky, which she used occasionally.

'Agreed Elke, I will call you when I have an arrival time in Leipzig.'

'Heidi don't chance taking the train, your enemies will be watching the stations. It is only one hundred and sixty kilometres from Leipzig to Berlin. I will pick you up in my car, a blue Volkswagen beetle, at the eastern entrance to the Brandenburg Gate at two o'clock. Wear a red woollen hat and dress yourself like a man with a black beard.', laughed Elke.

Heidi hit back, 'Have you always been keen on espionage Elke?

'Yes, it is one of my hobbies. See you at two, goodbye.'

The traffic was busy for early November at the Brandenburg Gate, one of the most famous tourist attractions in Berlin. Today it was heavily populated with visitors, letting their imaginations run riot as they visualised the Nazi rallies of the 1930s, culminating in the ranting voice of Adolf Hitler. Elke missed seeing Heidi at first but second time round she spotted the red hat and abruptly pulled over in front of a Mercedes driver who pumped his horn vigorously at the blue Beetle. Heidi opened the door, threw her rucksack in the back, jumped on board as Elke sped the car away from the centre of Berlin.

Glancing sideways at her new passenger Elke laughed, 'Well Heidi I've got to congratulate you on the lengths you have gone to disguise yourself especially the black wig and beard to hide your mop of red hair!'

'Thanks for coming to my rescue Elke. I'm sweating like hell under this outfit and I can't wait to remove it.'

Elke gave a cautionary response, 'Don't do anything yet, wait until we are past Schonfield Airport and on to the motorway. There are speed cameras, but I will keep under 100kph – the last thing I want is getting stopped and explaining why you are travelling looking like that. We'll be in the car for about two hours so tell me everything,'

Heidi tearfully began to relate how she had come to call Elke, 'I've been a complete idiot Elke. I got in tow with Fritz Kahn, a well-known drug pusher in Berlin who employed me as a mule to deliver drugs to wealthy customers. In return he supplied me with drugs to satisfy my habit. The customers paid me euros which I brought back to Fritz. One day he gave me a large consignment for Heinrich Perlstein, the pop singer who was hosting a birthday party. Perlstein, who you know is an extraordinarily successful performer and has made millions from records, concerts etc. I delivered the goods, and he gave me a large package containing almost one hundred thousand euros. I do not know what got into me, but I decided to run off with the money. When I failed to return, it was not long until Fritz phoned me to find up where I was. I had snorted some cocaine and was feeling high enough to laugh down the phone and tell him I had stolen his money. He replied by saying if he did not have it back by the morning I would die. I have ignored his threat because even if I did return the money, he would still kill me. That's how Fritz Kahn and his gang operate.'

Elke could not contain herself, 'Heidi, you're starting to scare me. Does this Fritz Kahn know anything about me, or have you ever mentioned Leipzig to him?'

'No, honest Elke.'

'So why are you going to Tallinn?'

'One of the girls I worked with in the 'Heiss Damen Club', Greta Horschal told me that she and a few other girls were going to Parnu, the closest port to Tallinn where they will board a large fish processing vessel call 'the Koidu-taht'. This ship frequently transports illegal immigrants to settle in the United Kingdom and delivers them via fishing boats into ports along the Scottish coast.'

'How many girls are making the trip Heidi?'

'I think Greta said there were five, including me.'

'This sounds exciting, give her a phone and see if she can find a place for me.'

Heidi reached into her bag and produced a phone which rang four times before a voice answered. 'Greta, Heidi here, I am on my way to Tallinn to join you. I am with my friend Svetlana Gorsky, who is interested in coming to Britain with us if there is room for us all on board. Do you think it is possible to accommodate her?'

'I will speak to Kurt Jansen who is organising the trip. I suspect it will not be a problem as these guys are only interested in one thing – money! Remember to tell your friend it will cost her fifteen hundred euros. See you when you arrive, we will be in the Youth Hostel on Vierte Strasse in the centre of Parnu. Goodbye.'

Elke had been listening to most of the conversation and broke the silence, 'Fifteen hundred euros! Well, all I can say is I hope we get a good breakfast for that kind of money.'

'Elke, I have sewn the money into the base of my case so don't let it out of your sight.'

Elke replied, 'Smart thinking, there's no way a bank would accept one hundred thousand Euros in cash.'

The girls arrive at Elke's student flat on the outskirts of Leipzig about four-thirty in the afternoon. They dumped their bags and headed out for something to eat at a local burger bar where they were able to relax and relate stories about their youth. They returned to the flat but not before Elke had satisfied herself there were no wardens about as guests to student's flats were strictly forbidden. While Heidi was taking a shower, Elke opened up her laptop and searched ''Koidutaht'. She gathered as much information regarding the vessel including all the technical statistics and a map of Koidutaht's layout which she printed off and put in her case.

The following morning both the girls were weary after sharing a single bed. They quickly packed their bags, engaged in a hot breakfast at the student's café and were soon on their way to Tallinn. Tallinn is 1600 kilometres from Leipzig and the girls had a discussion to decide how they should travel. It would take nineteen hours by car, less by train but that meant passing through Berlin where Heidi might be spotted so they settled for the two-hour flight to Tallinn followed by a 110 kilometre bus journey into Parnu. The bus trip was very relaxing as it stopped at the Kernu Mansion, a beautifully restored country mansion where they could get out and stroll round the grounds. From there it was on to the Jaanihanso Cider Factory where they enjoyed a few free samples before calling in to an alpaca farm where Heidi bought a sweater.

The youth hostel was just off the stylish centre of Parnu where they met the other four members of their group Greta Horschal, Anna Berkovitch, Alena Koresky and Sophie Baumen. Apart from Greta all the girls seemed nervous and went to their rooms immediately after their evening meal. Heidi and Elke (now known as Lana) went out to a bar which Lana welcomed as she wanted to know more about the Koidutaht and its crew. Greta explained that the Koidutaht was a factory fish processing ship with a large crew. She had been given the opportunity of an illegal entry into the U.K. by Kurt Jansen who was friendly with the vessel's captain Igor Shertsov whom she had never met.

'What do you know about Igor Shertsov Greta?' enquired Lana.

'Not very much really but Kurt Jansen who I have known for years says he's okay and runs the Koidutaht with a rod of iron.'

'So, we better keep out his way.' chipped in Heidi.

After another couple of drinks, the trio went the way of their companions to their single rooms. Elke got out a note-pad on which she wrote down 'Igor Shertsov'. A short time later lying in bed she recounted her role as a MI6 agent, which excited her, but was countered with the disappoint-ment that Mohammed al-Basiri was not returning. The only clue she had to how he disposed of the drugs hauls was what had written in his diary – 'TOGVOR SHIEL PAN-TURA', which she also wrote on her pad. For the next half hour, she attempted to make sense of the coded message and was about to give up when it she suddenly cracked it and unravelled the message as IGOR SHERTSOV AT PARNU. Mohammed al-Basiri had plans to contact or meet up with Igor Shertsov in Parnu so obviously a new drug route was being established and the Koidutaht was the vehi-cle chosen to administer it.

All she needed now was some proof.

The next day the girls all relaxed exploring the attractions of Tallinn which led them to the Old Town where they had a tour of the towers and walked the two and a half kilome-tres round the walls. On the way they passed many red topped towers which served in medieval times as protection for the city. Later they climbed up Toompea Hill where the Estonian Parliament legislates, before taking a tram to Kadriorg to visit Peter the Great's gorgeous palace and the manicured parks surrounding it. The day passed quickly as did the evening meal that followed and soon it was time to meet up with Kurt Jansen, a thirty- year-old obese man with blond greasy hair and a badly pock-marked face. At seven -

thirty prompt Jansen arrived in a Volkswagen mini-bus with blackened-out windows and loaded the girls into the vehicle for the short journey.

Before getting off the mini-bus Jansen turned round in his seat and addressed all the girls, 'Ladies, we've arrived at the Koidutaht, but before I let any of you out can you please all have your fares ready.', he laughed to himself before continuing, 'Today your trip costing is fifteen hundred euros each.'

The girls had been expecting this and went into their handbags and produced the money which was passed down the bus to the driver. Jansen checked over the money then opened the doors. The girls descended from the bus directly opposite a gangplank, which they climbed up onto the ship where they were met by Boris Andropov, the first mate of the Koidutaht.

'This way ladies, Captain Igor Shertsov is waiting for you.'

Chapter 7

The British Airways flight from London Heathrow landed on time at Edinburgh Airport with the low winter sun blinding passengers as it shone through the windows. Hugh McFaul gathered his coat, hat and briefcase from the overhead locker and exited into the airport. At the top of the walkway he was met by a tall, burly gentleman with a smile on his face.

'Good morning Mr McFaul. Detective Chief Inspector Grant McKirdy. Did you have a good flight?'

Slightly taken aback, Hugh asked, 'How did you know who I am?'

'We've not met before, but I was senior investigating officer in a murder enquiry we had here in Edinburgh when Professor Allan Phair was stabbed to death. It involved members of my team going to Belfast to interview a lady you are familiar with – Mhairi McClure. I saw a video of your friend John Johnston's father's funeral which you featured in.'

Hugh relaxed, 'It certainly is a small world.'

McKirdy grinned, 'When you've been doing this job as long as I have you keep all sorts of recall in your head.' Moving off from the top of the stairs he added, 'Come this way out through the VIP exit, I've got a car waiting out the back.'

Detective Sergeant Ian Lomax jumped out the police car as McKirdy and McFaul approached and after the formal introductions they headed off to Fettes Police Headquarters.

Grant kept the conversation going, 'Have you been to Edinburgh before Mr McFaul?'

'No, first time and please call me Hugh.'

'Well I hope you enjoy our city. I'll give you a little commentary as we go along. On your right we are passing the world headquarters of The Royal Bank of Scotland which went into freefall due to bad management when the financial crisis erupted. Many ordinary staff who had bought shares to boost their pensions lost a fortune, but nobody went to prison, as they would have had it been a bank robbery. Inflicting mental cruelty on citizens largely goes unpunished.'

Hugh sided with the D.C.I. 'Yes, I read about that, but the tragedy was that all directors helped themselves to inflated salary packages and pensions, which was the same at The Bank of Scotland. Wouldn't it be great Grant if the public sector gave us 'Golden Goodbyes' when we had failed to stop the crime rate increasing?'

Hugh's remarks brought a chuckle from the two police officers.

McKirdy continued pointing to his right, 'Over there is Murrayfield Stadium where we will be looking to overcome your rugby team in the Six Nations Rugby in January. Personally, I prefer football and my team, Hearts, play at Tynecastle Park which is just to the left of Murrayfield.' Turning to his driver he instructed him, 'Ian, take a left here over Ravelston and down to Fettes.'

At the top of Orchard Brae which leads down to Police Headquarters at Fettes Hugh asked, 'What is that lovely sandstone building down there which reminds me of Hogwarts in the Harry Potter films?'

'Fettes college, one of a number of private schools in Edinburgh. Tony Blair is a former pupil. If you have ever read any James Bond books you will recall Ian Fleming chose Fettes as his hero's alma mater. You are right about Hogwarts, a lot of people have commented on that probably because J.K. Rowling, the author of Harry Potter, lives in Edinburgh.

'Well I learn something every day. I'll test my colleagues back at MI6 head-quarters on Fettes College when we have our next office quiz.' replied Hugh jokingly.

The car drove up the hill to the entrance to Fettes Police Headquarters, a flat-roofed seventies building with all manner of security systems to prevent attack from intruders. Hugh and Grant got out leaving D.S. Lomax to remove the vehicle to the car park at the side of the building.

McKirdy signed his MI6 counterpart into the Building and proceeded through to a meeting room, ordering Detective Constable Avril Luxton to organise coffee and biscuits as he did so. The two security officers had no sooner removed their coats and placed their working papers on the highly polished wooden table when they were joined by Lomax and Luxton. Grant introduced Avril to Hugh McFaul before addressing the meeting:

'Thank you for taking the time to come up to Edinburgh today. Hopefully, our discussions will enable us to unravel the mystery of Miss 'X' who I now understand we should refer to as Svetlana Grotsky.'

Hugh intervened 'Svetlana Grotsky was the pseudonym used by the victim when working for MI6. Her real name was Elke Kohl.'

'Thanks for that correction Hugh. Until MI6 contacted us, we were having great difficulty in identifying Elke. We have established from forensics pretty much how she died, by being thrown into a freezing hold of freshly caught fish. What we are struggling with is the motive for her death. Based on forensic information our teams of detectives have been out around Scotland, interviewing fishing boat captains but this has not thrown up any clues. We are aware that there have been several instances where fishing ports have been suspected of trafficking drugs, but no charges have been laid.'

Hugh came into the conversation at this point, 'D.C.I. McKirdy your theory about drugs could be correct. Elke

Kohl, who MI6 recruited a few years ago when she was studying for a term at Durham University, was employed to look for any criminal activities in the Saxony area. Saxony is situated in what was East Germany, and although the two countries merged in October 1990 there are still some dubious characters on the loose there. Some of them served in the Stasi, the East German Secret Police. In terms of our operation in the German theatre Elke's role was miniscule but she did send us reports on a regular basis. Usually they were about leading business figures who were staying at five-star hotels which she frequented and offered overnight companionship to anyone who required it.'

'A sort of Mata Hari!', blurted out Lomax.

McFaul gave the young detective a stare then continued, 'If you say so. In Elke's last report she gave a perfectly good account of a liaison she had with an Afghan, Mohammed al-Basiri, who she suspects of being a drug dealer. In her opinion, al-Basiri was attempting to set up a new drug trafficking trail to send hashish and heroin to Western Europe and the United Kingdom in particular. He was only going to achieve this with the help of former Stasi senior police officers and from our point of view worrying, as it means they may have connections to Russian agents or worse the Russian Mafia. Her last report was about 30 days ago, and we have heard nothing since from her, until she turned up on Joppa Rocks here in Edinburgh thousands of miles away.'

'Have you run any checks on Mohammed al-Basiri or better still managed to get a photograph of him?', asked Grant.

'We did make enquiries, but his name does not come up on our extensive suspect lists. My thoughts are he was using a false name when he stayed in Leipzig. We know the dates he visited Leipzig, but not the hotel he booked into. I have left my assistant Moira Graham phoning all the top hotels to see if we uncover where al-Basiri stayed. When Moira gets a successful reply, she will request a copy of the hotel's close circuit TV records, coinciding with the time when Mohammed al-Basiri checked into the hotel.'

Ian Lomax spoke up, 'That's excellent sir, let's hope we get a photograph soon.'

Hugh continued, 'There's every chance that al-Basiri is connected to the al-Qaeda who supply hashish to the Russian mafia in return for weapons but also to plan terrorist attacks in the West.'

Grant McKirdy shuffled uneasily in his seat, 'Which means that it is vital we solve our local case and establish who is responsible for Elke Kohl's death in Saxony or wherever, and how they managed to transport her body here. Did Elke have many close friends?'

'Yes apparently, she was popular with her student friends in her first year at Leipzig University, but they noticed a change in her when she returned from her spell at Durham. MI6 may have to take the blame for that. Dr Raymond Robertson, who interviewed Elke, considered her to be highly intelligent and someone who could make a career as an Intelligence Officer. She in turn saw military intelligence as an opportunity to involve herself in the world of espionage and satisfy her desire to travel extensively while getting the buzz of adrenaline flowing through her veins. I must say that is a slightly naïve way of looking at it, most of what we do is rather boring, checking out movements of suspects who, the large percentage of will never be activated by their controllers. She did spend some time in Berlin in the summer holidays after she finished school. She worked in an advertising agency and according to her university friends had a good time. I intend going over to Berlin and Leipzig to see if I can get any new leads. That's all I have to report at present so tell me how things are going at this end?'

'The three officers looked at each other before D.C.I. McKirdy spoke up, 'Slowly, I am sorry to say. We expected to have this case wound up by now. As I said earlier with the favourable forensic report which we received it seemed to narrow our suspects down to the fishing industry. We immediately arranged to see Admiral Pearson Arbuthnott, Chairman of the Sea Fishing Authority in Leith which is only a few miles from here. The Admiral was very cooperative and gave us a complete dossier of all ship movements in Scotland. Our teams have investigated everyone on the list but, apart from a few of the fisherman's untaxed vehicles on the quayside, nothing relating to the case.'

'Grant, I can understand your disappointment. From our perspective MI6 takes fatalities very seriously as the police do also. Keep up your investigation and I in turn will report back to you when I get back from Germany. If you have time, I would like to visit Joppa Rocks, so I have a complete picture of Elke's unfortunate demise.'

'No problem Hugh, we'll have lunch first, then I'll drive you down there. It is only a few miles down the coast. Then I can drop you off back at the airport.

Grant and Hugh made their way down to the Leith Docks area which had become a trendy part of town and settled for the Shore Restaurant overlooking the Water of Leith. The Shore is a classical popular old watering hole with an extensive menu which served up an excellent lunch, washed down in Hugh's case, with a couple of large glasses of red wine. The two men got on very well with Grant relating his experiences of policing Edinburgh for thirty years and Hugh revealing his experiences in Kenya.

They had left the Shore Restaurant and were driving round the docks when Grant suddenly braked and pulled into the side of the road. 'Now that's interesting Hugh. See that white-haired gentlemen ahead crossing the road? That's Admiral Pearson Arbuthnott of the Sea Fishing Authority who I mentioned to you earlier. He is about to enter the local casino, which is unusual for this time of day, when you would only expect to find Chinese restaurant owners who work at night or punters with a serious gambling habit. It is maybe worth me finding out if he has a problem.'

'Let me know the outcome Grant.'

The drive continued and as they came round the bend at Seafield Road Hugh could not believe what he was seeing. 'I didn't realise Edinburgh had a beach that stretched for over a mile.'

'Portobello beach was a seaside resort about eighty years ago when they had a pier and was largely ignored by the local council until about ten years ago when they start cleaning it up and now it's become popular again. Joppa lies at the far end of Portobello.'

Five minutes later Grant stopped the car where Elke's body was discovered. Hugh got out the car and went over a patch of grass to look down on Joppa Rocks. The wind was blowing strongly making Hugh hold on to his hat as the grey waves crashed on to the rocks.

Hugh stood in silence thinking to himself, 'What a cruel world we live in. Elke's death has to be revenged to bring some dignity back into her life.'

Chapter 8

Hugh reported next morning to Richard Hartley at MI6 in London. Hartley smiled when he entered the room, 'Morning Hugh, how did you get on in Edinburgh?'

Hugh sighed, 'Not a lot of progress to report but I got on well with D.C.I. McKirdy and his team. They have not come up with anything new, but Grant McKirdy is not likely to give up so I am sure that I'll be seeing him again before long. I think the next move for me would be to go to Germany and visit both Leipzig and Berlin where Elke worked one summer in an advertising agency.'

'Yes,', said Hartley, leaning back in his chair and studying the ceiling, 'I was going to ask you, when you are in Leipzig, to call on Elke's parents and give them our condolences. I am uncertain if they were aware of Elke's role at MI6 and we are duty bound to offer them a 'death in service' payment. I will get personnel to supply you with the suitable correspondence for your visit.'

'Very good Sir. By the way I thought Edinburgh was a beautiful city. It must have been a great place to go to school.'

'Yes Hugh, I have happy memories of Loretto which is in Musselburgh, known as 'The Honest Toun' but we frequently went to Edinburgh for school outings and rugby matches.'

A week later Hugh and Campbell Anderson flew to Leipzig mid- morning where they had booked into the Leipzig Ibis for the night in the centre of city. Rather than go direct to the hotel they hired a BMW 5 Series and set off for Elke's parents' house in Naumburg a short drive from Leipzig/Halle airport. Hugh had made an appointment to see them and had established they both spoke English which saved him having to book an interpreter. They managed to find Elke's address in this very pretty town, famous for housing the Hildebrandt organ listed as the biggest in the world. The Kohl's lived in large townhouse on three floors which had become too big for them as the children had now left to find their way in the world.

Frau Inge Kohl, a stylish lady in her mid- fifties answered the door and led her two visitors through to the lounge where her husband Heinz was listening to classical music which he turned off when they entered the room. All four shook hands before sitting down in leather backed armchairs.

Hugh started the conversation, 'I'm Hugh McFaul and this is my colleague Lieutenant Campbell Anderson. Please accept our deepest condolences on the death of Elke who neither of us met personally but I did read her reports which she sent to London regularly. Did you know of her involvement with the British security services which began when she visited Durham University a few years ago.'

Inge kohl replied, 'No Mr. McFaul, this has come as a complete shock to us. We had no idea what Elke was doing in her spare time which was spent mostly in the halls of residence in the university.

Hugh carried on, 'Elke's remit was to observe any movements of any new characters who arrived at the university who she thought would be of interest to ourselves. Primarily we were looking for individuals who could have connections to the Eastern Bloc and may attempt to infiltrate the university. Elke was highly thought of by my colleagues who recruited her, and it was no surprise when she self – expanded her remit to include in her reports more about leading businessmen who were staying in the five-star hotels in Leipzig. It is difficult to talk about this part of Elke's story but it appears she took it upon herself to entertain some of the visitors who -', Hugh struggled to explain it, - 'paid for her services.'

Both parents gasped at the last remark with Heinz screaming out, 'This can't be right! Elke would never done anything like that. She was a good girl, raised by us to respect other people in line with the teachings of the Lutheran Protestant church which she attended every week before she went to university.'

To take some pressure off Hugh, Campbell Anderson continued the questioning, 'Are either of you familiar with a gentleman called Mohammed al-Basiri?'

The couple looked at each other, shrugged their shoulders before jointly answering, 'No -what is he to do with our daughter?'

'We are not altogether certain, but we have reason to believe he could be involved in supplying drugs from Afghanistan.'

'Oh my God! And you think Elke was mixed up in the drug trade!', exclaimed Frau Kohl.

Hugh could see this conversation was taking a nasty turn and intervened, 'No Frau Kohl, certainly not. We have no evidence of any wrongdoings on the part of Elke. Our purpose for being in Germany is to gather evidence to bring those responsible for her death to justice and right now the only name in the frame is Mohammed al-Basiri! Believe me, MI6 takes the removal of any of our agents, regardless of rank very seriously and will not let this case rest until we solve it.

Heinz Kohl, whose eyes had watered with emotion, raised his arm, 'Apologies gentlemen, my wife and I are finding it difficult to cope with Elke's passing. Have you any idea how she managed to be found in Edinburgh?'

Hugh responded. 'Sorry to say that remains a mystery. Elke did not arrive through the normal channels as we have checked all the airports, trains and ferries.'

Hugh chose not to mention the traces of fish flesh under Elke's nails for fear of upsetting her parents any further. Instead, Campbell came in to interrupt the silence which hung over the room, 'We are following up any scraps of information we can find. I understand Elke worked in Berlin for a short spell after she left school. Do you know which part of Berlin she lived and who any of her friends were?'

Frau Kohl relaxed and said quietly, 'Yes I still have her address. The only girl I can remember talking about was called Heidi Lotheram. Give me a minute and I will look for that address.

'While your wife is looking for the address Herr Kohl, would it be possible to see Elke's room in the hope we may stumble upon something which could help our investigation?', asked Hugh.

Heinz nodded his head, 'Come this way. I show you.'

Elke's room was a typical young girl's bedroom, brightly decorated with a floral bedspread. On her dressing table there was a selection of make-up treatments which confirmed Elke took a pride in her appearance. Shelves containing books, mostly of an educational nature were prominent but Campbell did notice a copy of Kim Philby's autobiography. Philby was a MI6 officer who sold secrets to Russia and sought political asylum there where he lived for the rest of his life. Heinz allowed the two security officers to do an extensive search of Elke's wardrobe and drawers, but they failed to uncover anything of interest to solving her murder.

They returned to the lounge where Frau Kohl was waiting with Elke's address from when she lived in Berlin - 21 Konigstrasse, Keuzberg. Hugh thanked the Kohl's for their assistance and was about to leave when he suddenly remembered something.

'Excuse me for saying this at your time of grief but Richard Hartley, our director told me to inform you that he appreciated the work Elke did on our behalf. In appreciation of her service you will receive an ex-Gratia payment from the British Government to use as you see fit.'

The Kohl's were both embarrassed and saddened by Hugh's words, 'Thank you', said Heinz, 'that is truly kind.'

Hugh and Campbell commenced their return journey back to Leipzig. Hugh spoke first once they were out of earshot, 'Thank goodness that's over, I felt deeply sorry for the Kohls. It must have come as a tremendous shock to them when the local police called at their door to say Elke had been found dead in Edinburgh, when they didn't know she wasn't even living in Leipzig.'

Cam replied, 'Not a nice situation, what do you want to do now?'

'We will go to the Lindtbaum Hotel and see if we can uncover anything on Mohammed al-Basiri.'

Lindtbaum Hotel was a five-star modern building rising to ten floors in the business centre of Leipzig. The impressive entrance hall had marble and bronze pillars, surrounding an atrium which housed several rectangular glass tables, each encircled by four red velvet bucket chairs. Hugh marched up to the reception and politely asked to see the manager. The attractive girl behind the desk asked, 'Who shall I say wants to talk to Herr Breitner?'

Hugh took a business card from his inside pocket and passed it to her, the card read, 'Lindsay Cameron, Managing Director, British Electronic Group' but was devoid of any genuine contact details. He had used this card on previous occasions when he did not want to disclose, initially, he was from MI6. Five minutes later Paul Breitner appeared at reception, a fresh-faced man with fair hair wearing a smart brown pin-striped suit, white and a pattered yellow silk tie. He smiled and introduced himself.

'Paul Breitner, I'm the manager of the hotel, how can I be of assistance to you?'

Hugh shook Herr Breitner's outstretched hand, introduced Campbell and asked, 'Is there somewhere private we can go without anyone listening to us. What we want to ask you has to remain confidential.'

Paul gave the two men a quizzical look then pointed to an adjacent empty glass enclosed compartment which they all filed into.

'Mr Breitner, Campbell and I are both from British Intelligence and we are in Leipzig today trying to find any clues which may us help solve the murder of one of our agents Elke Kohl. Miss Kohl often posed as a 'Hostess' for businessmen visiting Leipzig and we have reason to believe she used this hotel to meet one of your guests a Mr Mohammed al-Basiri, probably about six weeks ago.'

The manager of the Lindtbaum was quite shocked by what he had just heard but he managed to control himself before re-acting to Hugh's statement, 'Mr Lindsay, we are an international hotel and our goal in life is to satisfy all our guests' requirements, sometimes that does include, shall we call it 'personal services' in their room. I shall be able to ascertain when and for how long Mr al-Basiri stayed with us.'

Picking up the phone in front of him he dialled reception twenty yards away, 'Estelle, could you please look up reservations for a Mr al-Basiri who was in the hotel recently and also who booked him in or out at reception and if they are currently working send them across with the detail. Oh, also check the CCTV for photos of Mohammed al-Basiri..'

'Thanks Herr Breitner', responded Hugh and making small talk added, 'Nice place you have here.'

Breitner nodded then spoke, 'The Lindtbaum is one of the best hotels in Leipzig. I have been here seven years, and this is the first time I have ever been visited by security people.'

Hugh was about to reply when a short, stocky-built forty-year old lady in a royal blue uniform entered the room carrying some papers.

'Ah Constance, you've found what we were looking for. Take a seat and let me see the paper,' casting an eye over them Breitner continued, 'Mr Mohammed is the type of customer I would like to have all the time. He hires a suite, has an expensive meal in our best restaurant then retires to his room where orders two of our most expensive bottles of champagnes from room service! A man who loves the high life! Good looking fellow, I don't know why he had to resort to using the services of a hostess.'

The intelligence officers both looked at the photos, Hugh interrupted Herr Breitner, 'Can I speak to Constance?'

'Of course.'

'Constance, were you on reception when Mohammed al-Basiri checked out?'

The receptionist nodded her head, 'Yes I remember him, because he was in an incredibly happy mood and when I said, 'Have a good day.' He answered, 'I don't think they'll come any better than this one. He then went out of the hotel and got into a hired car.'

'I don't suppose you know where he was going?'

'No sorry.'

'Well thank you both for your help. In one of the photographs he is with a lady called Elke Kohl. Did she leave with Mr al-Basiri?'

'No, she left the hotel about one hour later.'

'Thanks for your help.', replied Hugh.

Constance returned to reception. Paul Breitner turned to face Hugh and Campbell, 'Sorry we couldn't be of more help. I wish you well and hope you catch whoever is responsible for the young lady's death.'

Campbell and Hugh left the splendour of the Lindtbaum and headed for the more basic surroundings of the Saxony Ibis Hotel. Cam was driving which gave Hugh time to plan out their next move. 'Well Campbell, what are your thoughts after seeing the Kohls?'

'Hugh today has been quite positive. We've been able to get a better picture of Elke's character and her secret life which the parents knew nothing about plus we have an address for where she lived in Berlin. Hopefully, that will throw up some clues as to how she left Germany. Paul Breitner was extremely helpful, as was Constance who remembered al-Basiri leaving the hotel in good spirits, using a hired car which saved us having to chase up all the taxi companies in the area. I think however we should get the office to check out all the local car hire companies to see if Mohammed uses them regularly – that is if he is using his own name.'

'Yes, like you I thought it was a reasonably useful visit and now it's on to Berlin where we can make our first call to Elke's ex-flatmate and also speak to the advertising company where she briefly worked for a short time. Right now, get your foot down, I'm ready for a good feed.'

'I thought you might want to go by Leipzig University and talk to Elke's fellow students.' Campbell suggested.

'Okay let's give it a go.'

The BMW did not take long to take get Hugh and Cam back to the university and after negotiating with the security men at the entrance they managed to get an audience with Fraulein Munster the Department Burser, who listened intently as they revealed the purpose of their visit. At the conclusion of Hugh's explanation of the events surrounding

Elke's death she phoned the halls of residence and managed to get two of Elke's classmates to join them.

Anna Altermann and Hilda Linden had both enrolled at the same time as Elke and in first year they were inseparable but had drifted apart in second year after Elke returned from her term at Durham. They were aware she had taken to getting herself groomed up but did not know what she was up to at nights in the top hotels in Leipzig.

Hugh brought the conversation to more recent events, 'Did Elke tell you she was going anywhere before she vanished?'

Anna shook her head butHilda, looking over her horn-rimmed spectacles offered an explanation, 'On the last day I saw her she told me she had been to Berlin to pick up a friend who she smuggled into the halls. She introduced us to her friend Heidi Lotheram who if I am being honest, Anna and I were not too keen on.'

'Why was that? Cam enquired.

'She was a bit dishevelled and, without wanting to appear snobbish, tarty. Her eyes looked glazed and during the evening she rolled up her sleeve unintentionally and I noticed her arm was punctured by needles.'

'Next morning did she hang around the campus?'

'No Sir, they both packed small suitcases and left. I don't know where, but they did not take Elke's car which is still in a parking space at the back of the building.'

Hugh turned to Fraulein Munster, 'Could we see Elke's room?'

'Yes of course. Girls could you take the gentlemen to Elke's room please.

Outside room 53 and Hugh thanked Anna and Hilda for their help and sent them on their way. Campbell and Hugh searched the room thoroughly and managed to find the keys to Elke's Volkswagen Beetle. A search of the car was disappointing apart from a paper napkin in the passenger door's side pocket Cam uncovered with the words 'Heiss Damen Club' emblazoned on it. He held it up to let Hugh see it.

'Good. Campbell, I think we'll be tasting a bit of night-life when we are in Berlin.'

Next morning the hundred-mile journey to Berlin passed very quickly as Campbell took advantage of the autobahn's no speed limit rules and put the BMW through its paces arriving in the centre of Berlin eighty minutes later

'Where to first Hugh?'

'I think we should start with Adenaur Hause, the advertising agency where Elke worked when she was here. Set the Satnav for Europlatz Building in Wilhelmstrasse, Cam.'

Traffic was heavy but after twenty-five minutes they found themselves outside a large glass-fronted building. They entered and took the lift to the eleventh floor where they met with Heindrich Grosser, a youthful forty-year-old. He remembered Elke as being one of the most efficient student temps that he had ever employed. He was very distressed when Hugh told him the purpose of their visit and regretted, he could not produce any helpful information for his guests apart from mentioning Heidi Lotheram as her best friend in Berlin.

Campbell and Hugh returned to their car where Hugh gave out his next instruction. 'The visit to Adenaur Hause went very much as I feared. Let's get over to Elke's old flat and see if we can get any additional information on Fraulein Lotheram who may be the key to uncovering Elke's destination prior to being washed up on Joppa Rocks. Once again engage your Satnav, this time for 21 Konigstrasse in Kreuzberg, a popular district for students.

21 Konigstrasse was a modern student accommodation block with a concierge on the front door who Hugh ap-

proached and asked for the whereabouts of Heidi Lotheram's apartment.

'Ein und funfzig', she replied pointing the visitors to the lift.

Room 51 was on the third floor. Hugh rang the bell and waited whist someone on the other side looked through the spyhole and asked in German, 'Whose calling?'

Cam answered in German, 'Wir sind freunds ab Elke Kohl, sprechen sie anglise?'

'Ya. '

Hugh reverted to English, 'Elke Kohl has been murdered and we are investigating the murder and wanted to talk to Heidi Lotheram.'

A couple of seconds later the door opened a fraction, a chain stopping it going any further to reveal a small slim girl in her early twenties who looked Hugh and Campbell up and down before taking the chain off the door. Hugh sensed the girl was nervous which might make it difficult to extract information, so he suggested: -

'I noticed there was a café at reception. Why don't we all go down there and have a chat – and could you please bring any photographs you have of Heidi?'

The girl nodded her agreement, retrieved her ski jacket, and followed the two MI6 Officers downstairs. While Cam ordered the coffees Heidi's flatmate introduced herself as Margaurite Dobereiner..

'How long have you lived in Konigstrasse Elsa?'

'About four years, I am from Cologne and after university I came here to work at one of the government departments.'

'Which one?'

'Department of Social Sciences.'

Hugh smiled back as Campbell returned with the coffee and biscuits.

Hugh addressed Marguarite once more, 'We're sorry to bother you but during our enquiries we have twice heard the name Heide Lotheram mentioned who, I understand, shares the flat with you.'

Marguarite hesitated then replied, 'Well she did up until a month ago. I came home one day, and she'd packed her bags and disappeared, and I haven't seen or heard from her since.'

'Oh dear, not what we wanted to hear.', Hugh said dejectedly, 'tell us what sort of person is Heidi? Where did she work and who were her friends apart from Elke Kohl?'

'When she first came to live with me Heidi was a nurse attached to one of the largest hospitals. She was great fun with a lively personality. That was probably about the time Elke was here. She changed dramatically when she got a job as a barmaid in the evening at the Heiss Damen Club to supplement her income. It is not an establishment which has a good reputation. Heidi started taking drugs and her habit increased to the extent she would not go to the hospital, phoning in to say she was sick. She appeared to be getting well paid as she was never short of funds to finance her problem. Sometimes when she was high, she would tell me about her activities at the Heiss Damen. These were often not confined to serving drinks, more acting as a delivery service for a local drug dealer.'

'Did she say who he was?'

'Not exactly Mr. McFaul, but she did refer to a guy who frequented the club often called Fritz Hahn.'

'When she left in a hurry, did she take a suitcase?'

'Yes, I noticed a small suitcase of mine was missing. Typical for Heidi, she was always borrowing something.'

'Have you any idea where she could have gone?'

'No, but when you catch up with her tell her to send back my suitcase – and her share of the rent!'

Her last comment brought a smile to the agents faces and their conversation to a close. Both men shook Margaurite's hand and thanked her for seeing them at short notice. What her comments did was not change the direction of the investigation, it was still full speed ahead for the Heiss Damen Club.

Hugh was concerned about going into premises, with a dubious reputation so he put a call through to Toby Masters, the British Ambassador in Berlin, 'Good evening Ambassador, Hugh McFaul speaking. Richard Hartley the Assistant Controller at MI6 asked me to contact you to let you know that Campbell Anderson and I are operating on your patch this evening. We are carrying out an investigation into the killing of one of our agents, Elke Kohl and tonight it is leading us to the Heiss Damen Club where we may meet some very unsavoury characters. Have you got a couple of security staff who could back us up if necessary?'

'Good evening Mr. McFaul. Yes, what time do you need them?'

'About 10.00, I don't think these places get going much before then.'

'Correct. I will ask Mike Connell and Arthur Shepherd to be there for 10.30 – how will they recognise you?'

'Tell them to look for a tall athletic figure wearing a yellow shirt and black casual suit. That will be my colleague Campbell Anderson – I will be having a quiet drink at the bar waiting for an approach from a local drug dealer.'

Ambassador Masters laughed. 'Sounds like an interesting evening – I wish my wife wasn't dragging me out to the ballet!'

The Heiss Damen Club was exactly as you would imagine, dimly lit, smelling of smoke with waitresses pacing about like a scene from the musical 'Cabaret'. In the middle of the club there was a small stage where a topless pole dancer moved her body seductively round the pole teasing her audience that she was about to discard her G-string. In front of her were round tables with red velvet bucket seats which were overlooked by booths able to house up to eight people. At the bar there were stools taken up with drinkers and others waiting anxiously hoping to acquire seats for the cabaret.

Hugh entered the club casually dressed and order a malt whisky with ice. As he was waiting for his drink a couple seated next to him slid off their stools to join friends who had arrived for the floorshow, so Hugh took one of their seats. The bar was circular, so Hugh was able to survey everything around him. Campbell arrived five minutes later and positioned himself on the opposite side of the bar so he could observe Hugh's movements. Campbell had no sooner lifted his drink when he was joined by the guards from the embassy who staged 'a long-lost friend act'.

'Great to see you John, let me introduce you, this is Harry who works beside me. Glad you gave me a call when you were in Berlin, it must be a couple of years since we met up at your sister's wedding.'

Campbell played along with the act, 'Must be, Sally had a little boy called Brian three months ago.', raising his glass he added, 'a toast to a good night.'

Across the bar Hugh ordered same again but this time engaged the barman in conversation using a broad Irish accent., 'Have you worked here long?'

'Yes', said the blonde heavy sweaty figure, 'about four years.'

'So, you would have worked with a young girl I am trying to trace called Heidi Lotheram.'

'Heidi used to work here part-time in the evenings but one day about four weeks ago she never appeared. The boss went looking for her, but no luck. Her flatmate has no idea where she has gone.'

'Well if she ever comes back tell her to call me. Here's my card, my name is Lindsay Cameron.'

The barman took the card and Hugh was contemplating what to do next when a large middle-aged man with greasy hair and a small scar under his left eye sat down beside him. He ordered a vodka and coke before speaking.

'I hear from Hector the barman who passed me you're calling card that you are looking for Heidi Lotheram. Can I ask you why?'

'And can I ask who I am speaking to?'

'Fritz Hahn, I own this place and a few other nightspots in the city. The reason I'm asking is because that bitch has a lot of money, which she stole from me Mr Cameron.'

'What line of business are you in?'

'If you know Heidi you've probably got a good idea and with your Irish accent you've come here arrange to purchase some powder to sell in Ireland. This British Electronic Group is more than likely a front, so why are you here in Berlin?'

'On the contrary, I was hoping to get some money from Heidi for a consignment she got a month ago which was arranged through her friend Elke Kohl. She has been distributing cocaine to some of your customers, right under your nose - if you do not mind the pun, so to speak. Did you know Elke Kohl?'

'Is this the same Elke Kohl who was found floating in the sea off Edinburgh?' asked Hahn.

'Yes'

'Well she didn't last long in the business. Yes, I met her a couple of times, good-looking girl. I offered her a spot as a pole dancer, but she was not interested. I wonder how she schemed with Heidi to set up an operation against me. We go through a lot of staff here. Last week one of the waitresses Alena Koresky handed in her notice and went off to Estonia of all places.', concluded Fritz.

'What is she going to do there?'

'Christ knows, at this time of the year it will be freezing!' exclaimed Hahn

before putting on a more serious face, 'Mr Cameron I was unaware of Heidi importing cocaine into my patch. Equally, operating from the U.K. you would not know that I control much of what goes on in Berlin. Take this as a warning, I do not want to see you here again.'

Hugh stared the gangster in the eye, 'Mr Hahn, I'm not used to being threatened so what if I refuse to adhere to what you just said.'

'How stupid are you? In this city if Fritz Hahn fends you off with a warning, many would consider you to be a lucky man, but if you want a sample of what might happen to you let me demonstrate!', Fritz snapped his fingers and three bouncers appeared out of nowhere, 'Take this piece of Irish shit out the side door and give him a beating.'

The three hoodlums made a grab for Hugh who knocked Hahn off his stool causing a split- second delay to their attack whilst signalling to Cam's group. They attacked the bouncers from behind putting them in an armlock whilst simultaneously denting their dinner suits with loaded Glock 7s. Hahn jumped to his feet ready to continue the fight but when he saw the firearms he backed off.

'Mr Hahn, as you see I cover all contingencies so don't ever try to threaten me again. I may want to continue servicing your patch, so always be on your guard. My men are new to Berlin, but I assure you they will kill you if I say the word! Now tell your goons to stay here while you get us a safe passage out of here.'

The party moved smoothly to the entrance, Cam, Mike, and Arthur keeping their weapons handy following Hugh and Fritz who led them to the taxi rank. Hugh turned to the Berlin drug dealer, 'Don't try and follow us, we shall be changing taxis quickly and staying overnight where you will never find us.'

He could say the last part with confidence as he had already arranged to return to the British Embassy by a side door and stay there overnight. Two miles down the road they transferred into another hired car.

Mike Connell let them into the embassy and took them up to a lounge the ambassador used for entertaining guests complete with a bar which Arthur Shepherd manned immediately. 'What can I get you?' he asked.

Hugh replied first, 'Oh it has to be a large Scotch.'

'And you Campbell?

'A large gin and tonic.'

The two Embassy staff settled for beers and they all sat round a polished oak table to reflect on the evening's proceedings.

Hugh raised his glass in a toast, 'Thanks everyone for your help tonight. It could have got quite nasty in the Heiss Damen if you guys had not been there. Fritz Hahn is a nasty, ruthless individual who is desperate to recover his money from Heidi Lotheram. After I told the barman I was looking for Heidi he could not wait to sit beside me and interrogate me as to why I wanted to talk to her. I played him at his own game making up a story that she had bought cocaine from me which she was distributing out to his clients and I was in town to collect my money.'

The other three laughed and Hugh continued, 'He got terribly angry on hearing that and told me never to return to Berlin. When I said I did not like being threatened he called in his protectors but fortunately for me you guys diffused the situation. He said he had met Elke Kohl and had offered her a job as a dancer which she turned down. Fritz knew about Elke's death and made a couple of disparaging remarks about her. Heidi had disappeared but this was quite common amongst his staff – the week before one of his girls, Alena Koresky walked out on him saying she was going to Estonia. Cam check out anything you can find on Alena Koresky in the morning.'

'Will do Hugh.'

'Mike, is there a café on the premises, I'm starving and would like a sandwich and a coffee before I turn in for the night.'

Connell replied, 'We have staff on here twenty-four hours so come on follow me and we shall take care of your requirements.'

Chapter 9

The forty -two-ton HGV, left Eyemouth with the five women from the Caledonian Princess on board and headed south down the A1 for a couple of hours. The refrigerated lorry, now with a heavy aroma of fish, pulled off the road at junction 44 on the A1 (M), skipped round Leeds and entered a warehouse in a run-down industrial area of Bradford. The door of the secret compartment swung open and the girls got out to be faced with six men in black balaclavas who they guessed were Asian judging by their brown hands. The startled girls screamed as the men grabbed them, hand-cuffed them and put tape over their mouths.

The leader of the gang shouted out instructions, 'Akbar' he said pointing at Heidi and Alena Koresky, 'blindfold these two, then take them to the toilet before you put them in the car for the three hour drive up to Glasgow. Mohammed, when they return get the other three into the van and over to the Kasbah.' The 'Kasbah' was situated in a more affluent part of Bradford where the gang ran a brothel to satisfy the wealthier Asian community who appreciated Caucasian women

The three girls were shaking with fright and Greta was hysterical rolling about on the floor until Mohammed kicked her in the stomach shook her back on her feet then slapped her face with all his might, 'Shut up! Anymore from you and you'll be dumped in the river.'

Hearing this all went quiet. Akbar returned with Heidi and Alena and led them to a waiting BMW 4 x 4 and loaded them into the rear seats alongside Ismail, another member of the gang who covered their faces with black hoods. Akbar produced a syringe which he injected into both Heidi and Alena putting them both to sleep. Neither girl struggled as they were unable to see what was happening.

Ismail removed the hoods muttering to himself, 'That will keep them quiet until we reach Glasgow.'

The two vehicles left the warehouse leaving the HGV full of fish to continue its journey to Billingsgate Fish Market in time for it opening at 6 A.M.

When Heidi regained consciousness the next morning, she was in a room which was spinning round. Her vision settled down to reveal she was lying in a bed which was extremely smelly. The bedclothes looked like they had not been changed for weeks. Heidi tried to turn round but was unable to do so as she had been handcuffed to the bedposts. The walls were covered in a beige floral pattern and the only window was blanketed out by a pair of heavy curtains. The only other piece of furniture was an old wardrobe with one door open due to a brass handle being missing. Alena who was also handcuffed was lying on a bed at the other side of the room still comatose from the injection.

Twenty minutes later she regained consciousness and immediately started wailing with fear which set off someone running towards the room. It was Hassam who had appeared to oversee abductions the previous evening. He approached Alena placing his thumb and forefinger on her face and squeezing tight 'SHUT UP!!' Hassam cried 'You are not going anywhere soon my friends have plans for you girls. We have paid good money for to Captain Shertsov and you are both going to earn it. Before I put anything in my shop window, I like to try the goods first so which one of you want to try my body first.'

Both girls let out a scream. Hassam produced cotton swabs which he wedged into the girls' mouths. They continued to make muffled cries and gyrate their angry bodies as Hassam began to remove Heidi's trousers and pants whilst disposing of his trousers. She continued to protest until Hassam slapped her a couple of the time and produced a large knife which he held close to her face.

'Enough!', he screamed in her ear, 'or I'll use this.'

Heidi knew there was no point in resisting, so she calmed down and suffered the indignity of this horrible man's abuses as he entered her body. It was all over in a short time. Hassam left the room leaving Heidi sobbing uncontrollably unable to wipe away her tears due to the handcuffs which were still tying her to the bed .What was further degrading was that Alena had witnessed this abuse which sent her into a frenzy at the thought she could be Hassam's next victim. Later that evening she was - before both hostages were sedated in preparation for their journey to the next den of iniquity.

Monteith Mansion, set in thirty acres of wooded farmland, had been built as a twenty-bedroom Victorian country house in 1880 by a leading Glasgow shipbuilder, overlooking the River Clyde near Kilmacolm. With the downturn in the shipping industry the house had gone through several owners, each one pushing it further into a state of disrepair. The 'nouveau riche' in the shape of several successful Asian businessmen had acquired the property for the purpose of developing the mansion into an up-market retreat for the wealthy to indulge themselves. All the décor and furnishings were to the highest standards with a spa facility which would be the envy of the top London hotels. The members were international and by invitation only to this very exclusive secret club. Nothing was advertised on the internet, recruitment coming from large conferences held in Davos and Monaco. Visiting members flew into Glasgow Airport nearby for a few days of debauchery and were treated to mixed sex experiences as Monteith was not a male-only establishment.

The sound of running water awoke Alena and Heidi who must have thought they had died and gone to heaven. They were both clad in white, thick towelling dressing -gowns lying on soft beds surrounded by green marble walls and their handcuffs had been removed. An Asian lady in a white silk kimono heard them stir and entered the room.

'Welcome, I'm Sadie, glad you have regained consciousness, you have been asleep for over twenty-four hours. After your journey, your bodies needed a good de-tox, so my staff took the liberty of cleansing you both. You have not eaten for a couple of days so lunch will be here shortly.'

Heidi interrupted, 'Good I am bloody starving!'

The lady in white continued, 'In the next few days you will be instructed in the art of seduction and how to keep our clientele happy at all times. This side of the complex is private, but you girls will be entertaining in the main part of the building.'

Alena spoke up, 'What do you mean by entertaining? Do you think Heidi and I are prostitutes?'

A gentle smile broke over the Asian lady's face, 'Girls I have bad news for both of you. You have been sold to my colleagues by Captain Shertsov and have ended up in a far better place than many who are re-sold into squalid parts of Bradford.'

'That's ridiculous we paid good money to Shertsov for a safe passage to Britain.'

'Maybe so but my superiors have paid a lot more.'

Alena was horrified at the thought of becoming a white slave, 'I won't do it, tell your bosses they're not on, I want out of here.'

Sadie stared at the two girls and coldly replied, 'Ladies I would ask you to re-consider if you want to get out of here alive!'

Her remarks only made the Alena and Heidi feel more helpless and their bodies shook with fright at what might lie ahead.

Sadie continued, 'I would advise you about trying to escape. The property has the very latest security systems money can buy. You would not be the first person to try but no one has succeeded. Come to the window and I will show you something 'pointing out of the window she continued 'See the three willow trees saplings on the left, they were planted over the bodies of the last three who tried to abscond.'

Heidi looked at the surrounding area for the first time. The beautiful view looked out on pine tree clad slopes with some jagged hills in the distance. The dark clouds were low, and the rain was only being delayed by a fierce blustery wind.

Heidi enquired, 'Very nice Sadie, where are we exactly?'

'All that will be revealed in time. Lunch is more of a priority at the present time. Follow me.'

At the end of a long corridor, covered in a Paisley-patterned green Axminster carpet, there were tall double doors which led into a dining room containing three large round tables covered with white linen tablecloths which were each set for ten diners.

Pressing a bell on the wall Sadie ordered the girls to sit down. A door at the other side of the room opened and two oriental girls came in wheeling two large trolleys upon which there were all kinds of culinary delight. Heidi and Alena did not have to be asked twice to tuck in – gorging themselves with chicken legs, a variety of savoury sandwiches backed up by a selection of soft drinks.

After satisfying their hunger Alena and Heidi were taken back down the hall into a large room which Sadie explained was the wardrobe department. Here they had access to some beautiful clothes to suit every would-be seductress as that was what their high- rolling clientele expected to see. Everything was happening too quick for the captives and they wondered what would happen next in this bizarre world they were entering into and their apprehension was not lost on Sadie.

Sadie sat them down, 'Girls, we run an upmarket establishment here as you can see from the designer clothes our staff have access to, and the beauty treatments that are on offer. Your job is to satisfy our customers. You are not alone, there are ten other girls who will be performing similar roles, but you will only meet them in the evenings at the casino. Most of our guests come here to gamble so do not be surprised if on occasions you are ignored, and your services are not required. You will each have your own room which will be locked every night to prevent any thoughts of escape so just accept your new surroundings unless you want to be, as I have already said, a permanent feature on the landscape.'

Heidi started to get twitchy as the sedation she had been subjected to was wearing off and her natural craving for drugs was emerging. She began to scratch her arm, sending a signal to Sadie to continue her induction.

'Heidi, I notice you are showing signs of withdrawal symptoms, fear not we have ample stocks of whatever you may require. Our drugs will only be made available to you at certain times of the day which will usually be after lunch to give you ample time to recover before our guests arrive. You will never be given an excess dosage as all the girls must be presentable to our clients. The exception we would deem permissible would be if a client, in the privacy of his bedroom, asked you to join him in his drug habit. Next morning, we would check that you were fit for work.'

The induction course continued for the next three days which took the tension out of the captives and prepared them for what they might expect from a client – but now the talking was over and it was now time for the real thing. Sadie escorted Alena and Heidi down in the lift to the dressing room on the ground floor. Alena had put on a tight figure-hugging black dress with a plunging neckline to show off her figure whereas Heidi was wearing a blue silk miniskirt with a white, low-cut, transparent blouse which demonstrated her physical assets to the full. Their entrance into the casino made the other ten escorts stop in their tracks and commence clapping as a way of welcoming them into the fold and making them relax. A girl in a long red evening dress approached them carrying a tray containing two glasses with what appeared to be champagne.

'Welcome, I'm Jane Baird,' she said, 'help yourselves. It's' non-alcoholic. We are not allowed to drink on duty.'

The girls each picked a glass and turned to the others, 'Cheers' toasted Heidi, 'but to God knows what!'

The other girls rallied round the newcomers outlining where they should go to obtain whatever the guests requested. The main attraction for guests was the poker tables where the wealthy pitted their skills against each other contesting hands for unbelievable amounts of money. The girls fetched drinks most of the night and it was only once players had been dealt out or used up their budget for the evening that they turned their attention to their hostesses. Alena and Heidi became increasingly nervous as they watched the others laughing and cavorting with the members. A small, overweight, Italian gentlemen, wearing an expensive suit approached the girls and without introducing himself asked Heidi to accompany him to his room. On the way there he introduced himself as Luigi Veron.

He laughed, 'I''m from Milan and I work in the fashion industry, What's your name?'

'Heidi, Heidi Gorsky from Berlin.'

'Have you worked here long?'

''No, I only arrived a few days ago. This is the first time I have been in attendance.'

By now they had reached Luigi's room. He unlocked his door, and they entered a beautiful bedroom. The décor was made up of different shades of red giving the room a very warm feel to it. Two sofas were separated by a round polished wooden drinks table which was situated just beside a cocktail cabinet full of alcohol. Behind the furniture was a large four-poster bed covered in satin sheets. Off the bedroom there was a luxurious bathroom with a double bath with an annex off which led to a dressing room.

'Pour yourself a drink Heidi while I go to the man's room.'

Heidi found the palms of her hand sweating and was relieved to pour herself a glass of cool white wine. A few minutes later Luigi returned to the room wearing a two-tone blue silk dressing gown and poured himself a large malt whisky then took a seat on the largest sofa and invited Heidi to join him.

'Cheers dear, sit down and talk to me before we retire to my bed. I have not had a good time on the poker table this evening, I need a little comforting. Would you mind removing your clothes as we talk, I love looking at the female form.'

Heidi had been groomed by Sadie for this moment. She stood in front of the little Italian and slowly unzipped her dress and stepped out of before quietly taking off her underwear to the approval of Luigi who was showing signs of an erection under his silk dressing gown. Luigi stared at Heidi's physique and suggested they retire to his bed.

'Don't be frightened young lady I have rules when I visit bordellos. What I require from you is stroking not sexual intercourse. I am happily married to the same woman for forty years and I would not betray her by having sex with another partner. However, we have an arrangement whereby she allows me to stroke flesh. Shall we begin?'

They both lay down and Luigi ran his hands across Heidi's thighs and up to her breasts while she returned by digging her nails into his thighs before running her hand up to his genitals. For a small man Luigi was very well endowed and Heidi found herself getting excited at the prospect seeing the little man explode his seed over her hands. Simultaneously his touch inside her body made Heidi gasp with delight. After climax they both lay back on the bed and talked for an hour. Heidi was about to return to her room when Luigi took an envelope out of a bedside table: 'Here Heidi, this is for you. Thanks for a lovely night and if I come back here to play poker, I will ask for you.'

'Thanks Mr Veron', Heidi replied taking the envelope which she later discovered contained two hundred pounds, 'Goodnight.'

Next morning Heidi was excited with her gift from Luigi and rushed down to breakfast to find out if Alena was in possession of a similar gratuity, Heidi found her sitting in a chair staring into her coffee cup with a paper tissue in one hand.

'Good Morning Alena, how did you get on last night?'

Alena turned her head to display a large bruise on her other cheek, 'Heidi it was awful, a large American took me back to his room and made improper advances to me and I panicked when he started groping my body and trying to remove my clothes. I screamed the place down and one of the girls called Monica came to my rescue. She calmed me down then placated the American by taking my place. He was going to report me to the management, but Monica was able to change his mind by suggesting we have a threesome. Realising I was still frightened she took the lead and satisfied him, but not before his hands had been all over me. Heidi, I do not think I can carry on like this. I am going to try and negotiate my way out of here.'

Heidi took one serious log look at Alena before speaking, 'Alena, I'm not sure you realise the seriousness of the situation we find ourselves in. Right now, there is no way out of here and you saying a word to Sadie will put you in mortal danger. We must perform for whoever comes along and at times it will not be pretty but sooner or later an opportunity will arise for us to escape. In the meantime, we must remove any suspicions from all those around us what we are planning to do. Do you understand me?'

'Yes' Alena sobbed.

'Good, I hope we have some better nights from now on.'

The next few weeks were busy times at Monteith Mansions with a steady flow of gamblers flying in to test their skills against some of the best poker players in the world and enjoying the 'Apres poker' services. Alena had calmed down and had taken Heidi's advice on board. Each morning over breakfast they discussed who they had been with to gather information as to what was happening in the world. Just as Heidi had predicted their opportunity to abscond from Monteith Mansions arose. One night some Afghans visited the casino and after a boisterous night one of them asked Alena back to his room. Alena was happy to accompany him as he was younger than her usual client.

Once in his room he wasted no time in being passionate and getting his carnal requirements over very quickly.

'That was lovely, let me get a bottle of champagne from the mini-bar and we can relax and talk before I get my next urge to be satisfied. Sorry, bad manners, I haven't even asked you your name.'

'It's Alena, Alena Karensky from Kiev. Have you been with any Russian girls before?'

'No, the nearest I've come was an East German girl who I believe was washed up on a beach in Scotland. Great pity, Elke was a really beautiful girl.'

'How did she get there? Have the police arrested anybody for her murder?

'To answer your first question, that's for me to know and you not to concern yourself about. As far as I know the police have not arrested anyone. Oh, by the way my name is Mohammed al-Basiri.

Next morning Heidi and Alena met for their usual briefings. Heidi went first but had nothing wildly exciting to report.

It was Alena's turn and she opened up with, 'Well last night I was in bed with a young Afghan whose company I enjoyed until we relaxed after the first of his three sessions. Whilst we were having a bottle of champagne during 'the interval' I asked him about other women he had bedded and whether there were any Russians amongst them? He said the nearest he had come recently was an East German girl called Elke whose body had been washed up on a beach in Scotland. The police have so far not been able to solve her murder.'

'Alena, what was this guy's name?'

'He called himself Mohammed al-Basiri.'

Heidi turned white and had to rush across the hall to be sick in the toilets. Alena got a fright and rushed after her to see what was wrong. She found Heidi on her knees vomiting into a toilet bowl. Some of the sick had come down her nose and Alena relieved her by getting paper tissues and a drink of water.

'Heidi are you all right?'

Heidi slowly got to her feet and leaned against the doorway for support. With tears coming down her cheeks she muffled an answer, 'I...I think the girl he was talking about was Svetlana Gorsky.'

'What !!' screamed Alena, 'How do you think that? We left her on the 'Koidutaht' getting friendly with Captain Shertsov!'

'Lana's real name is Elke Kohl and she told me when we travelled up to Estonia that she had taken to soliciting in some of the top hotels in Leipzig. On several occasions she met up with a young Afghan drug dealer whose name was Mohammed al-Basiri.'

'Why did she travel using a false name?' asked Alena.

'I haven't a clue.' Heidi lied, 'but this could be the chance we need to take get out of this place.'

'How?'

A more composed Heidi answered, 'Next time you are in bed with a client watch where he lays down his phone. When he goes to the toilet text to '999', 'I have info on Elke Kohl.' If we both do it the police will trace the call and be on to this place immediately.'

'Would it not be better to phone?'

'Possibly but a lot riskier, and if we're caught it will be a shallow grave for the both of us.'

Chapter 10

'Our man has just walked in.' confirmed Bob Salkeld to his fellow undercover cop Linda McTiernan.

Her eyes focused on Admiral Pearson Arbuthnott who they had come to survey at the casino in the heart of Leith's docklands. The Admiral went straight to the cashier placed a bundle of notes in front of her which she exchanged for gambling chips in a little plastic container with the casino's logo on the side. Without any hesitation the naval commander made his way to the blackjack table. The detectives gave him time to settle in as they played some roulette and slot machines where Linda managed to win the jackpot of one hundred pounds which drew the congratulations of all the gamblers nearby. Rather than use local Edinburgh police officers who might be recognised by the local underworld who tended to frequent casinos, the undercover officers had been sent over to Edinburgh from the Fife constabulary to report on Admiral Arbuthnott.

For the next few hours Bob and Linda observed the fortunes of Pearson Arbuthnott who was having a good night which was just as well since he was betting some very serious money and had things gone the wrong way he would have lost considerably. This was not lost on Linda who remarked, 'The Admiral must have a good pension or inherited wealth to be prepared to gamble for these stakes.'

'Or he is a compulsive gambler,' suggested Salkeld, 'look he's taking a break. Let's follow him to the bar and see if he mixes with anyone.'

Pearson Arbuthnott ordered at the bar, 'A nip and a half-pint please and barmaid have one for yourself. I am having an exceptionally good night.'

'In that case Admiral you can get one for me and my friend.' said a voice from behind.

Pearson spun round and saw somebody he had not seen for several weeks. It was Geordie McNab accompanied by his chief minder 'Maniac' McLagan.

'Oh Geordie, I didn't see you there, tell this young lady what you fancy, and we could have a chat.'

After taking their drinks, the trio retired to a quiet corner of the bar.

'How are things in the nautical world Admiral?', asked McNab, 'still keeping her Majesty's fishing fleet safe and in top order.'

'How about yourself?'

'The scrap metal business has been going well and my other interests are giving me a good return, thanks to yourself. That is what I wanted to talk to you about. I have had an offer to import more produce from Afghanistan using a fishing trawler that sails out of Peterhead. If I named the boat would you be able to remove it from your records like we do with the 'Caledonian Princess?'

Admiral Arbuthnott shook his head before answering quietly, 'No, definitely not, I should never have entered into our last arrangement which I now want to buy my way out of.'

McNab looked around him before replying, 'No chance Admiral I'm holding all the aces as far as you're concerned. One word from me to the Royal Navy and you can probably kiss goodbye to your pension. I was watching you playing roulette and you have upped the betting stakes so the commission I pay you seems to be agreeing with you. I will give you a week to think about it. I'm doubling your money. If not your current source of income will be terminated. Oh, by the way. Forget about going to the cops if you want to avoid a visit from Maniac McLagan here.'

The bodyguard put on a menacing smile.

The Admiral stood up, gulped down half of his drink and threw the remnants of it into McNab's face and shouted 'Go away McNab!! Anymore from you and I'll be going in Fettes to see the Chief Constable!' and stormed off. Arbuthnott headed straight back to the tables in a rage, which seemed to affect his judgement resulting in him getting more desperate and raising his stakes in the hope of recovering his losses. His bad luck made him drink excessively and become more aggressive resulting in the croupier calling the General manager to the table.

'Admiral Arbuthnott, I think it is time we got you a taxi.'

'Get your hands off me Mr. Sneddon. I'm one of your best customers.'

Smiling at the other punters round the table he replied, 'Unfortunately not tonight. Come with me Admiral.' he concluded taking his arm and signalling one of the bouncers to assist him.

'Where shall I tell the taxi to drop you off?'

'1 Doune Place, in the New Town.' Pearson slurred

Unfortunately, Linda and Bob were too busy gambling Linda's new acquired winnings to witness the incident with Geordie McNab but did see the Admiral heading for the exit.

'Linda it looks like Admiral Arbuthnott is leaving the premises, but not of his own free will, so we can call it a night.'

'Suits me Bob, I have managed to get some photos on my mobile which we can check out in the office tomorrow and see if anybody recognises anyone of note.'

The whole bar had looked in McNab's direction as he was drying himself with a handkerchief after Admiral Arbuthnott left. He was having difficulty containing his rage. Smiling to hide his embarrassment McNab coldly instructed his bodyguard, 'Maniac, you can decide how you do it, but the Admiral is about to go off on his farewell voyage!'

Chapter 11

D.C.I. Grant McKirdy was looking over the weekend's criminal activities when there was a knock on his door and Bob Salkeld entered accompanied by Linda McTiernan. Grant put what he was reading into a file and gave the two Fife detectives his full attention.

'Well, how did it go last night? Did Admiral Arbuthnott show up?

'Yes Sir, he had a long night at the tables. Initially he seemed to be in a good mood and was winning quite a bit of money. After taking a break at the bar he returned to the roulette table and his luck deserted him. In his attempt to cover his losses he increased his stakes further to no avail which made him consume excessive amounts of whisky that changed his personality considerably. He became abusive towards the croupier, who called the manager Mr Sneddon. He arrived within a few minutes and escorted the drunk admiral off the premises.'

'Sounds like the actions of a desperate man. Tell me was the casino busy?'

It was Linda who answered, 'Yes quite busy Sir. On a personal front I won a hundred pounds on a slot machine.'

'Good for you. I take it you will be donating your prize to a police charity', the D.C.I. replied. As Linda's face fell, he added, 'Only joking!'

Linda saw the joke and got back to business, 'I managed to take some photos on my mobile as I pretended to make phone calls. Do you want to see them?'

'Certainly. Well done Linda. Now let me see if any of our local mafia are money laundering their ill-gotten gains.'

Linda passed over the phone and McKirdy examined the pictures. On slide three he let out a gasp: 'Geordie McNab and his bodyguard Alistair 'Maniac' McLagan having a night out on the town! McNab is a hood who fronts himself as a local scrap metal dealer, but we have been watching him closely as we suspect him to be behind a major drug ring. I was not aware he is a gambler, but I will get D.S. Lomax to confirm with the manager how often he frequents the casino. Thanks for coming over the Forth Bridge to assist us. Before you go Linda, can you email your photos to Fettes. We are currently involved in trying to solve the murder of the young lady found on Joppa Rocks a few weeks ago. As you know we gather all sorts of information, relevant and otherwise. As one of my bosses said to me when I first started, 'gathering evidence is like having a packet of twenty fags, the last one you smoke gives you the most satisfaction – and in our game the last piece of evidence uncovered usually leads to a conviction.'

After their departure McKirdy sent for Lomax, 'Ian, you know, DC's Salkeld and McTiernan carried out surveillance on Admiral Arbuthnott down in the casino at Leith. McTiernan cleverly took photographs of the clientele and it showed showed Geordie McNab and his bodyguard in attendance. Get on to the manager and ask him how often McNab is at the casino – and the same thing goes for Admiral Pearson Arbuthnott!

Ian Lomax made the call to Sneddon at the Royal Casino, 'Hello Mr. Sneddon, Detective Sergeant Ian Lomax here. We are carrying out a money laundering exercise and we had a couple of undercover officers surveying the casino last night.'

'Really!' replied Sneddon in a concerned tone, 'Do you not think you should have warned me they were coming.'

'Well if we had they wouldn't have been undercover!' exclaimed Lomas, 'Don't worry yourself Mr Sneddon, we carry out these exercises all the time. What I wanted to discuss with you is Geordie McNab who our officers reported being in the casino last night. Talking off the record,

McNab is well known to us and we wondered how regularly he comes to the Royal Casino?'

Sneddon attempted to protest, 'Sergeant Lomax, that is confidential information which we never release.'

'Sir can I remind you who you're speaking to. Withholding information from the police is a serious offence. We could, of course, follow up a tip-off about criminal behaviour being carried out at the Royal Casino and raid the premises. Now publicity of that nature is not good for business.'

Sneddon frowned, 'Mr. McNab is a regular in the casino, usually at the weekends. He is someone who keeps to himself and never causes any problems.'

'Thank you. Mr. Sneddon, that is extremely useful. Oh, before you go our officers reported you had to forcefully remove a client form the premises last night who we believe was Admiral Arbuthnott. Why was this?'

The manager was taken aback at what he just heard and hesitated before answering,

'Your officers are very observant. I'm afraid the Admiral had too much to drink brought on by a bad night at the tables.'

'Has this happened before?'

'I have to admit it has. The Admiral has a gambling problem. I had to speak to him several weeks ago about his account which had become considerably overdrawn.'

'How much is considerable Mr Sneddon?'

'Over ten thousand pounds.' Sneddon lied, not wanting to mention the figure of fifty thousand or Geordie McNab's involvement.

'Wow!' exclaimed Lomas, 'that is serious. Did you get your money?'

'Yes, the Admiral cleared it. He comes from a wealthy family so presumably they came to his rescue.'

'Must be good to have rich relatives Mr. Sneddon ', lamented Lomax, 'it never happened to me, thanks for your help. Goodbye.'

Lomax went next door to report his conversation to his boss, 'Grant, the manager at the Royal Casino confirmed that this is a regular haunt for McNab. He also mentioned the Admiral Arbuthnott is a compulsive gambler who notched up a five-figure debt with the casino which was cleared by a wealthy relative. Last night he made a big loss and became obnoxious to the staff and was escorted off the premises. Sneddon, the manager made apologies for him by saying the Admiral had too much to drink.

Pearson awoke with a thumping headache and poured himself a large whisky. He was still wearing the same clothes he had when falling out the taxi last night. His hands were shaking when he thought about his behaviour in throwing a drink over Geordie McNab who he knew would seek revenge. Should he go to the police? No –not unless he wanted to go to jail. The phone rang and Pearson grabbed it hoping to get his aggression out on some poor call centre cold-caller.

'What do you want?', he bellowed down the phone.

A deep voice answered, 'Sore head this morning Admiral, 'Maniac' McLagan here - Geordie McNab's friend. I thought we might meet up to try and reconcile our differences after last night's contretemps.'

'Morning Mr McLagan, I must apologise for my action, but I stick by what I said. I will not have anything further to do with Geordie McNab.'

'I have to say Admiral that is not a very advisable line to adopt!'

The old mariner reacted angrily, 'Are you threatening me?'

'Yes, you could say that. Watch yourself crossing the road there are a lot of reckless drivers about, don't go into any high buildings with balconies and watch what your drinking – you never know it may be laced with some toxic substance which may not agree with you!'

'You bastard!' screamed the Admiral and slammed the phone down.

'On the other end of the line, 'Maniac' smiled to himself, 'Now the fun begins.'

For the next two weeks Pearson Arbuthnott was bombarded with life threatening incidents. The first time he noticed someone shadowing him, was when he came out his house crossed Gloucester Place and descended the steps into Stockbridge. Two youths followed him closely and one of them said out loud, 'I suppose we could kick the old bugger down the stairs.' They laughed and ran past, disappearing into the Xmas shoppers leaving the Admiral shaking with fear. Another day Admiral Arbuthnott stepped out of his office at lunchtime to get a sandwich at Ocean Terminal which meant crossing a road. He looked both ways before starting to cross but did not allow for a black sports car travelling towards the roundabout at speed then going round it anti-clockwise just missing him. Constant phone calls from 'Maniac' describing how he was going to harm Pearson and reminding him to watch what he was drinking at the casino as it was easy to spike his drinks. The harassment started to affect Pearson's concentration at the tables and his liability to the Royal Casino increased back to the previous levels, pre McNab's assistance.

All this was turning the Admiral into a nervous wreck and he couldn't see how he was going get out of his current predicament: 'If I go to the police and tell them about doctoring the marine data I will be sent to prison; If I don't settle my gambling debts I will be sued and perhaps made bankrupt and then my house, which is mortgaged to the hilt would be re-possessed.; I am up to my neck in credit card debt struggling to pay the interest on my balance every month; If I continue to sit here in fear McNab or that horrible man McLagan will pay me a visit which will leave me in considerable pain, nursing some broken bones. The whole things a mess, I don't know what my ex-wife would think, and my Admiralty colleagues would disown me. I have no choice I shall just have to do the honourable thing.'

'The Honourable Thing' was to take his loaded shotgun out of the cupboard under the stairs, place it under his chin, and blow his head off!!

The blast from the firearm shattered the silence in the New Town and the residents of Doune Place appeared from behind the long drapes which are familiar to the Georgian townhouses of one of Edinburgh's most expensive areas. Archie Humbert, the solicitor who lived above the headless retired naval officer, phoned the police and withing minutes the area was crawling with police cars and an armed response unit. A door to door search ensued and when there was no response from Admiral Arbuthnott, the order was given to break down the thick wooden door behind which was the blood- splattered remains of Admiral Pearson Arbuthnott!

'Congratulations 'Maniac'. My ferret in Fettes just tipped me off that the bold Admiral has sailed off to the roulette table in the sky!'

A shocked Maniac replied, 'Nothing to do with me, boss. I never touched him honest, I only threatened him.'

'I know', agreed McNab, 'he committed suicide by blowing his head off. All I can say is your strategy has worked, no chance of him shopping us to the cops. Goodnight, see you tomorrow.'

McNab was grateful he had the services of Maniac McLagan which made him feel a lot more secure.

Alistair 'Maniac' McLagan was born in Craigmillar on the east side of city, a rough area where there was often street fighting after the pubs closed. School did not suit his life-style which often left him up on burglary charges and spending his school holidays in a young offender's institute.

 It was at one spell in St. Joseph's Borstal in Haddington that one of his teachers, Mr Gibb, suggested he join the army. Military life suited Alistair as he enjoyed the physical combat where he could make use of his considerable strength. His regiment, the Royal Scots were sent to Iraq during the First Iraqi War. It was here that he earned his nickname 'Maniac' by fearlessly attacking and capturing Iraqi strongholds against the odds risking his own life and ending the lives of others, on several occasions.

His dark side led to him threatening some other members of his platoon and extorting money from them which was re-ported to the regiment's High Command. Maniac's indis-cretions led to him being court-martialled out of the army and, back into civvy street. With his record, seeking em-ployment proved difficult and the only work available to him was to sign on as a labourer at McNab's Scrap Metals. Geordie McNab took time to study Maniac's CV and rec-ognised how he could use him more productively chasing up bad payers in his ever-expanding drug dealership busi-ness.

Domestically McLagan had settled down and lived quietly in a respectable area of the city with his wife and two kids.

Chapter 12

'Grant McKirdy, who's speaking?' asked the sleepy detective eyeing his alarm clock reading 3.15 a.m.

'It's Ian sir, one of my friends who is on nightshift at Fettes has just rung me to say that Admiral Pearson Arbuthnott has committed suicide at his house in the New Town.'

'How?' a shotgun under his chin and pulled both barrels.'

'Christ, what would drive a respected member of society to do such a thing. Look thanks for letting me know, there is not much we can do about it tonight, as the forensics will be all over it just now. Pick me up at the house at eight thirty and we will go straight to the suicide scene. Thanks once again for letting me know Ian, I'll get back to sleep.'

Sleep didn't happen and McKirdy spent hours trying to work out why Pearson Arbuthnott had topped himself.

D.S. Lomax and D.C. Luxton pulled the unmarked police car up outside their boss's smart sandstone villa in Belgrave Road, Corstorphine at 8.30 as instructed.

'Nice house, you won't get that property on a Chief Detective Inspector's salary.', commented Avril.

'No, the boss married into money which helps.'

Grant McKirdy joined them and was ready and raring to make the short journey to the New Town. They managed to find a parking space in India Street and walked round the corner into Doune Place where there was already a major police presence. The three detectives made their way into the ground floor flat which was beautifully furnished. By New Town standards it was a small two- bedroom apartment very suitable for someone without a family. The police officer at the entrance to the building issued them all with light blue boiler suits before they were allowed to enter the lounge which still contained the Admiral's body.

Pathologist John Mason was surprised to see a deputation from the murder squad, 'Morning Grant, what brings you here? Suicides are not usually on your radar.'

'Morning John, we recently interviewed Admiral Arbuthnott when we were carrying out investigations ino the Joppa Rocks case. He also featured a couple of weeks ago when two of our officers were surveying a local gangster down at the Royal Casino.'

The Admiral's decapitated body had been thrown out of his chair by the force of the blast from the shotgun and was now crumpled on the floor soaking in a large pool of blood. His mutilated skull lay covered in a white linen cloth a few feet away.

Dr Mason reacted, 'That's interesting Grant. I haven't discovered anything untoward here. It looks like the subject placed the shotgun under his chin and fired off both barrels which sent his head landing over there. I met his neighbour from upstairs, Mr. Humber, who told me he knew the deceased had possessed a shotgun for years. He used to go shooting but had not been doing so recently.'

'Okay we'll have a look around and try and find some reasoning for the Admiral's action. Avril, see if you can find any telephones and get all the recent calls checked out. Ian, you and I will start going through all the drawers and cupboards and see what that throws up.'

The detectives went about their assigned tasks for the next three hours then took a break for coffee and sandwiches at the Christopher North Hotel. The hotel lounge was quiet which was not unusual for late mornings and they managed to find a quiet corner to discuss their progress. They delayed their formal conversation until the coffee and sandwiches had been served.

'Right Avril, what have you uncovered?'

'Well Sir, the Admiral Pearson had both a mobile and a landline. Both have been well used recently and I have checked out some of the numbers. The most common outgoing call was to Bradshaw the Bookie in Frederick Street where he presumably had an account for his sports gambling. His mobile phone on the other hand featured many incoming calls, which always took place, day, or night. I tried calling the numbers back but most of them just rang out or it was a dead telephone line.'

Grant scratched his chin before replying to what he had just heard, 'Avril look into the Admiral's background and produce a character dossier of the man. His name is quite a mouthful so let's call him 'A.P.A.' in future. Somebody has been bothering him and hopefully we'll know who before too long.'

'Ian, how did you get on?'

'I checked out his bureau. Packed full of unpaid bills for everything from rates to, would you believe, the local paper shop who he hasn't paid for two months. A.P.A.'s bank statements were even more interesting; he's twice re-mortgaged this place by way of an equity release but already he's slipped two months behind on his re-financing repayments. He has two credit cards, Visa and Mastercard both of which are showing balances at their credit limits with only the interest portion of them being serviced every month. The man was a financial disaster waiting to happen and I think what I have just told you was possibly responsible for his death.'

'A sad situation but one that does not explain the high level of phone calls Avril was telling us about. It makes me think that he might also be owing money elsewhere and he was being leaned on. I'd a good look through his wardrobes which revealed that the Admiral was a bit of a Beau Brummel buying lots of quality clothes and shoes which may account for part his high credit card balances. I wonder if he had any outstanding balances at the Royal Casino, Ian give your friend Mr. Sneddon a call and check it out.'

Later that afternoon once the casino was open for business D.S. Lomax phoned John Sneddon, 'Good afternoon Mr Sneddon, D.S. Lomax here. I am phoning to let you know Admiral Pearson Arbuthnot committed suicide sometime during the night by putting a shotgun to his head.'

'Good God!! that's horrible. I can't believe it, such a nice guy when he was sober. How would he get depressed enough to do that? Did he leave a note saying why he has shot himself?'

'No. We've recovered evidence that he was seriously in debt which may have pushed him over the edge. Which leads me to ask if you can tell me what is the state of his account with the Royal Casino?

'Give me a minute Mr. Lomax while I look it up.

Lomax heard Sneddon click on to his computer and fifteen seconds later come up with an answer.

'The current balance on the account is £11,330, I was going to talk to him about it, but he has not been in the Casino for over a week. Looks like I will have to write this one off.'

'You said last time his rich relatives settled the bill. Do you not think they would do it again?

Sneddon laughed, 'Would you be responsible for a dead man's debts when you didn't have to Sergeant Lomax?'

'No, I wouldn't. Thanks for your help.'

Andrew Turner arrived for work as usual but sensed that the office was quieter than normal. Two ladies in the admin staff were standing holding a conversation with paper handkerchiefs in their hands.

'What's up this morning?' Andrew enquired.

'Oh Andrew, a terrible thing has happened, Admiral Arbuthnot has killed himself.'

'Killed himself, are you sure?'

'Yes, the police are in seeing Mr. Jeffries (the Deputy Chairman) now. I think they are trying to establish if he was under any pressure at work.'

Andrew thought to himself 'Well that would be the first time. The Admiral only got this job on who he did know, rather than what he did know. Now I wonder what will happen to my extra money he gave me every month. However, it means no more dodgy deals although my wife might not agree when I tell her there is a cut in the housekeeping. I could change my records back to include the 'Caledonian Princess' or maybe I should try and find out who the Admiral was dealing with and increase my share of the spoils.'

Chapter 13

Two weeks after deciding on their course of action to escape from Monteith Mansion the opportunity arose for Heidi and Alena to get a message to the outside world.

A party of rich South Afrikaans farmers had flown into Scotland on a shooting trip and their host Sir Fraser Urquhart had arranged an overnight stay at the Mansion. They were a well-mannered party who loved a drink and soon they were all quite drunk and looking for some female company.

Heidi was picked out by Morne Le Grange, an exceptionally large red-faced individual in his early fifties who looked her up and down as though he was at a cattle sale before taking her arm and heading for the bedrooms. Alena was approached by a younger oily skinned weaselly chap who smiled, clicked his heels, bowed and politely introducing himself as Pete Erasmus then asked the way to her room. Both the girls gave their clients an outstanding performance of carnal varieties which worked the visitors into submission. Before doing so they located the gentlemen's mobiles by feeling their clothes and laying them at the side of the bed.

Pete Erasmus was the first to submit to exhaustion and snort his way into a deep sleep. Alena quickly took his phone into the bathroom, punched '999' into the mobile and texted 'Help me! I have info on Lana Gorsky.' She replaced the phone on the bedside table climbed back into bed and gently stroked her client to extend his slumbers.

 Heidi had taken on a bigger challenge than she imagined. Morne Le Grange was turning out to be a bull of a man who had the energy of an elephant. Heidi was beginning to fear she was going to miss the opportunity to get her message out. Her chance arose when drink took its toll and the big

Afrikaner made his way to the toilet. Heidi grabbed the mobile and took it under the covers, dialled '999' and a voice answered.

'Emergency services what do you require? Police Ambulance or Fire Brigade.'

'Police. I must be quick. Help me please I can give you information on Elke Kohl's murder.'

Heidi heard the toilet flush and quickly tried to restore the mobile to its rightful place. In her rush the mobile slid off the bedroom table and landed on the floor, smashing the casing against the tiled floor. Morne heard the crash and came rushing out of the bathroom.

'What has happened to my phone?' he roared, picking the broken mobile up off the floor.

'I'm sorry sir, I was trying to see the time and the phone slipped out of my hand.'

'Well it's a bloody expensive slip, that mobile cost me eight thousand Rand (£500) so I shall be looking for the management to deduct it from my bill. Now c'mon let's get back to what I'm here for.'

Nervously Heidi resumed her duties, frightened by the prospect of Le Grange reporting his damaged phone to Sadie, who would in turn speak to the owners. If anyone were to look closely at the 'Most Recent Calls' her punishment would be severe and possibly terminal. Her only hope was that the operator at Emergency Services picked up the brief message.

Two hours later Heidi returned to her room passing Alena on the way who merely nodded to her which was confirmation she had also dialled the police. Feeling exhausted and dirty she ran a shower which she had just stepped into when there was a knock at the door and Sadie strode in. Heidi grabbed a towel and wrapped it around her body.

Sadie wasted no time in getting to the point of her visit, 'We have received a complaint from Mr Le Grange who has reported you smashed his mobile phone.'

'Sadie, I'm sorry it was an accident. Mr Le Grange had gone to the toilet and I stretched over to see the time and knocked over the mobile.'

'You are not supposed to digress from what you are being paid for. We shall have to compensate Mr Le Grange by refunding his bill, but the cost will be borne by you out of the tips I know you have been receiving from satisfied customers. Any repeat of tonight's accident could have a bearing on your long-term future at Monteith Mansion.' Moving closer she gently rubbed Heidi's bare shoulder 'If on the other hand I could give you protection from harm.' she added shifting her hand down to Heidi's left breast and removing her towel which fell to the floor.

'Just enjoy me Sadie, but let it be our little secret. Why not come into the shower with me? Or shall we save it for another night.'

Sadie smiled, 'I'm busy tonight but will be back later in the week for a full session Heidi.' Sadie broke away but could not resist having a long French kiss with her new partner.

After she left Heidi steadied herself from fainting at the thought of how tonight could have gone so horribly wrong. Now that she had Sadie clamouring for her body, she felt she had hopefully bought sufficient time to get an answer to their '999' calls.

The two emergency calls had been received in the early hours of the Tuesday morning and the operators were confused at getting two calls from different mobiles, one texted and the other vocal. Both were reporting to have information on murders that on the surface were two entirely different victims – Lana Gorsky and Elke Kohl. The calls were forwarded separately to the murder squad for the attention of D.C.I. Grant McKirdy.

Next morning D.C.I. McKirdy arrived at the office switched on his computer and went to the vending machine for a coffee. He had fifteen emails in his in-box but could not believe what he was seeing under the headings 'Lana Gortsky' and 'Elke Kohl.'

Opening the first one, he let out a triumphant scream, 'You beauty!! The bloody breakthrough we have been looking for! Ian, Avril get your butts through here!'

The two officers knew that tone and rushed through to the D.C.I.'s office and arrived as his printer was running off copies of the Emergency Services Reports.

'Look what was received a few hours ago. Two messages first one a text stating, 'Help me. I have info on Lana Gorsky', the second call was from a lady claiming to have information on Elke Kohl. I will let you hear it. He played the message from Heidi, 'Police. I will be quick. Help me please, I can give you information on Elke Kohl's murder.'

Everyone listened intently, Lomax suggested, 'Foreign accent, could be Scandinavian.'

'German would be my bet.', Luxton guessed.

'We'll leave the accents to our linguistic department. I'm more interested in where the calls were made from? and why they arrived here within hours of each other?'

'Do you think it's someone's idea of a sick joke? asked Avril.

'No Avril, I can't see how someone would use two phones to name two ladies who hardly anyone outside this building knows anything about.' answered Grant.

The observant Lomas chipped in, 'Have you noticed the mobile numbers on both these messages they start with '++27' which is not in the UK where all our numbers begin

++44. Avril hand me that telephone directory on your desk and I will find out what ++27 corresponds to.'

The other two looked on as D.S. Lomax leafed his way through the telephone directory before stating, 'Here it is ++27 is South Africa and the 51 in brackets refers to Bloemfontein in the Orange Free State.'

A disappointed McKirdy muttered 'Oh no, how the hell do two callers in South Africa get mixed up with a murder committed somewhere between Leipzig and Joppa?'

Ian didn't answer as he was still reading the phone book, 'Sir there is an asterisk next to the dialling code for South Africa which states that mobile phone communications do not stretch internationally as far as the UK. Anyone visiting the U.K. is advised to buy a sim card on arrival.'

 Now we are getting somewhere. Avril dial the number for the phone which left the verbal message and see if they respond.

Avril did as she was instructed and held the phone away from her ear so the others could hear the response but there was none forthcoming as the device was out of order.

'Try the other one.' a frustrated McKirdy ordered.

This time it did ring for a long period until a voice answered, 'Sorry there is no one here to answer your call at present. If you would like to leave your name and telephone number, we will get back to you as soon as possible.'

Covering the mouthpiece Avril waited for the D.C.I.'s next command.

'Tell him you have an urgent message regarding travel arrangements back to South Africa.'

After she had passed on the message McKirdy addressed the others, 'Ian see if you can find out anything about these numbers from the telephone providers and Avril you keep trying that number every twenty minutes.'

The phone D.C. Luxton was trying to connect to was turned off in Pete Erasmus' pocket as he tried to make up for lost sleep on the bus taking him deer shooting in Perthshire in the Trossachs of Scotland.

D.S. Lomax had contacted all the South African mobile phone suppliers, who quickly identified the owners of the mobiles and their addresses. Ian then made calls to the each of their houses.

Mrs Erasmus treated his call with caution until Ian identified himself and explained the unusual nature of the call which had been reported into police headquarters in Edinburgh. Pete's wife confirmed that he and six others had gone on a shooting trip to Scotland but did not know who was hosting it. Ian thanked her for the information and asked her to get Mr Erasmus to phone him as soon as possible. Next it was contact with Morne Le Grange's family which took longer as Le Grange was a widower and it was several hours before he called Ian back.

'Mr Lomax, Hennie Le Grange here, I'm Morne's son, you left a message on our answerphone to call you. How can I help?'

'Thanks for phoning back, I am Detective Sergeant Ian Lomax of Police Scotland. During last night we received a text sent from your father's phone from someone claiming to have information on a murder we are investigating.'

'What! Dad phoned me a short time ago to check how things were going on the farm, but he didn't mention anything about a text or losing his phone.'

The D.S. did some thinking on his feet, 'Tell me Hennie, did your dad call you on your mobile?'

'Ya'

'Could you go into your recent calls and confirm that call was made from his own phone.', Ian waited as Hennie checked his mobile's data.

116

'Sir, the last call was not from Dad's number. It was listed as 05190 894333 which I know belongs to another farmer called Pete Erasmus.'

'Hennie, you just beat me to it, that number checks out with our information on Mr Erasmus.'

'Sir are they in some sort of trouble?'

'At this stage we don't know anything but if your dad phones again get him to call me immediately on this number. Hennie do you know who is hosting the shoot?'

'Yes Mr. Lomax, it is Sir Fraser Urquhart who has an estate in Perthshire. I will certainly get my dad to phone you if he calls. Goodbye.'

Grant McKirdy came up to Lomax's desk, 'How's it progressing Ian?'

'Pretty good Sir, I phoned both the numbers. Pete Erasmus' wife wasn't able to give me much information but will get him to phone us. My second call was more fruitful, I spoke to Hennie Le Grange who told me his father is on a shooting trip being hosted by Sir Fraser Urquhart somewhere in the Scottish Highlands. His dad had phoned him earlier, so I asked him to verify the number it was received from and it turned out to be Pete Erasmus mobile.'

'Good work Ian. Get a telephone number for Sir Fraser Urquhart plus any data we have on him and I will call him.'

Half an hour later the three Edinburgh Murder Squad investigators got together and studied the data Records had produced. Sir Fraser Urquhart was listed as being a Highland landlord with an estate stretching thousands of acres. The land had been handed down through the generations, having been given to the Urquhart family who contributed to the defeat of Bonnie Prince Charlie's Jacobean army in 1745. The address was listed as Urquhart House, near Auchterarder.

The D.I. made a call to the landlord's residence, which was answered promptly in an upper-class accent by Morag

Mackinnon, Urquhart's property manager, 'Good day, Urquhart house, Morag Mackinnon speaking, how can I help?'

'Morning, this is Detective Chief Inspector Grant McKirdy of Police Scotland speaking, can I speak to Sir Fraser Urquhart?'

'No, I'm afraid Sir Fraser has taken a group of South African tourists out stalking deer this morning.'

'Will I be able to get him on his mobile?'

'No D.C.I. McKirdy, mobile phones are not allowed on the shoot as they can affect the hunt if their ringtone goes off unexpectedly.'

McKirdy was beginning to get annoyed by Ms Mackinnon's condescending attitude, 'Well when he makes contact get him to phone me immediately, as it most important I speak to two members of his shooting party! In the meantime, my colleagues and I will make our way up to Urquhart House as I want to carry out interviews with the respected gentlemen today.'

Ms Mackinnon was beginning to realise the seriousness of the call and took a more apologetic tone, 'Sir I will tell Sir Fraser as soon as he phones but as that might not be for several hours I will send one of the gillies out in a Range Rover in the interim to find him and relay your message.'

'Thank you, Ms Mackinnon, I look forward to meeting you later.'

McKirdy put down the phone and turned to his staff, 'You heard what I said to Ms Mackinnon so get yourselves ready for a trip up to Perthshire. Even without putting the 'Blues' on we should be able to get there in under two hours. This is potentially the biggest breakthrough we have had in months, so I want to milk it as soon as possible. Right it is one-thirty now, I suggest we be ready to leave at two o'clock. Hopefully one of the gillies will have traced the hunt by the time we get there, or we will have a wait on our hands.

Chapter 14

D.S. Lomax drove the Audi 6 out of Edinburgh and on to the M9 towards Stirling switching to the A91 at Dunblane before coming off at Auchterarder and following a country road for ten miles. On the way up D.C.I. McKirdy received a call.

'Hello', said a voice in a deep polished public-school accent, 'am I speaking to D.C.I. McKirdy?'

'Yes, McKirdy speaking.'

'Sir Fraser Urquhart here. Morag got a message to me saying you are coming up to see two of our guests. Can I ask their names?'

'Morne Le Grange and Pete Erasmus.'

'Can we delay this a while. The two gentlemen in question are still out on the moor and I would not like to terminate their enjoyment.'

McKirdy sighed before replying, 'Sir Fraser I'm sorry to be a spoil sport but we require their assistance in a murder enquiry.'

'Oh, I see. Leave it to me then and I will bring them back to the house. See you when you arrive.'

Ian Lomax steered the car between the metal gates of Urquhart House on to a long driveway leading up to a large stone property which had two turrets at either end. Ian parked the car and by the time they got out of it they were met by a rounded middle-aged lady with grey hair tied in a bun. She was wearing an Urquhart tartan skirt topped by a brown crew-neck jumper over a white blouse.

She held out her hand, 'Morag Mackinnon welcome to Urquhart House.'

McKirdy shook her hand and introduced Ian and Avril.

'Follow me', said Morag, 'and I'll get some coffee organised. Sir Fraser phoned a few minutes ago to say he is about ten minutes away.'

The Murder squad entered the house and gazed in awe at the large baronial hall with the walls filled with Highlanders' shields, (known as targes),pikes, claymores, flintlock pistols and helmets. They were shown into a huge wood panelled drawing-room which had a large white marble fireplace at one end, and which contained a couple of large sofas, plus several well-cushioned armchairs.

True to his word ten minutes later Sir Fraser skidded his green Range Rover to a halt and jumped out with the two Boer farmers. The trio marched into the drawing-room just in time for coffee. Sir Fraser was younger-looking than the detectives had perceived, athletically built with darkening blonde hair and blue eyes. He was wearing a tweed hacking jacket over a twill checked shirt with britches and brogues to complete the country squire look.

'D.C.I. McKirdy, I'm Sir Fraser Urquhart and these are my two guests Morne Le Grange and Pete Erasmus. What is all this about? I love good cloak and dagger mysteries.'

'Pleased to meet you,' Grant reciprocated, 'this is Detective Sergeant Ian Lomax and Detective Constable Avril Luxton.'

Everyone shook hands and settled down in their chairs.

Grant took a gulp of coffee and cleared his throat before speaking, 'Thank you all for seeing us at such short notice. Avril will be taking the notes of our meeting if that is okay with yourselves.' The three opposite nodded their agreement so McKirdy carried on, 'Several weeks ago the body of a young girl was washed up on Joppa Rocks at the East end of Edinburgh. She had been beaten by more than one individual, sexually assaulted and thrown into a hold of live fish where she died of exhaustion and hyperthermia.'

The three gentlemen opposite screwed up their faces at the thought.

The D.C.I. continued, 'We struggled to identify the victim and how she managed to get to Scotland from her home in Leipzig, Germany. Her identity has been clarified but we are still in the dark as to how she got to Edinburgh. Last night the Emergency Services unit in Edinburgh received two calls, one text and one verbal which we have traced as coming from mobile phones owned by Pete Erasmus and Morne Le Grange.'

The two Afrikaners reacted furiously to each other in Afrikaans before returning to English. Morne Le Grange a huge man who in his young days could have been a rugby prop yelled, 'Good God, that is not possible! My mobile phone is broken. Stay here and I will show you!', he shouted before storming out of the room.

The slim figure of Pete Erasmus was a lot calmer than his counterpart. 'Here is my mobile. Do what you want with it, I can't understand why it was used to phone the police.'

Ian Lomax took the phone from Pete and fiddled about until he reached 'Messages', 'There it is! That's the message which was sent at two-thirty this morning.' He passed the mobile back to Pete, to let him read in disbelief the text Lomax had discovered.

At that point Morne came back into the room and thrust his mobile into Lomax's hand, 'See man, my mobile is kaput so how could I send a call to the police?'

Grant McKirdy took control of the discussion, 'Gentlemen, can you tell us what your movements were last night?'

The two looked at each other before Pete took the roll as spokesman, 'We flew into Glasgow airport at four o'clock then took the short trip to Monteith Mansions where we had arranged to stay overnight and play some high stakes poker against some international opposition. The game finished about midnight then we retired to our rooms in the company of a hostess.'

'Hostess!' exclaimed Avril, 'you mean prostitute.'

'No, I mean hostess. We did not have to pay the management for their services, but I did give my hostess a tip.'

The D.C.I leaned forward in his chair, 'What are the names of these 'hostesses'?'

Pete Erasmus replied, 'The lady I was with was called Alena.'

Morne went red in the face, 'Mine was called Heidi.'

'Did Heidi come from Berlin Germany, Mr Le Grange?'

'We didn't talk too much but I think she mentioned Berlin. I went to the toilet at one point and that is when she must have phoned you because when I came back my mobile had fallen off the bedside table and smashed.'

McKirdy asked. 'How did you two get introduced to Monteith Mansions?'

Pete answered, 'We'd gone down to Sun City in South Africa to play poker and this Asian guy overheard us saying we were going to Scotland on a hunt for reindeer. He recommended Monteith Mansions and gave us a contact card to make a booking.'

Lomax piped up, 'Do you still have the card?'

'Yes, it is in my luggage. I will be able to get it for you.'

Pete disappeared upstairs for five minutes and returned holding the card, 'There you are inspector.'

Grant studied the card which read: MONTEITH MANSION, (Former home of shipping magnate Blair Monteith), THE BRAES, KILMACOLM PA13 4AB.

He turned back to the two visitors, 'Gentlemen establishments like Monteith Mansion are frowned upon in Scotland. It is legal to play poker but not when they are supplying hostesses on the side. We could charge you for doing so but I shall overlook it this time as you have been most co-operative and provided us with a line of enquiry which may assist our investigation. My decision is subject to you agreeing, that under no circumstances you speak to anyone about this meeting or contact Monteith Mansion. The same goes for you Sir Fraser, do you all understand?'

The three nodded their agreement.'

'Good, then we'll be on our way. Enjoy the rest of your holiday and good hunting.'

Chapter 15

Grant McKirdy used the return journey back to Edinburgh to organise his next move.

'What we have just heard was extremely useful. We must plan an assault on Monteith Mansions before anybody discovers Alena and Heidi have tried to alert the police. Avril, get on to Police HQ and get logistics to obtain as much information as they can on Monteith Mansions using Google maps or any other service.

I will set up a meeting tomorrow morning with Commander Mark Donald of the Armed Response Unit to devise a plan of attack, code name 'MM'. I would like to go in with all guns blazing as soon as possible.'

Lomax commented, 'It will be interesting to find out who is running MM and how long they have been offering 'Hostesses' to fatigued poker players or anyone else for that matter. It has all the signs of a white slave gang and we all know how ruthless they can be. The two callers will be wetting themselves with anxiety hoping we received their calls for help.'

'Do you trust the three we have just left to keep their mouth shut.' asked Avril.

'Yes, they have too much to lose if they don't. It would not go down well if the Orange Free State Times reported two of their citizens had been involved in a sex scandal. That part of South Africa is very strictly protestant and God fearing!' assessed D.C.I. McKirdy.

Next morning Grant McKirdy was studying a map of Monteith Mansions when his office door opened.

'How are you this good morning?', asked the jovial Commander Mark Donald, 'Have you got something my boys can get their teeth into?'

'Morning Mark, nice to see you. Yes, I'm just looking over the plans for the target building. Pull a chair up and come round this side of the desk and see what you think is the best plan of attack.'

The Commander joined McKirdy who went on to fill in the details of the murder enquiry before returning his attention to the lay-out of Monteith Mansions.

'MM as we will refer to it is situated in twenty -three acres of heathland near Kilmacolm in Renfrewshire.' informed McKirdy 'it's a large sandstone house which is protected by security cameras and the entrance has hydraulic bollards and large wrought iron gates.'

Mark interjected, 'Well that rules out smashing an armoured vehicle through the gates, it would never get past the bollards.'

'Quite.' agreed the D.C.I., 'Protection systems like that usually indicate that the occupants in there are up to no good. The gardens are well maintained with a big lawn at the back of the house. There are a couple of doors out to the garden which could provide simple entries for your men, but the front doors look as though they are re-enforced and could prove difficult. Inside there are roughly thirty rooms counting the kitchens although our targets Alena Koresky and Heidi Lotheram are more than likely to be upstairs in the bedroom area. What is your thoughts Mark?'

The Armed Squad supremo scratched his ginger beard which hid the jowls of fat on his red face, 'Do we know what kind of resistance we shall be facing? Will any of the staff be carrying firearms?'

'I can't say Mark. The only two communications we have had were the mobile calls - but experience would tell us to operate on the basis they will be.'

'Grant, my immediate analysis in order to achieve the element of surprise we should launch our attack in the early hours of the morning when people are normally in their deepest sleep. Kilmacolm is not far from Glasgow Airport so they are used to aircraft flying about so we could get quite close to the gardens by our helicopter which holds twelve passengers. If the pilots put their headlamps on, it will do two things a) provide light for my men to speed towards the rear entrances b) cause confusion within MM which may make them panic for an escape through the front gates which means they will dismantle the bollards. I'll have another squad of officers positioned at the gates to enter when this happens and cut off any exit anyone tries to take.'

'Mark, that seems to cover all bases. You have summed the situation up beautifully. I'm treating this incident as 'Red Alert' as we're seriously concerned for the safety of the two girls who are being held hostage. If possible, I'd like to engage an offensive this evening if that were within your radar.'

Commander Donald hesitated, 'Leave it with me. I will have to make a few logistical calls – helicopter availability etc – and I will get back to you, but I am confident that we can meet the timescale. Email me over a copy of the lay-out of MM so I can brief the men. Planning is everything in armed response to make sure we keep casualties to a minimum. I'll give you a call as soon I have everything in place,'

'Very good Mark, my team will be nearby ready to enter the building and make arrests. Will you fly in the helicopter?'

'Christ no! I hate these bloody things. I, like you, will not be far from the entrance!', the Commander chuckled and left the room.

McKirdy summoned Lomax and Luxton to his room to inform them about his meeting with Commander Donald and

127

prepare them for what could be a long night, subject to getting a positive response from the Armed Response Unit.

'Any questions?'

'When can I go home and get my beauty sleep?', laughed Avril.

Not to be put off the D.C.I. answered back cheekily, 'As soon as you can find an empty cell in the jail downstairs but only after I get the go-ahead from Commander Donald.'

Two hours later Grant's phone rang, and he picked up the handset,' D.C.I. McKirdy speaking.'

'Grant, it is all systems go for 4.00 A.M. tomorrow morning. I will be in position near Kilmacolm at 2.30 a.m. to control operations from an unmarked van. Keep in touch with me when you are in the area. I've had to inform the local police chief we're carrying out an operation on his patch, to avoid any interference from the local constabulary. Don't be shy, when you are near us, as we have a coffee machine on board.'

'Good news, Commander I look forward to seeing you in Kilmacolm.'

Grant signalled Avril and Ian into his room. 'That was Armed Response on the phone. Everything is in place for a raid on MM tomorrow morning at 4.00 a.m. I have agreed with the Commander that we'll join him in the control vehicle, so we monitor the operation as it progresses which means being there at 2.30 a.m. I think we'll make a lot of arrests so Avril phone Strathclyde and arrange for staff and transport to assist us with probably fifty arrests.

The time is now five o'clock, go home and try and get some sleep. Ian you will be driving so you can pick up Avril first and be at my house for 1.00 a.m.'

'Very good Sir, will Mrs McKirdy be supplying the bacon rolls?' asked the D.S.

'Now there's a good idea. I'll suggest it but I won't promise anything.' McKirdy replied.

The weather was foul as D.S. Lomax steered the Audi through the sleet, which was battering the window, pressed on by the cold north wind. The curtain on McKirdy's darkened front lounge moved to indicate he had heard the police car approaching. The front door opened, and he marched quickly down the path carrying his briefcase and into the rear seat of the Audi.

'Evening Sir, have there been any further developments since this afternoon?'

'No nothing Ian. What a horrible night, I would not like to be up in a helicopter tonight, damned cold I should imagine.'

'I think the adrenaline will keep them warm Sir' Ian smirked 'but we could have a problem as the car climbs up the M8 to Shotts as it is bound to be snowing.'

Ian's weather forecast was accurate. Just after the Harthill Service Station the slush turned to snow causing the rear-drive Audi to slip in the frozen ruts caused by other vehicles, especially the HGV lorries. Many travellers on the M8 consider Shotts to be the barometer of Scottish weather. Once you are passed it the weather improves and that was the case for the detectives as their car sped through Glasgow over the Kingston Bridge and taking the A8 cut-off to Greenock. The B789, sign-posted the way to Kilmacolm and Grant, who had been taking a nap in the back of the car acknowledged he had seen it by calling Commander Mark Donald.

'Mark, we've just come off the A8 and are heading for Kilmacolm. Where are you located?'

'Before you enter the town there is path on your left, take it for a mile then turn right down a farm road and we are in a cutting to your left. Extinguish your headlights as soon as you see us.'

Ian located Armed Response's operations vehicle first time and the trio evacuated the warm car to face the elements. The D.C.I. knocked and opened the door and entered. Mark Donald was sitting in front of a lap-top placed on a make-shift desk. Behind him, two officers were sitting with head-phones on talking to colleagues at different locations.

Grant shook hands with the Commander before asking, 'How are we doing Mark?'

'My airborne team are on their way to Glasgow Airport and the others who will be backing them up at the entrance to Monteith Mansions will be here soon. The two officers here are in radio contact with each of the groups and I am monitoring them on this laptop. Once I give the word the helicopter will take to the air, for what will only be a ten-minute journey. The pilot knows to make a quick descent down on to the back lawn close to the house with his head-lights blazing. This should cause panic amongst the occu-pants and give my men cover as they make for two rear doors.'

'Well, let us hope it all goes to plan.' wished D.C.I. McKirdy.

An hour later the ground troops arrived, and their leader, Inspector Magnus Murdoch, came aboard the Operations vehicle to investigate any last-minute changes to strategy. Commander Donald was happy to report everything was as outlined in the orders he had passed out earlier so Murdoch departed as quick as he had entered.

Grant, Avril, and Ian took advantage of the coffee mak-ing facilities which Mark provided. As they sat down at the opposite end of the van from the two monitoring officers Grant went into his briefcase and brought out a package, 'There you are bacon rolls all round – don't say I'm not good to you.'

The D.S. and D.C. smiled their appreciation.

At 3.50 Mark Donald issued the command to the leading officer of his airborne squad Pilot Alfie Flaherty, 'Move now Flaherty. Team leader Inspector Ogilvie good Luck I'll follow you into the house once you have cleared it for us.'

Switching off the transmission Commander Donald turned to D.C.I. McKirdy, 'Right Grant get back to your car and follow us to Monteith Mansion. My men will monitor the helicopter's progress, but we shall be in a position to see it landing.'

It only took five minutes for Ian Lomax to position the Audi near the gates of the big house and rendezvous with three large vehicles with blacked out windows ready to transport the accused to the Glasgow constabulary jail cells. He turned off the Audi's engine and the murder squad were enjoying some silence for a few minutes.

Suddenly they heard the loud drone of a helicopter as it dived down and landed on the lawn at the rear of Monteith Mansions. The headlamps from the aircraft lit up the building as simultaneous its doors opened, and a dozen armed response officers scurried towards the house at speed smashing through the glass doors and setting off the burglar alarm. Lights started illuminating rooms in the house as the occupants wondered what was happening. Once inside the patrol made their way systematically through the house, shouting at the top of their voices, 'Police!! Police!! Come out of your rooms with your hands above your heads and lie on the floor where we can see you!'

A thorough search of the bedrooms produced guests in varying states of undress, some wearing as little as a towel round them to protect their modesty and others still in their pyjamas. A couple of the management staff had tried to do a runner but were apprehended at the front gate. The whole operation was over in ten minutes and by the time McKirdy and his team entered Monteith Mansions everybody had been herded into the main lounge.

Grant McKirdy held up his hand as a gesture for silence as he looked round the room at the assembled company which was about sixty strong.

'Ladies & gentlemen, my name is Detective Chief Inspector Grant McKirdy and the gentleman to my right is Commander Mark Donald from the Armed Response team. Our purpose for raiding Monteith Mansions is we believe several illegal acts are being carried out here. There are people in this room who we believe can assist us with a murder enquiry. Everyone present will be interviewed by members of my staff, only briefly tonight, but many of you will be liable to longer spells of interrogation later. Before we begin can I ask Alena Koresky and Heidi Lotheram to step forward. A murmur broke out in the room as the two girls stepped forward, both barefooted, wearing towelling white dressing gowns with the 'MM' crest on the breast pocket.

Grant went to meet them and shook their hands and quietly said, 'Many thanks for your bravery in contacting us. We'll arrange to take you back to Edinburgh where you will remain in custody tonight and be interrogated tomorrow regarding the murder of your friend Elke Kohl.'

The girls broke down in tears at the mention of Elke's name and Grant signalled to Avril to assist him.

Sadie broke ranks and charged towards Heidi with a knife in her hand, 'Heidi, you bitch! You cheated on me after all I have done for you!'

Heidi saw her coming and jumped out the way, as two-armed response officers closed in on Sadie and diffused what could have been a nasty situation.

Grant made a further announcement, 'Okay everyone, go back to your rooms and get dressed. On your return, we will conduct a brief interview to establish the purpose of your stay at Monteith Mansion. For those of you who we think are of further interest to Police Scotland we will escort you to the buses we have outside to take you into Glasgow where you will spend the night. Heidi you and Alena will come with us back to Edinburgh.'

Heidi and Alena returned in casual clothes each with their little suitcases and still beaming at the thought of being rescued. McKirdy entrusted them to his security officers who put them in the rear of an unmarked police van with D.S. Lomax for company.

'Ian get the girls settled in at Fettes and make sure we have armed officers outside their cells in case there are any reprisals from the Monteith Mansions management, who we don't know much about at the present time. Arrange for them to have a sleep in and have lunch at midday. I will make sure we have interpreters present when we start our interrogation at 4.00 p.m.

'Now Avril I better get you home, it has been a long, but remarkably successful day and hopefully more positive revelations tomorrow.'

Avril had lived in Marchmont with her parents but recently moved to a flat in nearby Bruntsfield, which took Grant McKirdy a bit out of his way. However, it gave him time to talk to his newest member of staff. She filled in Grant with her current lifestyle, buying expensive clothes, purchasing a new car, and moving to her own flat which she shared with a friend. After he dropped her off, he smiled to himself thinking how the young were full of big ideas. He was relieved when he turned into his driveway and fell into bed at 9.45 a.m. exhausted.

The previous afternoon Geordie McNab received a call on his private mobile, 'Mr McNab, the Ferret speaking. McKirdy is doing a raid tonight somewhere in the West of Scotland following two tip-offs from girls claiming to have information on Elke Kohl's murder.'

133

McNab felt a cold shiver down his back, 'Thanks for letting me know and if you hear anything else get back to me.'

Geordie sat back and considered his options. If these girls, whoever they are, do have information on how Elke died then the police will be able to uncover Captain Igor Shertsov, the Caledonian Princess activities, and eventually his drug ring which could result in a long prison sentence. Thinking about it the only evidence which links him to the Koidutaht is Peter Fraser and Martin Watson and the crew of the Caledonian Princess.

He picked up the phone and made a call. 'Peter, Geordie McNab. What are you up to this week? I thought we might meet up for a drink.'

'Sorry Geordie, this is my busy time I'm just getting the boat ready to set sail the day after tomorrow and there are just aren't enough hours in the day. Have you got another consignment coming in already?'

'No, not from yourselves but there is another supplier on the scene who will be sending produce this week. When you get back give me a call and we will have a night out. How's Martin? is it your usual crew making the trip?'

'Certainly are, they have all been with me for years, we're one big successful happy family.'

'Long may it continue Peter, see you soon.'

McNab did not put down the phone. Instead, he contacted Maniac McLagan and asked him to come and see him as a matter of urgency. The following evening Maniac drove to the outskirts of Eyemouth parked his car and took a rucksack out of the boot. He made his way down to the quayside keeping to the shadows whenever possible until he spotted the Caledonian Princess. Maniac's army training had taught him to be patient and he did not come out of the shadows for half an hour which convinced him there was nobody on board. Making his move, Maniac swiftly boarded the boat and moved to where he thought was the most effective area to place an explosive, based on the knowledge he had of the Caledonian Princess' layout. He chose to hide the bomb under loose cables in the engine room situated in the middle of the trawler and set the timer for two days in advance. He departed as silently as he arrived and was soon heading back to Edinburgh using a series of the same country roads which brought him to Eyemouth avoiding the speed cameras on the A1.

Maniac called McNab, 'Job done Boss. I placed the bomb in the Engine room underneath some old cables with enough explosive to send it to the bottom of the sea.'

'Well done Maniac', congratulated Geordie McNab, 'the Caledonian Princess served us well, but I've managed to set up a new courier called The Northern Lights which sails out of Peterhead. I will have to make a trip over to Parnu to meet up with Igor Shertsov and introduce him to Dave Holden, the skipper of The Northern Lights. We have no plans to bring in any illegal immigrants, but it may do no harm for Holden to meet Kurt Jansen should the occasion arise.

I will want you with me in Parnu to watch my back. Shertsov is a nasty bugger so you'll be in good company McLagan! We can take the wives over to Malaga for a week's holiday, all inclusive, and once we settled them down in the hotel we can fly up to Tallinn for a couple of days and do the business.'

'It will be a real holiday for my wife if I'm not there and she can drink as much as she likes! All that will be missing is a holiday boyfriend, but she knows better not to get involved with the opposite sex.' said Maniac in a threatening tone.

Chapter16

Police Scotland officers were busy the morning after the raid on Monteith Mansions. In Glasgow teams of officers were involved in eliminating those who were a danger to the public and the unsuspecting who'd just come for a good time, which had gone horribly wrong. All the bookings for Monteith were done covertly making it different from most establishments who used a guest signing -in book. This delayed the investigators from building a picture of the clientele which they were desperate to know about.

The charges broke down into hree different categories:-

1. The murder of three sex slaves who were allegedly buried in the grounds of Monteith Mansions.
2. Procuring 12 women and enslaving them into providing sexual services.
3. Running gambling facilities without a licence.

In Edinburgh Grant McKirdy prepared to interview Heidi and Alena separately with the help in Heidi's case of Gwen Mackie a German interpreter and Pamela Dudgeon who spoke fluent Russian, Alena's native tongue. Accompanied by a female police officer, Heidi was escorted into Room A1 still dressed in the same clothes she'd been wearing when she arrived at Fettes Police Station. However. she had showered and applied some make-up and looked relaxed.

The D.C.I. invited her to so sit down and began his questioning:

'Heidi, it is probably better if I start by telling you what happened to your friend Elke Kohl. Her body was washed ashore on Joppa Rocks on the outskirts of Edinburgh. Our forensic teams reckon she died after being thrown into a trawler's fish hold and most likely died of exhaustion and hyperthermia. What we want to know, is how she got there?

And we are hoping you can provide us with that information? If you could start by telling us how you met up with Elke.'

Heidi was shocked at what she had just been told and wiped away some tears before giving her version of events.

'I met Elke when she worked in Berlin and we became good friends. When I had a dispute with Fritz Kahn, the bar owner of the 'Heisse Damen Club' I phoned Elke and asked if I could come to Leipzig and stay with her. She came up to Berlin and picked me up as she thought it wouldn't be safe to travel on public transport as Fritz's gang may be looking for me.'

D.C.I. McKirdy interrupted. 'Why would he be looking for you?'

'I owed him some money.'

'How much?'

'One hundred thousand Euros.'

'Good God! How did he have that type of money?'

'He's a drug dealer who sent me to pick up a package from a pop star and I decided stupidly to run off with it.'

'We'll put that aside for now. Go back to what happened next with Elke.'

'I told her one of the girls from the club, Greta Horschal, had secured a passage on a boat to be smuggled into Britain. She decided to join me, so we flew from Leipzig to Tallinn then took a bus to Parnu. There we met up with Kurt Jansen and four other girls, Greta Horschal, Anna Berkovitch, Alena Koresky and Sophie Baumen who'd each paid fifteen hundred euros for the trip. The next day we boarded a large fish processing ship called The Koidutaht. We all met Captain Igor Shertsov and the first mate Boris Andropov who led us to cabins where they fed us. He told us the Koidutaht was a fish processing vessel with seventy-five staff on board, but we never saw any of them. We all settled down for the night and when I woke in the morning Elke had gone. An hour or so later Boris came into our cabin and asked for Elke's case which he took away. I asked what was happening and he said, 'Elke and Igor are getting on very well, so she has decided to stay on board.'

'Several hours later a fishing boat came alongside, and we were transferred to it and told it was heading to Eyemouth on the East coast of Scotland.'

Again, McKirdy butted in, 'What was the name of the fishing boat?'

'The Caledonian Princess'

'Go on.'

Heidi took a sip of water, 'Conditions on board were cramped and two days later we arrived at Eyemouth but were kept in the cabin until darkness when we were transferred again, this time on to a refrigerated van. The van was driven by an Asian man who we only knew as Mohammed. He drove South to Bradford and dumped us all into a warehouse. This was when we started to panic, the other three girls Sophie, Greta and Anna were bundled into a locked van and I don't know where they were taken. We were left with the leader of the group called Kassim who....' Heidi began to cry, 'raped both of us!'

D.C. Luxton comforted Heidi and gave her a drink of water before McKirdy continued his questioning.

'Heidi, I know this is not easy, but we must know how you ended up at Monteith Mansions.'

Heidi nodded her head then replied, 'We were drugged and put into a car and the next thing I knew was when I woke up in Monteith Mansion. Alena and I did think about planning an escape, but we didn't have a clue as to where we were. Sadie, the lady who controlled all the twelve hostesses sensed our mood. She asked us to look out the window at three trees which were planted in the garden and told us these marked the graves of hostesses who had tried to escape in the past.'

'Ian, take a note of that and get the forensic team to carry out a dig.', instructed McKirdy, 'carry on Heidi.'

'We were well treated in Monteith Mansions in terms of food and clothing but every night we had to carry out sexual acts on the guests who had flown in to play some serious high stakes poker. Their mood changed depending on how they had performed at the table, occasionally we had to indulge in a threesome. Sadie, our governess took a shine to me, so when I broke Mr. Le Grange's mobile phone she smoothed it over with the management in return for 'Some tender loving care.' Alena and I were on tenterhooks not knowing whether you'd gotten our messages. Thank God you did, we shall be forever grateful to you.'

Grant continued 'A rescue like the one carried out last night is what we are in policing for. Is there anything else you would like to add?'

Heidi shook her head.

'We'll have to ask you and Alena to remain in custody for a few days during which you will be interviewed by the Border Force to see if you'll be allowed to stay in this country permanently. You'll be allowed to go into Edinburgh and see the sights, but only in the company of female police officers. Please don't try to escape as we will fitting you with electronic trackers to you.'

McKirdy continued, 'I want to know more about the money you stole from Fritz Kahn, but we can leave that until tomorrow. That's all for now, Avril can you arrange for two female plain clothes officers to let Heidi see our city please.'

Heidi left the interrogation room and Grant returned to his office. His first action was to call Ian Lomax.

'Ian, Heidi gave us some good information regarding how she got from Estonia to here. First port of call, if you pardon the pun, is Eyemouth to check out 'The Caledonian Princess' which should be on the list of boats you got from Admiral Arbuthnott. Secondly contact Yorkshire Police and inform them that we have reason to believe that there is an Asian gang operating a sex trafficking ring on their patch. Give them the names of the three girls who were dropped off in Bradford after coming off the Caledonian Princess. I'm going to interview Alena Koresky although I think a lot of her evidence will be similar to Heidi's.'

Grant's words proved to be true. Alena Koresky was a lot younger than Heidi and not nearly so streetwise. She was hesitant with her answers and required the assistance of the translator Pamela Dudgeon on several occasions. However, there was one important piece of information she provided:

'One evening I was entertaining a young man from Afghanistan and he told me he knew Elke Kohl and how she had been murdered.'

D.I. McKirdy leaned forward in his seat, 'Do you have the name of this man?

'Yes, Mohammed al- Basiri.'

'Now there's a name I have heard before somewhere.', replied Grant chewing the end of his biro.

His thoughts were interrupted by Ian Lomax appearing into his office carrying a wad of computer sheets, 'Sir I have scoured the list of ships movements we got from Admiral Arbuthnott and there is no trace of a vessel called 'The Caledonian Princess.'

'Are you sure Ian?'

'That's what I thought you would say Sir, so I brought in the data to let you see for yourself.'

'No need for that Ian, I believe you. Arbuthnott must have removed it for some reason. Phone the harbourmaster's office in Eyemouth and verify the Caledonian Princess' existence.'

Five minutes later. 'Eyemouth Harbourmasters office Edmund Ferguson speaking.'

'Good afternoon Mr Ferguson, I am Detective Sergeant Ian Lomax speaking to you from Police Scotland in Edinburgh. Can you confirm to me that you have a fishing trawler named The Caledonian Princess which normally berths in the harbour?'

'Yes, the Caledonian princess is registered at Eyemouth and has been for a number of years. Why do you ask?'

'I'm investigating an enquiry which might involve the skipper of the boat. Can you tell me for how long The Caledonian Princess sailed out of Eyemouth?'

'I've worked in the office here over twenty years and the Fraser family have owned the boat about fifteen years. Old man Fraser died three years ago and Peter Fraser, his son, became the skipper.'

'Is the Caledonian Princess in Eyemouth at present?' asked Lomax.

There was a shuffling of papers which could be heard over the phone before Ferguson replied, 'No she sailed last night and probably won't be back for four or five days. You could always try and get the skipper on his mobile.'

'Have you got a number for him?'

'Yes, it is 07777 145645'

'Thanks for your help Mr Ferguson, we'll maybe give Mr Fraser a call.'

Ian Lomax hung up the phone and turned to his boss.

'Well at least we've established The Caledonian Princess exists. Do you think we should give Peter Fraser a call?'

'No, I'd rather we didn't alert him just now. We can arrange to meet him on the quayside at Eyemouth harbour complete with sniffer dogs to see what he has been up to. In the meantime, I'll update Hugh McFaul at MI6 on our progress.'

Chapter 17

'Afternoon Hugh, Grant McKirdy here. How are you doing?'

'Busy, the Arab Spring is causing us a lot of heartache as we try to evaluate who's backing who and what splinter group Whitehall should be supporting.'

'We domestic cops don't have that problem. I'm phoning to give you an update on the significant progress we are making into the death of Elke Kohl.'

'Really delighted to hear it.'

'We received two Emergency Service Calls a few days ago both saying they'd information regarding the murder of Elke Kohl. We traced the calls from two mobiles belonging to a couple of South African tourists who've been gambling and enjoying the company of women who we've since uncovered have been kidnapped and forced into prostitution in an establishment near Glasgow.'

'The South Africans co-operated fully with us and we raided the hotel they'd been staying in and made several significant arrests. The two girls Heidi Lotheram and Alena Koresky were rescued and have since been interrogated by my team with the use of interpreters. They've come up with some names that we believe may have been responsible for the death of your agent Elke Kohl.'

'Six girls boarded a fish processing factory ship 'The Koidutaht with the help of a Kurt Jansen at a cost of fifteen hundred euros each. The following morning Elke had gone and one of the sailors Boris Andropov came and took her case saying she and the captain Igor Shertsov had become an item. They, in our opinion, are responsible for the murder of Elke Kohl.'

'That's brilliant news Grant. I'll look at our records and see if we have anything on Shertsov, Andropov and Kurt Jansen. We would like to see them brought to justice but that's a decision for Assistant Controller Hartley to make.'

D.C.I. McKirdy cautioned, 'Do not be in a hurry to take revenge just yet, there are a few other issues you should be aware of. You may remember when we were down in Leith, I pointed out Admiral Arbuthnott who was making his way into the Royal Casino.'

'Yes, I do, a tall man with silver hair and a beard to match.'

'Correct Hugh, well a couple of weeks ago he blew his head off with a shotgun. It appeared to be suicide, but I'm not convinced as he was owing money to the wrong people. He was up to his ears in debt.'

McKirdy continued, 'When we were cross-examining Heidi and Alena, they both described the fishing trawler which brought them to Eyemouth as The Caledonian Princess. The boat's name does not appear in any of the data we obtained from the Sea Fishing Authority. This adds strength to my theory that Arbuthnott was removing vessels from the records which would then enable it to wanderfreerly in the North Sea without anyone knowing its whereabouts.'

'An Ideal situation for smugglers to take advantage and bring in contraband or livestock in the shape of illegal immigrants.' commented the intelligence officer.'

'Something else we found out from Alena Koresky was she entertained a young man from Afghanistan, who knew how Elke Kohl was murdered. His name was Mohammed al-Basiri.'

'Basiri!!' exclaimed Hugh, 'he's the guy Elke spent time with at the Lindtbaum Hotel in Leipzig. We've a photo of him on record.'

'Hugh, he has managed to slip into the country, so you better get your colleagues at MI5 to put his name and photo out as he is unlikely to be here on a holiday. Going back to the Koidutaht's crew, we now believe they could be involved in drug trafficking and we would like to carry out further investigations to flush out local drug dealers in Edinburgh. Everything we discussed today will be submitted to you shortly in a formal report.'

'Okay Grant, I look forward to receiving your report then I'll talk to Richard Hartley.'

The shipping forecast on BBC Radio 4 had warned vessels in the Dogger Bank area of a Force 7 north-easterly which had now arrived alongside The Caledonian Princess as it was buffeted by the cruel sea. Martin Watson who was taking the night watch was in the wheelhouse steering the boat and watching as the spray from the waves battered the glass in front of him. The rest of the crew were below decks sleeping preparing themselves for a busy day ahead dropping their nets in the hope of getting a big profitable catch to take back to Eyemouth. He made himself a coffee and was just stirring the sugar in his mug when the huge explosion burst through the boat, splitting The Caledonian Princess wide open. No one on board had any chance to escape and as it sank almost immediately into the turbulent icy waters of the North Sea.

Ian Lomax decided to call into the Sea Fishing Authorities offices unannounced to see Andrew Turner and clarify with him as to why The Caledonian Princess had been deleted from the data sheets he had sent to Police Scotland. Turner was not pleased to see D.S. Lomax as he was not used to meeting people in his job as he always worked in the background.

'Good day Mr Turner I'd like to ask you why a vessel called The Caledonian Princess was not registered on the data you sent to Police Scotland?' asked Lomax.

The young computer geek's face went red before he answered, 'Admiral Arbuthnott told me to take The Caledonian Princess records out the system. He never fully explained why but it was the morning after he had a bad night at the Royal Casino that he asked me to change it.'

'And you never thought to tell us! Do you realise how much police time you've wasted? We've had teams of officers touring round fishing ports interviewing the crews of all trawlers in and around the Firth of Forth. If we find out that you were involved in altering the data, you could be facing a compulsory sentence in Saughton Prison.'

Lomax calmed down before continuing, 'I take it this was the only boat removed from your records?'

'Yes Sir.'

'I will leave it there for today, but you will be called upon soon to come into Fettes and make a full statement. Goodbye.'

After D.S Lomax left Andrew Turner retired to the toilet where he sobbed his eyes out at the thought of what he had let himself get involved in.

Two days later D.S. Lomax received a call from Edmund Ferguson, Eyemouth's Harbourmaster.

'Sergeant Lomax', he began, 'I thought I better call you to say that we have lost contact with The Caledonian Princess. She hasn't been in touch with us for two days. We raised a call to alert the Coastguards and they in turn conducted a helicopter search of the Dogger Bank area where the Caledonian Princess was heading. There was a force 7 gale the other night but that is something Peter Fraser and his crew were well used to coping with. There are no signs of any debris yet, but sometimes it takes the sea a few days to give up their dead.'

Lomax was taken aback by Ferguson's statement, 'That's shattering news Mr Ferguson. I'd planned to come down to Eyemouth and interview Peter Fraser and his crew following an incident which was reported to us.'

'What was it about? Maybe I can help you.'

'Thanks, but at present I would rather not say. I appreciate your call and if you hear anything further please contact me immediately. Goodbye Mr Ferguson and thanks for letting us know.'

'I will do Sergeant Lomax.'

D.S. Lomax wasted no time in entering D.C.I. McKirdy's office with Avril Luxton who he'd collected on the way, 'Sir, Eyemouth Harbourmaster's office has just phoned me to say that The Caledonian Princess has disappeared off the radar. The coastguard has been alerted and a helicopter has flown over the area with no success so far.'

'I don't like the sound of this Ian. Fishing trawlers just don't disappear. A few years ago, one did, when its net got entangled with a nuclear submarine that was in the area although the Ministry of Defence denied it. I think there is a more practical reason for the ship going missing. It cannot be engine failure or a fire otherwise they would surely have sent out a SOS. My thoughts are there has possibly been an explosion on board and our problem is finding out who or what caused it?'

'Grant, this has scuppered my plans to meet The Caledonian Princess when it returned to port and have it searched thoroughly using sniffer dogs for any signs of illegal drugs.'

'A great pity Ian, but as the Bard Robert Burns said, 'The best laid schemes o' mice an' men gang aft agley.'

Chapter 18

Meanwhile McKirdy was wasting no time tidying up the loose ends from the Monteith Mansion raid.

Heidi Lotheram, along with her interpreter Anna Alterman, was summoned to interview Room 6 where she was faced with D.C.I. McKirdy and a lady who introduced herself as Catherine Ruane from Border Force.

As usual McKirdy kicked off the proceedings,' Good afternoon Heidi, Cath Ruane is from Border Force. The decision to allow you to remain in the U.K. will probably depend on the answers you give her during this meeting so think carefully and choose your words wisely.'

'When I last interviewed you, you admitted to stealing a parcel of money from Franz Katz, a drug dealer based in Berlin. The figure of one hundred thousand euros was mentioned. Can I ask you where that money is now?'

Heidi smiled and almost giggled, 'It is in the false bottom of my suitcase. I cannot believe that Police Scotland would have allowed me to come into one of their main police stations without searching my case thoroughly.'

An embarrassed D.C.I. McKirdy responded. 'There was so much going on through at Monteith Mansions that bag searches were at the bottom of our list but it is very observant of you to make that point.'

Cath Ruane moved the meeting on, 'Miss Lotheram you have entered the U.K. illegally. Why did you do that at great risk to yourself when, with Freedom of Movement in the European Union, you could just have hopped on a plane in Berlin or anywhere else in Germany and arrived safely?'

'Ms Ruane, Mr McKirdy has just mentioned I stole a large sum of money from one of the biggest drug dealers in Berlin, Franz Katz. He has one of the largest intelligence webs in Germany and if I had made a move to use public transport to leave the country, he'd have known about it and come after me. Katz has a reputation for eliminating anyone who upsets him.'

'Your CV does not enhance the case to allow entry into the U.K. My department has been heavily criticised for allowing undesirables from Eastern Europe to enter the U.K. and set up illegal practices. However, provided you hand over the stolen money to the British Government or a charity we will allow the application for permanent residence to be consider at our next intake meeting. D.C.I. Mckirdy has been impressed by the brave action you took, at risk to your own life, to pass information which could lead to the arrest of Elke Kohl's killer. The next meeting of the Immigration Entry Board is not for two weeks. In the intervening period you will be placed in a safe house along with Alena Koresky. The safe house is supervised twenty-four hours a day by security staff. Do you understand Heidi what I have just said?'

The grateful young German replied, 'Thank you Miss Ruane, I will not let you down.'

McKirdy called a halt to the meeting and arranged to meet up again with Ms Ruane and Heidi as soon as they had heard back from the Immigration Board.

Chapter 19

Following his arrival at Eyemouth on board the Caledonian Princess Mohammed al-Basiri drove out of the town and down the A1 for an Hour. He then took the A69 from Newcastle to Carlisle before joining the M6 until he reached the turn-off for Blackburn, then on to his final destination Nelson. The Lancashire town was traditionally a mill town which later produced bedding and furniture. Since the 1980s the make-up of the population had transformed with a large influx of Asians changing the character of the town.

He parked his car just off Leeds Road and entered a house by the backyard which would not have been out of place in the TV soap 'Coronation Street'. Al-Basiri knocked on the door and waited as it was unlocked by Ismail Goulan who greeted him with a traditional Asian hug.

'Welcome brother, did you have a good journey from Estonia?'

'No, I'm not built for sailing. I was sick as a dog for three days and could not look at the food when it was presented to me. However, I've arrived now without anyone, apart from those involved in distributing my hashish, knowing I am in the country. I have orders to plan a major incident in the U.K., so Nelson is a good base for me to travel about looking at possible targets to inflict devastation upon the infidels.'

'You must be hungry after your journey. I have prepared a lamb Rogan Josh which my wife will serve to us presently. After our meal we can have a chat and I will tell you about our base here in the North of England.'

By the time Mohammed left Nelson three days later he had a very concise appreciation of the strengths of the Jihadi warriors in Lancashire. Next, he was off to Scotland to carry out more reconnaissance to see if the Jihad ideology had the same significance as the North of England. He was welcomed with open arms and given a room in a flat in Glasgow's Maryhill district. From there he was able to visit a large cash and carry business who he was hoping would contribute financially to the cause. It was one of the merchants Anwar Segoura who invited him to have a night out at Monteith Mansions to enjoy as he put it 'the company of a nice white wicked infidel girl.'

After Glasgow, al-Basiri headed for the Midlands and met up with his Jihadist brothers at Handsworth. The West Midlands town had become heavily populated by the Asian community and Mohammed was again welcomed into the local al-Qaeda sympathiser's home where they discussed co-ordinating an attack on a major British landmark.

'What is the target you have decided on?', asked Mussa al-Kariba.

'The thought of our leaders is that it should be something of significance which would get us global coverage and be remembered for a long time. When the Twin Towers in 2001 were attacked it was phenomenaly successful and will live in the hearts of the world for a long time. If our brothers had accomplished their planned attack which was to fly a jet plane into the pillars at the front door of the White House, an image that would have represented a complete demise of the West in our followers' eyes.'

'So, what should we go for now?' enquired Mussa.

'The British are very protective of their Royal Family so we must avoid attacking any of their residences they use regularly. The consequences for the Asian community would be horrendous if any senior members of the Royal Household were killed. There is an exception to that thought but I will keep that target to myself for now.'

'Tell me Mussa, how are we placed for engaging young men who would like to become martyrs for the cause and join Allah and the pleasures of the seven virgins?'

'In the Midlands, some young men who have been radicalised at mosques in the Birmingham area would do anything to kill the infidels.', Mussa verified.

'Tomorrow you must take me a tour of the area and introduce me to those you think best to further our cause. We shall need access to bomb-making equipment and a supply of Semtex. The funding for the project will be made available to you from me, on the success of my drug trafficking profits.'

Chapter 20

Hugh McFaul received the Police Scotland report along with the latest news about the disappearance of The Caledonian Princess and arranged a meeting with Assistant Controller Richard Hartley. McKirdy report had been emailed to Hartley in advance so Hugh did not have to go through it line by line.

Hartley rocked back and forward in his swivel armchair, hands clasped contemplating his next move, 'Good news from Edinburgh Hugh. Things have moved on a pace and we now know who was responsible for Agent 1425', Hartley always liked to address his staff by their roll number, 'we now must decide How? Where? and When we dispose of them?'

'I wouldn't be too hasty Sir. There has been a late development since Police Scotland's report was sent. The Caledonian Princess with five sailors on board has disappeared off the radar, presumed sunk. This would appear to be connected to the activities carried out on board The Koidutaht. The sinking of The Caledonian Princess has denied the police any access to a first -hand account of what really took place that night. Grant McKirdy is convinced that a local drug cartel is involved, and he would like us to hold off terminating the supply route until we are in a better position to follow the drug trail the whole way through. This includes how they're sending their proceeds out of the country to safe tax-free havens.'

'Okay Hugh I'll take your advice and hold off going after Captain Igor Shertsov and his first mate. Regarding tracking the money made by the Scottish dealers, I think I know someone who can assist us.'

'Who would that be, Sir?

'You remember Mhairi McClure, the IRA's financial wizard who was sentenced to twenty years at Her Majesty's Pleasure and is now in prison at Askham Grange in Yorkshire.'

A week later Richard Hartley and Hugh McFaul made the journey up to Askham to visit Mhairi McClure. HMP Askham Grange is one of the smaller all-female prisons hosting only one hundred and fifty prisoners, some of whom go on day release to nearby businesses. The Governor Helen Malcolm was surprised to get a call from MI6 asking to come and interview Mhairi McClure. She had not long been under her care after being transferred from HMP Bronzefield.

Richard was his usual charming self, making small talk over coffee with Governor Malcolm before taking the short trip along the corridor to an interview room. Two minutes later the door of the room opened and in came Mhairi McClure accompanied by two prison officers. Three years older since Hartley and McFaul had previously seen her, Mhairi was now in her mid-forties but had kept her looks and slim figure by working out in the prison gym. Inmates in open prisons did not have to wear a prisoner's uniform and Mhairi looked smart. dressed in a black cotton blouse, grey slacks, and her hair pulled back in a ponytail.

'Good morning Mhairi', said Hartley putting out his hand for a handshake which she ignored. 'Very well, you know Hugh McFaul so there is no need for an introduction. Guards can you leave the room. We know Miss McClure and what we want to discuss with her is highly confidential and a matter of National Security.'

The guards looked puzzled but did as they were told and left the room.

Hartley opened the conversation, 'How have you adapted to prison life here in Askham Mhairi?'

Mhairi sneered at the two intelligence officers across the table, 'No thanks to you two who were responsible for putting me in here.'

Hartley reacted angrily, 'Miss McClure you put yourself in here because you never got over the death of your fiancé. You took out your revenge on one of our senior officers, Colin Inglis, who we later found out had been a bad egg, so your action was partially justified. Had you stopped there you might have been shown some clemency, but you subsequently caused the deaths of a further six people in your attempt to escape capture.

'You co-operated with us two years ago and in return we shortened your sentence by eight years. Another situation has arisen. We have a situation where I think you could be of use to the security services. What sort of work have you been engaged in recently?'

'I have continued to use my computer skills and have written some programmes for Her Majesty's Prison Service, which is how I was transferred to Askham Hall. However, there is still a lot of room for improvement in my opinion.'

'Good. Do you still keep an eye on the financial markets, and would you be able to place money laundered funds in safe tax havens around the world?'

Mhairi shrugged her shoulders, ''Yes, I suppose so. To me working the financial markets is like riding a bike. So, what dirty little scheme do you want me to carry out for MI6?'

Hugh McFaul took over from his boss, 'One of our agents has been murdered, the victim of a horrible death by suspected drug dealers based in Edinburgh but operating throughout Scotland. The dealer we know is handling considerable sums of money which he sends offshore. What I want you to do is pose as financial expert offering him better arrangements than he has at present. We know where he hangs out so by using your charms, I'm sure you will be able to get his trust.'

'What's in it for me?'

'At the very worse a holiday away from Askham to Edinburgh. We'll put you up in a five-star hotel and supply you with a wardrobe to look the part of a financial high-flyer. If you are successful, we'll arrange to have your prison sentence cut further.'

'So how do you know I'll not try and escape when I'm in Edinburgh?'

Hartley smiled, 'Oh that's easily answered. You'll have a microchip inserted into your body which is like having your own Sat-Nav, so we'll know exactly where you are day and night.'

The prisoner sulked at the idea of having the microchip inserted into her body but continued to ask questions, 'How long do you think your project will last? When is it going to start? Is there any travel involved?'

Hartley raised his hand to summon an end to Mhairi's questions, 'Hold on, I'm sure you'll have plenty of questions but to answer what you just mentioned; at this stage we don't have a specific timeframe for our project; no timeframe has been decided yet; regarding travel we think it's unlikely although the gang we're monitoring are international. If you did have to travel anywhere, we'd supply you with a bodyguard who'd have the dual role of protecting and monitoring you. Well, that is as much as I can tell you at present. Are you interested in helping us?'

Mhairi sat back in her chair before replying, 'There's one important factor you've omitted to confirm – what my sentence would be reduced by?'

Richard Hartley had expected the question, 'The truth is Miss McClure at present I can't answer that question, partially because I have no idea to what level of contribution or value you will bring to the project. Any reduction in your time in prison will be increased by an incentive bonus tied to the successful outcome of the operation. Any system we use to measure the benefit you brought to the project will be expressed in years.'

'Not quite the reply I was looking for Mr. Hartley. However, you acted honourably in the past, so I would love to experience the outside world and Edinburgh is dear to me as I once had a boyfriend from there.'

'Thanks for your positive agreement to join us. As soon as we have lined up the suspect, we will arrange for you to go to Edinburgh for a briefing session prior to facing our target. Hugh, go and tell the guards we've finished our meeting.'

The guards appeared back into the room and everyone said their farewells, only this time Mhairi McClure did shake hands.

On the way back to London the two MI6 officers discussed today's events which they thought had been an excellent success.

Hugh raised a couple of doubts in his mind, 'Sir, do you think we can trust Mhairi McClure? And will the Service not view us using a convicted terrorist as a weakness on our part?'

'Whether we can trust McClure there is not a problem. We told her she would have a tracker fitted. What I didn't tell her there will be another device fitted which can leak a poison to kill her instantly.'

After a brief silence Hartley continued, 'This is not the first occasion military intelligence has made use of criminals.'

'My father told me the story that during the Second World War a Scottish safecracker of Lithuanian parents called 'Gentle' Johnny Ramensky, because he never resorted to violence. He was enlisted into Commando 30 the equivalent of the S.A.S. and parachuted in behind enemy lines. He opened Safes as far apart as Rommel's HQ in North Africa to Herman Goering's headquarters in Schorfheide Germany. He also took part in the Italian Campaign where he blew open fourteen Embassy strong boxes in one day. His

157

actions provided the allies with secret Nazi intelligence. At the end of the war he reverted to civvy street where he returned to burglary and spent most of his time in prisons, some of which he escaped from.'

'Sounds like quite a character Sir.'

'Yes, Hugh he was, unlike the lady we are about to release into public life who has assassinated individuals when she needed to.'

On return to London Hugh McFaul sent a message to D.C.I. McKirdy to keep him in the loop about expecting a visitor in the shape of Mhairi McClure. Her name brought back memories to Grant as he had gone across to interview her in Northern Ireland ten years ago in connection with the murder of Allan Phair, an Edinburgh academic who was stabbed to death in Edinburgh.

Chapter 21

Mohammed al-Basiri had completed his U.K. tour of al-Qaeda strongholds who were just waiting for his command to swing into action and create mayhem upon unsuspecting British citizens. He had returned to Nelson where he enjoyed the local environment and climbed up Pendle Hill where in medieval times witches had been burned at the stake. He debated with himself what site would create the greatest impact for his cause but decided to leave the final decision until he returned from Edinburgh where he had arranged to meet his largest customer in Scotland - Geordie McNab.

The Balmoral Hotel at the East end of Princes Street was busily seeing to all their guests breakfast requirements when Geordie McNab, dressed in a smart grey herring bone business suit approached reception and asked for Mr al-Basiri.

'He's waiting for you in the lounge sir - if you are Mr McNab.'

Geordie nodded and a member of staff led him through to where al-Basiri was reading an Arab morning newspaper. Mohammed stood up and towered over the shorter muscular-built McNab before shaking hands.

'Can I get you a drink Mr McNab?' he asked.

'Yes, I'll have a pot of tea and a scone if there is one available.'

Al-Basiri did not quite know the meaning of the word 'Scone' but signalled a waiter to assist him.

The waiter smiled at McNab, 'What flavour of scone would Sir like? Plain, Cheese or Fruit?'

'Fruit' replied the scrap dealer.

The pair returned to business with Mohammed commenting 'Mr McNab it is a pleasure to meet you at last, I have enjoyed our business arrangements to date and hopefully we can expand on this in future. Tell me about your current operation here in Scotland?'

McNab poured himself a cup of the newly-arrived tea before answering, 'Keeping my answers in business speak, currently we import products through yourselves which are distributed via my scrap metal vehicles to agents placed mostly in the Central Belt of Scotland. Their clientele is largely working class so prices are not as high as it would be in London.'

'Have you ever considered expanding into England? I've toured around a bit since I arrived last week, and the North of England looks a good area for our products.'

'Maybe so, replied McNab, 'the population in the Greater Manchester area is three times the size of Scotland, but it is already run by some pretty ruthless gangs, in Manchester and Liverpool who I don't fancy or need to take on. Just recently we've been questioned by the police who were investigating the body of a young woman washed ashore locally.'

Al-Basiri lowered his voice, 'I take it we're talking about Elke Kohl. I was on The Koidutaht' the night she was murdered.' I recognised her from Hotels in Leipzig where she posed as a prostitute. I think Igor Shertsov took the correct action when he found her scouring round his ship with a torch in her hand. There is every chance she could be a policewoman or a secret agent for the German Government.'

'The killing didn't end there Mohammed', admitted Geordie, 'I got a tip-off that the police were going to be waiting for the Caledonian Princess docking at Eyemouth so I arranged to have a bomb planted on board which sank the boat. To date no debris has floated to the surface.'

'Unfortunately, that is par for the course in our business', sighed al-Basiri, 'Do you have any other trading problems?'

'No, I have managed to replace the Caledonian Princess with the Northern Star so I shall be able to keep up trading arrangements with you. On the receipts end my charges for laundering money have increased recently so I probably need some help in that department. I'm planning to go over to Estonia to introduce the crew of the Northern Star to Igor – maybe you should come over too, Mohammed.

'I'll think about it Geordie. I have never been in Edinburgh, so I'm going to play the tourist today and take in all the sights. Where do you think I should begin?'

McNab quickly answered, 'Go out the front of the hotel on to Princes Street, turn left and take the first on the left and you will see all the open-top buses waiting to show you the city.'

'Thanks Geordie, I'll take your advice and be in touch with you soon.'

Across the city at Police Scotland's Fettes Headquarters D.C.I. McKirdy was contemplating his next move. His investigation had been halted by the disappearance of The Caledonian Princess. The co-incidence of the ship going missing just when he had arranged to search the trawler bugged him. Had there been a leak from his department and if so to whom?

His prime suspect was Geordie McNab, but he did not want to rope him in just yet, preferring to wait until Mhairi McClure reported on the drug peddler's money laundering activities.

Grant had not told D.S. Lomax or D. C. Luxton about Mhairi's expected arrival or anything about her identity. As far as they were concerned, she had been foisted upon them by MI6 who were investigating money launderers in Edinburgh. Most importantly of all he made them unaware that he knew Mhairi as both of his detectives had not been in the department long enough to remember what happened ten years ago.

Two weeks later McKirdy was at Edinburgh Airport as the passengers from British Airways 11.30 a.m. flight from Heathrow came through the arrival gate. He spotted Mhairi immediately walking smartly to the carousel to pick up her case. She had been taken out of Askham two days earlier, whisked into London for a complete makeover physically and sartorially. The result was she was transformed back into an older version of the clever, attractive woman Grant had known from a previous time. Walking alongside her strode the athletic figure of Cam Anderson who was to be responsible for her security while she was in Edinburgh. Mhairi had been given a new identity and was now to be known as Veronica Benson.

Grant stepped forward and tipped his hat, 'Good morning Veronica and welcome to Edinburgh.'

Veronica stepped back as though she was inspecting the Guards, 'Grant McKirdy, Jeez are you still keeping Edinburgh safe from the likes of me!', she laughed then shook the detective's hand before continuing, 'this is the latest man in my life Campbell Anderson.'

'Please to meet you Campbell, Hugh McFaul speaks very highly of you.'

'More than I would of him!', exclaimed Veronica.

Grant cut her short, 'If you want to enjoy your stay in Edinburgh living a life of luxury there will be no more remarks like that.'

Veronica realised she had crossed the line with her scathing words causing her to blush and mumble, 'Sorry.'

The trio made their way to the waiting police BMW and set off for the Sheraton Hotel in Lothian Road where rooms had been arranged facing on to Edinburgh Castle and Princes Street. Along the way Ian Lomax acted as tour guide for Veronica, who had never been to Edinburgh, and Campbell, who could not remember much about the Capital having only been here on a drunken rugby tour.

The newly arrivals registered in as Veronica Benson and Graeme Devonshire, Cam's nom de plume when he was engaged in field operations. After the luggage had been taken to their rooms Veronica and Cam followed Grant into a meeting room, leaving Lomax to guard the car in the courtyard at the rear entrance of the Sheraton.

Grant had arranged coffee and shortbread biscuits for the visitors before starting his debrief: 'Veronica have you enjoyed the last few days in London being pampered and readying yourself for the task ahead?'

'Apart from having my body abused by a surgeon sticking a tag into my arm and being pummelled by masseurs to remove the pale drawn look of a prisoner. Yes.'

'This is Wednesday so enjoy the city for the next two days as I don't think we shall be seeing our man until sometime over the weekend. The man I'm referring to is Geordie McNab a local drug dealer and although he did not kill Elke Kohl it was the activities of his organisation which led to her death. The actual killers reside in Estonia.'

Grant went into his briefcase, took out a folder which he opened and produced a photograph of Geordie McNab, 'This is the man who we want you take into your confidence and get him to talk out his business. You will not be wired up, but Campbell will, so keep close together. McNab is on twenty - four hours surveillance so we shall know when he makes his way to the Royal Casino so be ready to move at short notice. Veronica, where would a man like McNab be likely to dispose of his illegal earnings?'

Veronica puffed her cheeks out before answering, 'It's hard to say. often difficult to say. If he's new to money laundering, he'll probably be quite happy to arrange a safe bank and not worry too much about what he is being charged. As they gain more confidence dealers usually are in contact with competitors and, provided they are not competing for the same distribution areas they will exchange information about disposing their money.'

'Well Veronica let us hope you can make Geordie McNab an offer he can't refuse. Tomorrow I'll arrange for plain clothes officers to take you down to Leith, where the casino is situated, so that you can familiarise yourselves with the area.'

'Have a good night on the town tonight but both MI6 and Police Scotland's orders after tonight are 'NO ALCO-HOL.'"

Campbell smiled and added, 'Well Miss Benson we better make good use of our time before the curfew comes down.'

Veronica laughed, 'Have no fear, my time in prison has not dented my Irish desire for enjoyment.'

Grant stood up, 'I must be going now. You both have my telephone number so call me if you need anything.'

Going up in the lift Veronica saw an advert for the Sheraton Spa, 'Campbell that looks good. They've got a swimming-pool, do you fancy a dip before our evening meal?'

'Sorry to be a spoiler Veronica but I don't have my trunks with me.'

'I haven't got a costume but I'm sure a place like this will sell them. I will go down and ask at reception and come back up and tell you.'

The elevator doors opened. Campbell stepped out leaving Veronica to descend back to Reception. Once she had disappeared Cam suddenly had a horrible sinking feeling he had just been duped by Veronica who was about to leave the building. He rushed down the stairs and arrived breathless at reception to find Veronica in conversation with one of the receptionists.

'What are you doing here Cam?'

Cam took a deep breath then lied, 'I just realised I had forgot to give you my trunk size.'

'I'm sure these Speedo's will fit.' Veronica replied holding up a pair of red and blue patterned briefs.

Ten minutes later Cam knocked on Veronica's door and she appeared like him in a white towelling robe and slippers to match, courtesy of the Sheraton. They made their way down to the spa then into the twenty-five metre swimming pool area, disrobed, showered quickly, and got into the pool. Cam was grateful for the exercise and did six lengths freestyle before joining Veronica who was demonstrating a slow swan lake breast-stroke action. As he approached her, she appeared to choke and started coughing and Cam's natural reaction was to pull Veronica towards him. Veronica had admired Cam's body and her fainted cough allowed her to get close to the first male she had touched for a few years. She quickly recovered, smiled sensually at Cam before sliding her hand down to the sizeable bump on his swimming trunks.

Cam drew back protesting, 'What do you think you are doing?'

'Sorry Cam, I was just testing if you were up for a bit fun. I have not had any 'fun' for a few years, and I couldn't resist trying.'

'Veronica, I take my work very seriously and it does not involve acting like James Bond!'

His words brought a conclusion to the swimming, but Veronica's frustrations did not dissolve there. As she waited for Cam, she read the list of treatments the Spa had on offer and asked the young, muscled attendant, 'Who does the full Body Massage?'

'I do Madam.'

'When can you take me?'

'As soon as my colleague returns from her tea break.'

Cam joined Veronica at reception who informed him, 'Cam this young man is going to give me a full body massage, so I'll meet you in the bar in a couple of hours.'

Cam was speechless and left Veronica to it.

Fifteen minutes later Veronica removed her robe and lay face down on the bed. Marco, the Turkish masseur applied warm oils to her back and legs moving his strong fingers into her body as she gasped with pleasure. Turning on to her back she requested, 'Now do my front and especially my groin.'

Marco smiled and obliged by starting at her neck and moving his hands over her breasts before stroking her pubic hair then slipping his fingers inside her. Veronica used her foot to stroke down the inside of his hairy leg then up to the swelling in his shorts. Marco stood up removed his shirt and shorts before proceeding to see to Veronica's needs as she devoured him for the next hour. When she was satisfied Veronica gathered herself together, thanked Marco for his time, shook his hand before returning to her room.

As she was leaving the spa she turned and spoke to Marco, 'Thanks for a lovely afternoon. You were just the tonic I needed. I do not have any money on me for a tip but put through a charge for an extra session and I will settle it.

Two hours later Veronica entered the cocktail bar with a big smile on her face wearing a silk floral blouse over black slacks which caught the eye of businessmen in the bar until they saw she was joining Cam. He had smartened himself up and dressed casually, in grey houndstooth slacks over a black sea island cotton shirt.

Cam greeted Veronica with an opening salvo, 'Did the body massage come up to expectations?'

'Absolutely! I feel like a new woman and ravenous for a good feed. You should try it sometime Cam.' she concluded with a twinkle in her eye.

166

'Enough of your temptress remarks. What can I get you to drink?'

'A Campari and soda – my perfect aperitif.'

'I 'll go for a large gin & tonic.'

The rest of the night passed off very amicably with Veronica commenting on how her life had changed from being a public- school educated socialite to ending up in prison with a life sentence. Cam played his cards close to his chest and made up most of what he said about himself, after all that is what good spies normally do for a living!

Chapter 22

The earphones informed Mohammed al-Basiri, 'We are passing on your left Holyrood Palace, where Mary, Queen of Scots lover, Lord Darnley, was murdered. On your right is the Scottish Parliament opened in 2001 to host the devolved Scottish Government who are responsible for taking care of many government departments, apart from defence, immigration, and foreign policy amongst others.

This was the sixth time Basiri had heard these words. 'An interesting place this Edinburgh.' he thought to himself 'I had not expected to find an opportunity to cause havoc here, but I'm staring at the perfect opportunity. On my left, Holyrood Palace where my men could fire rocket launchers into from Arthur Seat, a nine-hundred foot extinct volcano looking down on the Palace. This would put a dent in the British Establishment and the Royal Family's official Scottish residence in Scotland.

Across the street the Scottish Parliament could also be reached simultaneously by the same procedure which would put the emergency services under even more pressure. It may not have the impact of the Twin Towers attack on New York in 2001 but it would remind the British that their fight against Islamic fundamentalism is still very much alive. Both these targets will be well protected so I will have to organise a diversion.'

The earphone continued. 'Next we shall be entering the Queen's Park which is a Royal park where the traffic is controlled by Royal consent, closed to all vehicles on Sundays and to commercial vehicles at all times.'

Returning to his thoughts Mohammed continued to think of the logistics of his bold plan.

'The Glasgow cell should be able to acquire weapons within a few days and keep them out of Edinburgh until the night before the attack probably disguised under deliveries of fruit or vegetables bound for the Edinburgh markets.'

'Now how can I bring the traffic to a standstill in Edinburgh?'

Scotland's capital city with its mostly white-collared industries isn't a hot-bed for budding al-Qaeda followers. Mohammed al- Basiri decided to retreat to Nelson. There he could make use of a safe house and move around freely among the local population undistinguished wearing traditional Asian clothes, which wouldn't be the case in Edinburgh. After making numerous coded messages it became apparent that getting a hold of rocket launchers would prove difficult to smuggle into Britain past Customs & Excise. This only delayed his plan and forced him come up with a new plan of attack.

Chapter 23

'D.C.I. McKirdy, we intercepted a call on Geordie Mc Nab's mobile. He's making arrangements to go to the Royal Casino on Friday night.' reported an excited D.S. Lomax.

'Good news Ian, I'll let Cam Anderson know and he can alert Veronica Benson to be ready to move once we know he is on his way down to Leith. As a rule, he doesn't go there until after ten o'clock so they will just have to sit around in the Sheraton and await our call. I will get Bob Salkeld and Linda McTiernan to make a re-appearance at the casino to give Veronica and Campbell cover in case they should need it. They are now known to the management and won't look out of place.'

'Will I let Avril know about Friday night Sir?'

'No, I'd rather keep this between us Ian. Avril has been putting in a lot of shifts lately and she deserves a night off to enjoy herself.'

'She certainly knows how to do that Grant, partying every weekend and going to Majorca regularly for Hen Parties. Oh, to be young and single again!'

'Too bad Ian', said his consoling boss, 'You'll just have to settle for taking the kids to the cinema for two hours of cartoons. You crack on and I will speak to Campbell Anderson.'

Anderson answered his mobile after three rings with his Sandhurst voice, 'Anderson speaking.'

'Hello Campbell, Grant McKirdy here, are you still managing to keep Veronica Benson under control?'

'Yes, we've been doing the usual tourist thing around Edinburgh, the Castle, The Scott Monument and so on. Last night we took your advice and took a taxi down to Leith to stake out the Royal Casino. When we were in Leith, we managed to board the Royal Yacht Britannia for a tour, before having an excellent Italian meal. Early in the day we took the tour bus round the City and down near Holyrood House we passed another bus going in the opposite direction. I know this sounds funny but one of the passengers on that bus reminded me of Mohammed al-Basiri. Can you get Hugh McFaul to send you his photo and check out the CCTV on the tour buses, the tour we were on left Waverley Bridge at 10.00 a.m.'

'I'll look into that for you Cam. I'm envious of this holiday you and Veronica are having, Police Scotland's idea of entertainment is a pie and a pint in a local pub. Anyhow, the reason I called. Surveillance has picked up a call from Geordie McNab's mobile that he and his bodyguard 'Maniac' McLagan are planning to go to the casino on Friday night. We do not have an exact time yet, but we will confirm it to you as soon as we know. Does that all sound okay to you Cam?'

'Yes, I will make sure Veronica has on her best bib and tucker to meet Edinburgh's Mr. Big, - who hopefully we'll be bringing down to size soon.'

'Good, be in touch on Friday night.'

Cam went down to the lounge where he found Veronica scouring the pink pages of the Financial Times. She had ordered herself coffee and signalled to the waiter to bring another cup for Cam.

'Just catching up with the financial markets. It is not a newspaper which is available to prisoners at Askham Hall. I prefer to be in a position where I can drop in a few one-liners on the state of the market which always impresses new customers.'

'Good thinking Veronica. I've just had Grant McKirdy on the phone. It'll probably be all systems go tomorrow night which should give you sufficient time to prepare for Geordie McNab and impress him into submission with your financial expertise.'

'Cam that last remark had a hint of sarcasm in it so it will cost you a glass of procecco – and get something for yourself!'

Cam laughed and headed for the bar for the last time today. He wanted a clear head tomorrow as this could be when they round up everyone connected with the murder of Elke Kohl.

Chapter 24

'I've been on to that bloody travel agent for two hours Geordie. You would think we were going to the moon instead of ten days all-inclusive in Malaga. I booked for the McLagans as well, so I'll leave you to get the money for that one.'

'When do we leave Ella?'

'24th March at 11.00 a.m. so no early rises for us.'

'Good I'll let Manic know.' replied Geordie, then talking to himself he added, 'No way will Maniac be paying for the holiday. I am grateful to him for sinking The Caledonian Princess and scaring Admiral Arbuthnott to death. With both of them parties out the way I can sleep at night.'

McNab caught up with Maniac as he was doing his rounds down in Drylaw, one of Edinburgh's toughest districts, 'How's things Maniac?'

'I'm doon in Drylaw where wee Alfie Armstrong owes us a couple of grand, for the gear we supplied two weeks ago. The silly little bastard he has spent the money on some stripper he met in the Doocot pub.'

'Is he with you just now?'

'Yes.'

'Put him on.'

A weak voice squeaked, 'Hello Mr McNab.'

'Hi Alfie, what have you been up to with my money?'

'As I telt Maniac I was seeing Marlene Crawford frae the Doocot. It is, honest, this wus the first time a've been with a real woman and she cost me a fortune! We went doon fir a weekend to London and honest to God she wus expensive, as ah say she cost me a bloody fortune. Actually, she cost you a fortune as she ran off with a' the money,' he stupidly chuckled.

McNab changed his tone, 'You stupid little bastard! You better get me back that cash in the next seventy-two hours or she will be the last woman you will be with, as Maniac will cut your balls off! Pass the phone back to Maniac.'

'Maniac, you heard what I said, he is got three days to repay me or he will suffer a lifelong injury. As a reminder break a couple of his fingers before you let him go.'

Maniac smiled at the unfortunate Armstrong now turning white with fear, 'With pleasure Boss.'

Chapter 25

A strong icy wind howled round the back courtyard of the Sheraton Hotel as the taxi arrived to take Veronica and Campbell down to the Royal Casino in Leith. Veronica was grateful for the fur coat and matching Cossack hat MI6 had supplied for her trip to Edinburgh to add credence to her character as a high-rolling financial guru.

Twenty minutes later they arrived at the Royal Casino and quickly rushed into the building to be met by a staff member who relieved them of their coats. An attendant escorted them through to the bar, pointing out as they walked where all the different gambling games could be found. As they arrived at the bar the couple thanked the attendant for their help and ordered a drink from the bar.

As Cam waited for the drinks Veronica cast her eyes over the premises. The casino was decorated in a warm red colour scheme with the wallpaper and soft furnishings almost matching. The furniture consisted of a mixture of velvet sofas and large armchairs designed to let you sleep off an over consumption of alcohol or sulk after an unsuccessful trip to the tables. A series of standard lamps at regular intervals were positioned to shine down on the rich dark coffee tables to enhance the relaxed ambiance. Two large wooden doors led the gamblers through to the gaming room where all the action took place. The croupiers were all actively taking in money from the punters, the men immaculate in black tuxedos and the females clad in tight fitting white blouses cut away to show off a bit of cleavage above black velvet trousers.

Cam and Veronica engaged themselves in polite conversation whilst people watching the assembled gamblers for a sign of Geordie McNab. A half hour passed and still no sign of him despite the Police Scotland unmarked car team reporting McNab and two of his heavies had left his house in

Barnton Gate which was only three and a half miles from the casino. Suddenly the wait was over, Geordie McNab made his entrance, looking every bit like the gangster he had dreamt of being all his life. He was wearing grey pin stripe suit, a black shirt and a white tie supporting a jewel-clustered tie pin. On his feet he had a pair of black-patent crocodile embossed leather shoes. McNab's receding hair-line was slicked back to complete the Godfather look. His two companions looked equally threatening in their black suits covering their scarlet silk shirts, completed with matching white ties.

Cam made a comment, 'He's smaller than I had imagined although extraordinarily strong, if you look at his shoulders and hands. He probably owes his build to throwing about large pieces of scrap   metal.'

Veronica couldn't keep her eyes of 'Maniac' McLagan 'He has a face you would just like to smack if you were brave enough. I have seen his type before when I lived in Northern Ireland. Big hard men who strut about inflicting fear into anyone who challenges them and always trying to start a fight at the drop of a hat, because that's what they enjoy doing more than anything.'

Cam asked, 'Do you miss Northern Ireland?'

'Yes', Veronica answered in a serious tone, 'I sometimes feel if I had my life over again, I would accept my fiancé being murdered and settle for an entirely different lifestyle. That way I would not have been led into aiding the Irish Republican cause, which got me involved in carrying out some hellish crimes which were totally out of character to those who knew me in my youth. But that is all behind me now, so tonight I need to concentrate on getting my prison sentence reduced.'

Cam reflected on Veronica's words. How did a smart, attractive, intelligent woman allow herself to become radicalised? Cam had never been in any serious relationships preferring to live the life of a womanising bachelor although he knew that could not go on forever. For the present he remained dedicated to serving Her Majesty's Secret Service.

'Come on Veronica, we have some work to do.'

The gamblers in the betting area cast an eye over the two newcomers, Veronica in particular, who was dressed in a purple figure-hugging silk cocktail dress with a slit at the side which rested well on her slim, toned physique. Her blonde hair was cut short and swept back over her ears and to complete the look she had a gold pendant hanging just above her cleavage. They both surveyed the lay-out of the casino before heading for the cash exchange to buy betting chips to use when placing their selections. Cam produced his bank card and both players got the equivalent of two thousand pounds each.

They decided not to join McNab and his colleagues at the roulette wheel immediately, instead settling to throw a few dice with mixed success – Veronica lost one hundred pounds while Cam won two hundred and fifty pounds.

Two players at the roulette wheel in the shape of Bob Salkeld and Linda McTiernan vacated their seats allowing Veronica and Cam to close in on Geordie McNab. The new players were welcomed by a few nodding heads from the others round the table as the croupier asked them to place their bets. Veronica placed one hundred pounds on 'Red' which came up favourably with an even money return. After her early success she became a little more adventurous and had a good run which attracted the attention of everyone round the table including Geordie McNab.

'If you don't mind me saying so Miss, you have an incredibly good system which I wish you could pass to the rest of us.' said a smiling McNab.

'Well Sir, in my line of work I study the odds mathematically and I trust I get the probability right.'

'You've lost me, what is it you do for a living?'

177

'My colleague and I are financial advisors who concentrate on the international currency markets and on providing tax avoidance solutions for our clients.'

McNab had bought the bait, 'That's interesting, I also do some dealings in the international monetary markets. Would you like to join me for a drink to compare notes?' putting out his stubby right hand he added, 'my name is Geordie McNab.

McNab found a quiet corner in the bar after telling his two bodyguards to leave him with his new friends

Veronica had accepted his handshake whilst turning to introduce Cam as Graeme Doncaster, a name he would answer to throughout his dealings with McNab 'I'm Veronica Benson, we both work for Farrer Financial Services, FFS to you. You will not see us in the phonebook, our clients, shall we say, are specialised and not always trading legitimately. Our remit is to find them suitable destinations for their spare cash if you know what we mean. Casinos are attractive networking establishments for us as many of the attendees are trying to cleanse the excess money they have accumulated.'

Geordie held up his hand, 'Stop there this all sounds very interesting. Let me go and get you a drink. What will it be?

'A glass of prosecco would be nice.' replied Veronica.

'As I am in Scotland a large Talisker Malt whisky is my tipple.' said 'Graeme'.

Ten minutes later McNab returned from the bar with the drinks and sat opposite Veronica and Cam. 'Tell me do you come up to Scotland often looking for business?'

'Unfortunately, no, Scotland only has eight per cent of the United kingdom's net worth so only has limited scope for us as many of our clients are based globally.'

'So where do you lodge your client's money?'

'We have just met you so I would not like to divulge too much information at this stage. However, to give you a glimpse into our world we operate with about twenty banks which are based in tax havens round the world, everywhere from Europe to Central America and the Far East. The trick is to transfer the funds quickly through newly registered companies who are transferring fictitious goods which the local Customs & Excise officers in these tax havens process as genuine, for a small fee.'

'What is it you do Mr McNab?', Cam asked.

McNab took a gulp of beer before answering, 'I have a large demolition and scrap metal business not far from here which I operate during the day, but the bulk of my income is not transparent.'

Veronica prompted him., 'You mean from criminal activities.'

'Well Miss Benson I like your direct style. Yes, my income is not quite kosher shall we say.''

'If that is the case it can only be the result of robbery, burglary or drug trafficking.' assessed Veronica.

'You could be right, but I am not admitting to anything tonight. I currently move money to Bermuda through an agent who 'Buys' scrap metal from me but not in sufficient quantities which means I am constantly storing cash. That is buried funds which I am getting no return on. The other thing which bothers me is Bermuda have an expensive processing charge so I would be interested to know what FFS would cost me.'

'Can I ask what your current transaction fees are costing you?' searched Veronica.

'Four per cent.'

'Wow! I can understand your concern. FFS would be looking to charge you half that price.' Veronica confessed.

Geordie looked over his shoulder before continuing the conversation, 'I am not comfortable about discussing this any further here. How long are you going to be in Edinburgh? We could meet up tomorrow and I could show you documentation regarding my present arrangements and you could see if there is anything you can do for me.'

'Graeme and I will be in Edinburgh for two days. Tomorrow morning, we have an appointment in Perthshire, but we should be back mid-afternoon. Where do you suggest we meet? Here's my card you can call me anytime once you have decided a venue.'

'Miss Benson, you will probably be coming back down the motorway over the Forth Road Bridge so why don't we meet in the Dakota Hotel in South Queensferry which is just off the motorway when you leave the bridge.'

Cam spoke up, 'We have Sat-Nav, so we'll be there okay. How about three thirty? Give us your mobile number and if we are running late, we will call you.'

Cam wrote down Geordie's number and the two parties headed back out into a bitingly cold East wind whistling through Leith Docks.

Back at the Sheraton Veronica and Cam had a quick debrief.

Cam kicked off the resume of the evening's events, 'I thought that went rather well and hopefully we can find out more about McNab's activities tomorrow. I thought your line about us having an appointment in Perthshire was a clever diversion.'

'I felt it aided our credentials, but we shall have to make a trip to Perthshire in the morning as Geordie McNab is likely to have us followed.', Veronica suggested.

'I will phone Grant McKirdy first thing in the morning and get him to have two of his local Perth-based officers to meet us for lunch.'

'Do you know anywhere in the area we can dine?'

'At MI6 we never scrimp and as we are posing as two financial high-flyers, I will book a table at Gleneagles Hotel for 12.00 noon.'

Next morning Cam phoned McKirdy and requested support. Grant's reaction was 'Lucky buggers, I've never been there.' He phoned Perth and was not surprised when two of his fellow D.C.I.'s Ralph Smith and Jack Hope wanted to take up the offer of a slap-up lunch, but Grant persuaded them that he needed officers who were not normally in the public eye. It was decided that Veronica and Cam would be joined by Alexa Gibson and Harry Anthony.

Geordie McNab was also active the morning after meeting Veronica and Graeme Devonshire. He took out Veronica's business card and phoned Farrer Financial Services. The call went through to a special phone in MI6's office and was answered by Norma, Hugh McFaul's personal assistant.

'Farrer Financial Services. How can I help you?'

'Yes, my name is George McNab' said Geordie in a polite Edinburgh accent, 'May I speak to Veronica Benson or Graeme Devonshire?'

'Terribly sorry Sir but they are both away on business to Scotland and won't be back for a couple of days. Would you like to leave a message for them?

'No thanks,' McNab put down the phone and thought to himself 'well they seem genuine.'

Veronica and Cam left the Sheraton ten o'clock sharp in a BMW 5 series and headed for the M9 motorway which took them out past Stirling then on to the A91 heading for Perth. They took the exit for Auchterarder and were soon cruising up the Gleneagles driveway with its famous golf courses on either side and parked outside the entrance. Cam kept his eye on the rear window throughout the journey and commented on the black Mercedes which always seemed to be about five hundred yards behind them. Gleneagles had long been the playground for the rich and famous from all over the world involved in all aspects of life from politics, entertainment to sports champions.

Cam went to reception to announce their arrival and get directions to the dining room. Alexa and Harry were already sitting in the cocktail bar anxiously waiting. Cam approached and introduced Veronica.

'Hello, I'm Campbell Anderson and this is Veronica Benson. I am assuming you two are Alexa and Harry from Perth C.I.D.

The couple smiled and shook hands as Cam continued, 'We're glad you could join us today. We are involved in trying to bring a nasty drug dealer to justice and we are certain he has had us followed here to see if our identities are genuine. We told them we were financial gurus from a fictitious company called Farrer Financial Services and that we had a meeting with two money launderers who wanted surplus cash sent overseas and that's where you two fit in.'

Harry laughed. 'As they say, 'there's no such thing as a free lunch'.

Cam raised his hand in defence, 'There is today – it is all on us. I said we were posing as financial wizards but that is not altogether untrue as Veronica is an expert in moving illegitimate cash and turning it into usable currency.'

Alexa cast a glance at Veronica, 'Well that's a topic which will keep us occupied over lunch!'

Her words proved to be true as Veronica gave a fascinating insight into how international criminals moved their money. The food as expected was five-star – Alexa convinced Veronica to start with Cullen skink (a Scottish fish soup) while the men had the liver pate, then it was on to fillet steaks all round followed by a selection of desserts. Cam was an excellent host supplying the Perth police with fine wine which Veronica and he refrained from because of their impending meeting with Geordie McNab later in the day. Two hours later they said goodbye to Alexa and Harry, who had been very good company and crossed the roundabout in the direction of their car, casting a quick glance at the black Mercedes where the driver, wearing a chauffeur's cap was kidding on he was sleeping at the wheel.

They had time on their hands so Cam took a different route back towards Edinburgh through Glen Devon which was more scenic and quieter which meant the Mercedes, if it followed, would be more exposed. Soon they joined the M90 at Kinross then travelled down to the Forth Road Bridge and marvelled at its sister bridge, The Forth Rail Bridge, one of the finest engineering feats ever built. Exiting off the motorway they descended into the pretty port of South Queensferry which housed a marina just off the cobbled streets. Cam guided the BMW down the slip road sign posted 'South Queensferry' and followed the Satnav instructions for a couple of minutes which took him into the Dakota Hotel car park The Dakota Hotel was a modern building with an outside covering of dark, almost black glass which made first time visitors wary of what lay within.

Before they arrived McNab had received a phone call, 'Hi boss Gogs here, I followed them up the road and they entered Gleneagles Hotel as though they owned the place. They did not emerge for a couple of hours but were shown off the premises by a smartly dressed couple who went back indoors. They drove back down Glendevon and that made it more difficult to follow but they are now on the M90 heading your way.'

'Thanks, Gogs. You have confirmed what I wanted to hear. Bye.'

As Veronica and Graeme entered the hotel Geordie McNab was waiting for them and ushered them to a private room just off the bistro bar. A waitress saw them go into the room and gave them a few minutes to settle down before knocking on the door to take their order for tea and coffees.

Geordie sat on a bucket-shaped red fabric chair on the other side of a black Formica topped table facing Veronica and Graeme.

'Have you had a good day? The weather's not been too bad for this time of year,' reaching into his satchel (which put Cam on alert) he continued, 'I've brought you what paperwork there is so you can see how I currently do things and if there is anything else you need, I will be only too happy to oblige if you can save me money.'

Veronica picked up the documents Geordie had passed over the table and started to examine them passing each sheet to Graeme as if for a second opinion.

'You are certainly moving quite a bit of cash Geordie. How is it accounted for at present?'

'Oh, usual money laundering practises – tanning shops, taxis which keep their meter going most of the day, but never leave the garage and almost anything that can wash the bad cash into good clean money. It's the surplus cash I need to get moved on so that I can pay for the drugs through international banks without having to trust couriers to do it for me.'

Graeme joined the discussion, 'Geordie who are your customers?'

'It varies, Edinburgh is a wealthy city with a number of independent schools full of kids with disposable incomes, so we charge them more. At the other end of the scale are the council estates full of the poor who need daily fixes to relieve them from the deprived conditions in which they live. The West of Scotland has a far higher population, but my supplies would be subject to competition from established gangs. We've entered into an agreement with them, whereby I supply the East of Scotland from Berwick to John of Groats and they take everything in the West.'

Veronica enquired, 'Do you ever get any offers to work internationally?'

'Yes, I am often asked to tender for demolition work in some African countries and Eire.'

'Good!' exclaimed Veronica, 'FFS has good contacts with Ireland and we can arrange for a company to set up a contract with you to supply scrap metal on a regular basis. You could disguise your surplus cash in metal boxes which our contact will get changed into Euros before investing the funds with tax havens. I'll instruct them to move it on quickly several times so that it becomes untraceable. You can use these new companies to purchase property or jewellery as an investment for your retirement.'

'At present you're giving the money to a local agent who is getting it out of the country to Bermuda, but from what I see, they are not trading on and finding a home for it to blossom. You are being charged a four per cent admin fee when we would charge just over half that, plus holding your funds in cash does not compare with the yield you would get from investing in property in the long term.'

Geordie McNab was impressed by Veronica's performance and there was only one thing on his mind, 'When can I start using your services?'

'We don't put anything in writing by way of a signed contract. We prefer to conduct our business by email. If you would like any customer references, we can supply them although you will appreciate the nature of our business does not lend itself to shouting about our abilities from the rooftops. When are you next expecting to have a tranche of cash which needs cleansing?'

Geordie outlined his work-in-progress for the coming weeks, ' 'The Northern Star', a fishing vessel from Peterhead will be delivering a shipment of drugs next week. So allowing for distribution by my army of couriers selling the drugs and collecting in the money, I would say three weeks.'

Cam asked a bold question, 'Do you ever meet any of your suppliers?'

Geordie's eyes took on a serious look, 'No, not normally but one of them did come to see me yesterday.'

'That must have been a bit risky for him, flying into the U.K. was it not?'

'No, he came in on a boat under the cover of darkness but whether he will return home that way I wouldn't like to say.'

(Cam smiled to himself, 'So it could have been Mohammed al-Basiri I saw from the open-deck bus tour window.')

Graeme continued his line of enquiry, 'It would make sense to re-trace his steps.'

'Well, that is not exactly possible' Interrupted Geordie. 'as The Caledonian Princess, the boat he arrived in, was lost at sea a couple of weeks ago. To go back the way he came, he would have to go to Peterhead and sail on the 'Northern Star.'

Veronica steered the conversation back to the agenda of their meeting, 'I'll confirm to you in the next few days the address in Ireland to send the scrap metal in Ireland and then it is over to you to do the manual work. Are you going to be available to be contacted at any time day or night?'

McNab responded, 'Yes Miss Benson but I have booked up a holiday to go for a week to Marbella on March 24. I'm taking the wife and kids along with my right-hand man Alistair McLagan and his family by way of a thank you.'

Veronica chuckled, 'That's magnanimous of you Geordie, I wished our bosses gave out holidays! Any jobs going?'

'No Miss Benson, I couldn't see you carrying out Maniac's duties. I don't think you would ever resort to any form of violence.'

Veronica smiled back and thought to herself – 'If only you knew the half of it McNab.'

'We'll leave it at that for today. You have my office number which I understand you used earlier today to check out our credentials.'

'You can't blame me for making sure Miss Benson of your identity. There are a lot of fraudulent criminals in this world.'

At that they all left the hotel for the carpark where Maniac was waiting for his boss in a Mercedes 500. Veronica and Cam shook hands with McNab as though they had completed a business deal and went their own ways.

Chapter 27

Cam wasted no time in contacting Hugh McFaul, 'Cam here Hugh Mhairi and I have just come out of a meeting with the local drug Lord, Geordie McNab. During our chat I asked him about suppliers. He admitted he had met one of them in Edinburgh yesterday which makes me think that it was Mohammed al-Basiri who I saw on the tourist bus. I think we have to step up surveillance on him and his likely al-Qaeda contacts.'

'Good work Cam, I'll give the search an amber warning and see if any of our whistle-blowers can link any possible attacks to Edinburgh. I'll be in touch as soon as I know anything further. Bye for now.'

'Sorry about that Veronica and referring to you as Mhairi, How did you think our meeting went with McNab?

'He's a bit out of his depth in comparison with the organisations I have served', observed Veronica, 'but all he can see at present is cost savings. He will try us out so you will have to set up an arrangement with a friendly scrap dealer in Ireland.'

Cam re-acted, 'I'll get our guys to put a request to Interpol who will use their influence with the Irish Garda who will come up with a contact.'

'As soon as he transmits cash to Ireland, I'll set up the necessary links to dispose of the money. This could take a couple of weeks before I have any funds to work with so what shall I do in the meantime?'

'Good question Veronica, I will let you know after I have consulted Hugh and Assistant Commissioner Richard Hartley.'

It was back to the Sheraton Hotel where Veronica went to the spa while Cam made his phone call to MI6 headquarters. Cam explained the situation and asked what he should do about Veronica?

Hugh set up a conference call with Richard Hartley, Cam, and himself. Hartley kicked off the proceedings, 'Not an easy one Anderson, I wasn't thinking about how long this would take. Come back down to London tomorrow and I'll find a safe house for her for a couple of weeks. If nothing happens by then it'll be back to HMP Askham Hall for Miss McClure.'

'Thank you, Sir I will break the news to Veronica over Dinner.'

Cam decided to take Veronica out for dinner for her last night and had booked a table at the Dome in George Street, a former banking hall which had been tastefully converted into a restaurant. The Dome had won prizes for its décor and was now a tourist attraction, especially at Christmas when it housed a twenty-foot Christmas tree reaching up from the middle of the bar in the direction of the stained - glass domed ceiling. Veronica was impressed and had taken Cam's advice and dressed for the occasion in the same rig-out which had created a stir at the Royal Casino earlier in the week.

The restaurant was busy with a mixture of Edinburgh's professional classes and tourists which gave the place a pleasant atmosphere. A waitress took their order for drinks and left them to ponder over the menu. Having made their selections Cam took the opportunity to advise Veronica of Richard Hartley's decision on her future.

He started by raising his glass, 'Cheers Veronica here's to a good night. This afternoon I had a conference call with Hugh and Richard Hartley about what we should do next - in particular, what your role should be. Hartley was pleased that you'd got Geordie McNab's trust and hopefully he will be back to us soon. Tomorrow we'll be returning to London where we've arranged to put you up in one of our safe houses sharing with security guards. You'll be there for at least two weeks, working on setting up havens for McNab's money. You will be able to walk about London freely as you know we've fitted you with a tracker.'

'Are you not scared I get it removed and vanish?'

'No Veronica', replied Cam coldly, 'What we didn't tell you is that we've actually inserted two microchips into your body, the other one contains a toxic substance which will kill you instantly. The problem you have is you don't know one from the other.'

Veronica took a gulp of much needed iced water, puffed her cheeks, and exhaled, 'You guys really do think of everything.'

Cam broke the silence that followed, 'Sorry to be the bearer of bad news Veronica.'

'So, what happens if McNab fails to call?'

'You will be returned to Askham Hall but with a reduced sentence.'

'Cam I was just starting to enjoy myself. I might have known it wouldn't last much longer.'

'Look Mhairi, sorry Veronica, I have been asked to submit a report on your performance which I think is very professional. There could be a chance to assist the department in the future as Richard Hartley is keen to utilise spies who are not known to the opposition. He constantly surveys all the universities looking for the next Mata Hari.'

Cam's words cheered Veronica up, and even more so with what he came up with next, 'While you are in lockdown in London I could see if they would allow you to spend some time with your mother probably at a quiet location in the Cotswolds. Would you like that?'

Veronica could not contain herself she stood up and leaned forward and gave Cam a big kiss. The other guests must have wondered what was going on.

'Sorry Cam, I did not mean to embarrass you. I would love to see my mother as she has only been able to visit me a few times in the last four years.'

Mhairi's father had died eighteen months previously and she had attended his funeral in Newcastle County Down under strict security and on the understanding the service was restricted to close family members.

The rest of the evening went off extremely well and the excellent meal was enhanced by some delicious wines and liqueurs. When the waitress came with the bill she chatted to the couple, 'What are you celebrating tonight?'

Cam answered, 'Nothing specific, but we've had a couple of successful business meetings.'

'Are you going down the stairs now to 'Why Not' our nightclub?'

'We don't know anything about it.'

'Well if you want, I can get you passes that entitle you to free admission as you have been using the restaurant, plus a safe passage into the VIP lounge as it is usually busy on Saturdays.'

Veronica fuelled with alcohol was excited at the prospect of some disco music, 'Come on Cam, I can think of nothing better to finish off our trip to Scotland!'

A waiter escorted the couple past the waiting queue and into the darkened lighting and the loud crescendo of the disco which thankfully muted slightly once they were in the VIP lounge. This area had a bouncer on the door, who Cam gave the once over and decided was a rugby lock- forward trying to earn some extra money. The lounge was nicely designed, very modern. Cam and Veronica settled down at a small table where a waitress came to take their drinks order. The clientele surrounding them were a mixture of well-heeled individuals and high-heeled attractive young girls on the hunt for the former.

After people watching for ten minutes Veronica convinced Cam to take to the dance floor. He turned out to be a bit of a mover which suited her style and she found herself being attracted to him. Soon the music slowed down, Veronica swayed into Cam's body as the alcohol began to make her amorous. Cam realised what she had in mind and suggested they head back to the Sheraton. Veronica thought her intentions were about to be satisfied so much so she cuddled into Cam on the short journey back to the hotel.

Cam picked up their keys from reception, handed Veronica hers, and said, 'Thanks for a good night. I'll see you at breakfast, then we will get the 10.00 train to King's Cross which should get us into the office mid-afternoon.'

Veronica's eyes widened as Cam turned and walked away towards the stairs as she muttered under her breath, 'You inconsiderate bastard!!'

For a Sunday, London was busy around Whitehall as the official car which met Veronica and Cam at King's Cross Station made its way to MI6 Headquarters at Vauxhall Bridge. Hugh McFaul was in his office when they arrived and called Campbell in for a debriefing session.

'Good afternoon Campbell, welcome back from what appears to have been a successful visit to Edinburgh. As you know, we don't normally engage ourselves with domestic criminals. However, there seems to be a bit more in this case with an Afghan drug producer turning up in Edinburgh having been smuggled into the country by boat. Also, the discovery that the Estonians who murdered Elke are engaged in the white slave trade adds to our anger to get rid of them once and for all!'

'Apologies, I'm going on a bit how did you get on with Mhairi? Did she do what you asked of her?'

'Yes Hugh, she acted very professionally and got the confidence of Geordie McNab which was excellent.'

'Good. Ask her to come through for a chat.'

Campbell Anderson returned to Hugh's room with Mhairi (being referred to as Veronica ceased once she was back in MI6 HQ,) who nodded to the man who had captured her in Sitges five years ago, but still did not shake hands.

Hugh had expected courtesies to be abandoned so after everyone was seated, he commenced proceedings.

'Morning Mhairi, glad you got back from Edinburgh in one piece knowing what we do about Geordie McNab and his associates. Cam has given me a favourable account of your performance which will hopefully lead to a satisfactory conclusion. I have arranged for you to stay at one of our safe houses which is out in a leafy part of Buckinghamshire near Chesham. You'll be given twenty-four hours protection and be able to work on Geordie McNab's money laundering scheme. You will be reporting to Beverley Thomson who will be your liaison officer should you require anything further from ourselves.'

Mhairi spoke for the first time, 'If I can stop you there Mr. McFaul. I have suggested to McNab that he arranges to send scrap metal over to Ireland to companies in the South, which I've used when I was moving funds out of Northern Ireland. McNab will disguise bags of pound notes within the batches of scrap metal which will be discounted by a friendly bank manager. Obviously, I can't contact them direct, as I am still on an IRA wanted list so you will have to give me an assistant to train in the art of moving money.'

'Okay we'll arrange for someone to come out to Chesham and be taught the system by you.'

Mhairi smiled for the first time, 'Thanks, how long do you think I will be in your safe house?'

'Well, Miss McClure, at this point in time that depends on Geordie McNab. I fear that if he does not call us in the next three weeks it is not going to happen. Is that enough time for you to set up a disappearing act for his surplus cash?'

'Yes.' Mhairi confirmed, 'can I ask, will I be confined to barracks at Chesham or can I go out and walk about?'

'No, you'll be able to walk freely within a certain radius which we will confirm later. 'I'd suggest you try not to escape as we have a tracker system fitted and a second device fitted which, if activated will release a toxic poison which will kill you in a matter of minutes.'

'Cam has already told me that. One further question. Can my mother visit me?'

'Only under supervision, by that I mean you would have to be wired so we can listen in to your conversation to ensure no secrets of our activities are leaked.'

Mhairi reacted, 'Not altogether satisfactory, but better than nothing I suppose!'

Hugh McFaul picked up his phone, 'Our meeting is over, can you send a car to take Miss McClure out to Chesham.'

After a few days in the comfortable safe house in residential Chesham Mhairi made a phone call to her mother Kate. She lived alone in a flat in Newcastle County Down on the Northern Ireland coast, after the death of her husband Jack three years previously.

'Mum, it's Mhairi, how are you doing?'

'Good God! Is that really you Mhairi? How are you managing to phone me from that number? Have you escaped from jail?'

Mhairi smiled to herself before replying, 'No nothing like that. I am on an assignment which has allowed me to work from a house in Chesham. They allow me to go out the house and move around freely under supervision so I'm phoning to see if you would like to meet up in Buckinghamshire. I thought about having lunch in Amersham which is only a few miles away and there is a nice hotel there, The Crown, which was used for filming 'Four Weddings and A Funeral.'

'Sounds wonderful, I can't wait to see you and get all your news. I'll phone the hotel you suggested and make a booking to stay overnight and confirm it to you. Oh Mhairi, this is so exciting, I can't wait to tell your Aunt Lizzie.'

Mhairi stopped her mother in her tracks, 'Mum, you can't. You musn't tell anyone about this call if you don't want me to be sent back to Askham Prison before we have even met! Do not phone me, I will contact you tomorrow to see if you have managed to get a booking in Amersham. I must go, Bye for now.

Kate McClure contacted The Crown and was given a room for two nights, commencing six days after Mhairi had been in touch. Mhairi was excited when she spoke to Beverley about her mother's visit as she had to receive official approval to leave the safe house. Beverley, who had built up a good relationship with Mhairi gave her consent and offered to arrange a car, to take them from Chesham to Amersham which she herself would drive.

On the day she had agreed to meet her mother Mhairi entered the smart Georgian entry hall of the Crown which featured high white pillars dominating the space. Her mother was seated in one of the floral-pattered armchairs with her eyes fixed intently on the entrance door.

Mhairi had chosen to wear a navy business suit enhanced by a light grey lambswool polo-neck sweater to protect her from the cold weather. She walked confidently into the Crown and on seeing her mother rushed forward and gave her a huge hug. Beverley did not accompany her into the hotel preferring to look round the antique shops in the town.

Mother and daughter broke from their embrace and wiped the tears from their eyes. Kate cleared her throat prior to suggesting, 'Mhairi, there's a comfortable lounge next door. Let us go through and we will order some coffee and have a good chin-wag.'

Mhairi took her mother's hand and they made their way into a beautifully decorated lounge with classic furniture to match. They found two comfortable seats in front of the blazing log fire.

'Well Mhairi', asked the older lady, 'tell me, how did you manage to be living in Chesham?'

'I am not able to tell you very much.' Mhairi admitted 'I have signed the Official Secrets Act, but let me just say that I have been asked by the British Government to use my knowledge of international finance to assist them with a difficult situation involving illegal money laundering.'

'So, what's in it for you dear?'

'At this stage I don't honestly know but my performance is being monitored and if we are successful in ending the activities of these criminals, I may well have my prison sentence reduced.'

'That is wonderful news!', expressed the excited parent, 'By how long?'

'Hopefully, a few years. However, it will be a while before I know the answer to that question. I was approached by the security services who visited me at Askham Hall six weeks ago. I was released into their care and spent time training in London before taking a trip up to Scotland for a few days. I have spent the last few weeks in a house in Chesham literally waiting for a phone call which is frustrating but not as boring as Askham Hall. Now that is you up to date, let me hear about life in Newcastle County Down.'

'Pretty quiet really, I miss your dad – it is difficult going out on your own, although because Newcastle is full of retirees, I have made a number of friends. I go to the Bridge Club once a week and have taken up grass bowls which I prefer to play indoors and not be subjected to the elements. if you are short of male company, there's also the tea dances, which I go to with my friend Reenie McGhee. You should see us, Mhairi, we're a right couple of old swingers bopping away to the music of the 60s!'

For the next two hours Kate and Mhairi reflected on the past laughing at the good times, shedding tears for the problems their troubled lives had brought them. Mhairi's fate had been decided when her American boyfriend was ambushed and killed by British soldiers outside Londonderry. His loss resulted in her taking on a completely new living agenda which eventually led to a twenty-year prison sentence. *

Soon it was time for lunch which they decided to have in the hotel after hearing and seeing heavy rain battering the windows driven in by the strong cold north wind. The lunch was excellent, three courses washed down by red wine after which they returned to their chairs in front of the fire for Irish coffee and mint chocolates. All too soon It was time to say goodbye and mother and daughter had a final hug for what could well be the last time.

As previously arranged Beverley returned to the car park behind the hotel. Mhairi met up with her twenty minutes later to begin the silent journey back to Chesham.

- To find out more you require to read 'Operation Large Scotch' and the sequel 'She's Not A Lovely Girl'

Chapter 28

'What's the plan Mohammed? Did you see anything in Scotland that would be of interest to our movement?'

Mohammed al-Basiri had returned to Nelson to plan his next terrorist attack based on what he had seen in Edinburgh.

'I am putting together a plan to cause serious disruption on the streets of Edinburgh, but to succeed I shall need your co-operation and possibly a young martyr.'

Ismail Goulan nodded to Mohammed's request, 'I have someone in mind, Bahram Yousef, who has been attending the local mosque since he was a young boy and has been frustrated by the inactivity in Nelson. He was considering going out to Syria but changed his mind as he thought his parents would alert the British security services and he would be picked up at Manchester Airport and imprisoned.'

'Does Yousef live locally?'

'Yes, just up the hill in Marsden.'

'Can you introduce him to me tomorrow?'

'Yes, if he is available. I'll give him a call right now.'

Ismail produced a mobile from under his robes and made the call. Mohammed could overhear the conversation and Ismail gave him a thumbs up signal indicating the meeting was on.

Next morning at ten o'clock a young innocent-faced boy of sixteen lifted the latch at the back entrance to Ismail Goulan's house and rang the back doorbell. Ismail answered the door and ushered the boy through to his front lounge where Mohammed al-Basiri was waiting for him. The room was decorated in dark red embossed wallpaper which surrounded the light rugs scattered on the floor on which sat a cream leather lounge suite. The room was dulled down further by the curtains remaining shut to prevent any unwelcome guests looking in.

Ismail signalled for Bahram to take a seat before introducing his two guests to each other and outlining to Bahram the reason for asking him to his house.

'Bahram Yousef, Mohammed al-Basiri', the two shook hands as Ismail kept talking, 'Mohammed has travelled here from Afghanistan with specific instructions to recruit a squad and launch an attack on the British establishment. To complete his plan Mohammed necessitates possibly using a martyr to activate a suicide bomb and he has given that honour to you - on my recommendation.'

Bahram felt a lump in his throat and a cold shiver run down his spine as he tried to deliver his acceptance speech, 'Al-Basiri I am honoured to have been chosen to carry out a sacrifice for Allah in his fight against the infidels. I shall require suicide bomb training and can't wait to join my seven virgins in heaven.'

Mohammed probed further into Bahram's character, 'How long have you been active in our movement?'

'Six years Sir, ever since my schoolteacher explained fully in teachings of the Koran and why Muslims should wage a Jihad against the infidels who have taken advantage of us for centuries.'

'Are your parents in agreement with your attitude towards Christians?

'No, my grandparents came here in 1948 after the repatriation of India. Our family have built up a large business in the ensuing years which makes them incredibly grateful to this country or, as I would call it subservient. They do not approve of terrorism and will be embarrassed, not to say horrified by the thought of their son being hailed as a martyr in al-Qaeda circles.'

Mohammed became slightly concerned by the boy's answer as he could be influenced by his parents and this could result in his plans being aborted. He would have to step up Bahram's radicalisation programme and in the final analysis, to prevent any possible terminations to his plans, resort to hypnotising him.

'Bahram, there are no specific dates yet for the attack nor can I reveal to you the target. Only I know when I shall require your help, but I will give you ample warning. This meeting is to be kept absolutely secret any talk of what we have discussed being leaked by you, will lead to your premature death – and there will not be any virgins waiting in the Hereafter for your arrival!

'That is all for now. I shall be back in Nelson soon and we can meet again and see how you are getting on with your field training.'

Bahram shook hands with two older men and made his journey back to Marsden with a great deal on his mind.

Back at Gouran's house Mohammed and Ismail discussed their discussion with Bahram.

'How do you think that went?' enquired Ismail.

'Like many young boys I have encountered in the past he is full of idealistic support for our movement which is very admirable. I am concerned he comes from a family who have prospered from the British way of life so I would like you to monitor him closely and also look for a suitable substitute martyr should we need one.'

Mohammed spent the next few days streamlining his plans for the Edinburgh assault. Using the internet, he studied the Edinburgh Street Map to find out more about the city and how to get his team in place without drawing attention to themselves. Approaching Edinburgh on public transport was a non-starter as they would more than likely be picked up on CCTV.

Ismail had given him the names of weapon suppliers and Mohammed had sent them coded messages requesting everything he needed. This was nothing new to al-Basiri who had gathered a reputation in the terrorist movement for being a leading strategist who did not leave the slightest detail to chance. Favourable responses to his requests were received within a few days which allowed him to return to Glasgow and the safety of Anwar Segoura's house.

From Glasgow he took an early morning trip through to Edinburgh disguised as a driver's assistant in one of Anwar's cash and carry vans. The driver was given instructions by Anwar to deliver his load, but also to obey any orders he was given by Mohammed. The traffic on the M8 was busy as usual and it was not helped by the severe wintery driving conditions which had vehicles sliding all over the road. This did not worry Mohammed who was used to the hazardous driving landscape of Afghanistan where the winters were harsh and the roads very uneven. Basiri's cynical mind told him that the Scottish Police would be too occupied with road incidents to be paying much attention to a delivery vehicle going about its routine deliveries.

The deliveries covered most of the city and Mohammed enjoyed seeing the contrasting the wealthy areas, Morningside and Barnton to the less fortunate districts of Drylaw and Craigmillar. The latter was their last stop and Mohammed asked the driver Hassam to let him off close to the Queen's Park. Hassam headed the van in the direction of Pollock Halls, Edinburgh University's Student accommodation campus. Mohammed stepped down from the van and for the next two hours climbed the slippery slopes of Arthur Seat, which many locals described as shaped like a crouching lion looking down on Edinburgh. It was bitterly cold, and he was glad he was dressed for the elements and chose not to clamber to the top but went along Salisbury Crags striding along the top looking down over a cliff-face which had been the scene of many Edinburgh citizens' suicides. From there, he continued travelling east on his way along the Crags until he reached St. Margaret's Chapel an eleventh century ruin once used for worship by Scottish royal families. All the time he was taking notes of the vista below him from which he would decide his angle of attack.

As promised, he returned to the heat of the van after two hours and Hassam, who was wondering why anyone would want to climb Arthur's Seat in those conditions began the journey back to Glasgow without asking.

Chapter 29

Mhairi McClure was relieving her boredom by playing solitaire on her computer. She had been locked up in a large villa with stables attached which had been converted into offices, set in several acres of land. The ringtone on the phone which was solely for her use startled her and the familiar voice on the other end of the phone engaged her concentration.

'Good afternoon Veronica, it's Geordie McNab. I'm ready to send my first consignment to Dublin. Have you managed to contact any scrap yards in the area who will accept my load?'

'Yes Geordie, it's in order. One of my assistants Beverley Thomson has spoken with O'Hara Metals who are based a few miles outside Dublin, and they will be expecting you.'

Geordie was a little edgy, 'Why are you not handling the transaction personally?'

Veronica had to quickly think on her feet, 'Although I have picked up your call directly it has been diverted to me here in the Cayman Islands where Graeme and I are meeting with some friendly bank managers.'

'Lucky you, the weather will be a bit better than here.'

'Yes, lovely sunshine with a warm breeze in the evenings. How are you getting the funds to Dublin?'

'We shall drive down to Holyhead and take the ferry into Dublin. Maniac McLagan will be accompanying my driver, Willie Bristow, as my security to ensure that the transaction is handled smoothly. I have instructed Maniac to remain with the loot until your friendly banker arrives and takes it off his hands.'

'Good idea Geordie, but I'm sure there won't be any hitches. I've used this route to move on money many times. I will put a call through to O'Hara Metals and get a time and date for your delivery. Liam Callaghan from Lumis Banken will come to O'Hara's yard and pick up your cash. I'll call you back soon with the final plans.'

Veronica put down the phone and went downstairs to Beverley Thomson's office. Beverley had been in the security services for fifteen years after leaving Bristol University with a degree in classics. She was a spinster with a frumpy appearance – Fair Isle woollen jumpers, tweed check skirts and brown brogues were the order of the day. She had never married, and many doubted if she had ever had a boyfriend.

Beverley's strengths were in organisation and communicating her way through awkward situations. Veronica had explained in detail how as Mhairi McClure she had laundered money into tax havens. Between them Veronica and Beverley decided that Beverley would contact O'Hara Metals posing as a friend of Mhairi McClure who she had met during her time in prison. MI6 fitted her up with a false identity of a prisoner who had recently been released from prison after serving five years for fraud in case the O'Hara's decided to check should they be suspicious.

Mhairi approached her desk and sat down opposite Beverley, 'I think we are in business. Geordie McNab has just been on the phone and he is ready to commence operations as soon as possible.'

'Excellent Veronica, why don't we phone them? You can listen in in case I stray from our prepared script.'

Veronica felt a tingle of excitement and burst out, 'Go for it, Beverley!'

'Good afternoon can I speak to Aiden O'Hara?'

'Speaking'.

'My name is Amanda Cosgrove. I was given your name by Mhairi McClure who I met whilst we were serving time in Askham Hall Prison. Since I've been out of prison, I've met with some of my old criminal contacts who want me to move some of their funds abroad. Mhairi told me she had utilised your services as a middle- man to receive funds which would be picked up from you by local financiers. Obviously, there will a sizeable commission in it for you.'

'Mhairi McClure! .Jeez, now there's a name from the past. I know who she is, but how do I know you are genuine?'

'You could contact Mhairi for a reference but that won't be easy because the authorities monitor all her calls coming into the prison and that would draw some unnecessary attention to yourself. What I think would be a better line of action for you would be to talk to Geordie McNab my client in Edinburgh who met my colleague Veronica Benson a few weeks ago. Veronica is presently visiting bankers in the Cayman Islands and has asked me to negotiate on our half.'

'Okay give me McNab's telephone number and I'll give him a ring.'

'Like yourself, Geordie is a bit cautious about talking openly. I suggest, when you phone him, you say the call is about Farrer Financial Services and he will probably relax and make arrangements for delivering his merchandise.'

'Okay you know the fella, so I'll take your advice.'

'Mr O'Hara let me know as soon as you take delivery so I can arrange the next movement of his funds. The scrap metal is coming over to Dublin on the Holyhead Ferry and the driver of the lorry will be accompanied by Alistair McLagan, Geordie McNab's senior security man.'

'I look forward to meeting them and I'll ask around to see if I can get them a return load which will cut down on their travel expenses.'

'That's awfully kind of you Mr O'Hara. I look forward to hearing from you.'

Beverley placed the phone on the receiver and exhaled deeply. Having concluded the conversation with O'Hara Beverley was so excited she resorted to calling 'Veronica', 'Mhairi', who reached out to offer her congratulations on a job well done.

'You were outstanding Beverley.' confirmed Mhairi, 'O'Hara bought in to your idea of not calling Askham Hall. I'd suggest that arrangements are made to monitor any calls to their switchboard for anyone wanting to talk to Amanda Cosgrove or myself. Everything is in place now and all we can do is wait for McNab's HGV to get across the Irish Sea.'

They didn't have to wait long, five days later McNab Scrap Metals Scania HGV drove through the gates of O'Hara Metals and stopped in the yard near the waste dump. Willie Bristow jumped down from his driver's cabin and went into the weighbridge office to seek out Aiden O'Hara. O'Hara had seen the HGV pull into the yard and came through to the front office to meet the new arrival.

'Good afternoon, you'll be Alistair McLagan from Edinburgh.'

'No', replied the short, sweaty, overweight driver, 'Mr McLagan's still in the cab. I'm the driver Willie Bristow, pleased to meet you.'

'Well go and ask Mr McLagan to come in while I put on the kettle for a cup of coffee. Just leave your vehicle where it is parked just now.'

Maniac accepted Aiden's invitation and joined him for a coffee in his office which consisted of a large oak desk with a large high -backed leather chair and two smaller leather backed seats in front of it. Around the walls there were Road Maps of Europe and boards with hooks, on which Tachograph recordings were latched to them.

'Did you have a good journey?' enquired the Irishman.

'Yes, although I found it a bit boring. I prefer to be driving myself and going a bit quicker than any HGV.'

'So, you're not a regular on the road?'

'No, I work closely with my boss Geordie McNab and act as his personal assistant.'

'How would you like your coffee Alistair?'

'Black with two sugars please.'

O'Hara placed the two mugs of coffee on the desk and opened a tin containing a variety of chocolate biscuits and gestured for Maniac to help himself.

'Now you've arrived I will give Mr Callaghan from Lumis Banken a call to say you are here and by the time he gets here you will have offloaded your consignment.'

'Willie my driver has begun to open up the hidden compartments which were only available from below the HGV. I'll go out and help him and it should only take twenty minutes to get them all out. Where do you want me to dump the scrap metal - I understand it's part of your commission for allowing the boss to move his assets?'

'You're right about that Alistair so you are!', said a jovial O'Hara, 'Just get Willie to move up the yard to where the crane is and it will lift most of the scrap and dump it with the rest of the metal waiting to be sorted out.'

Maniac and Willie recovered the sacks of money from the hidden metal containers and guarded them in a room next to Aiden O'Hara's office until Liam Callaghan arrived in his green Range Rover accompanied by two security men who Maniac reckoned were carrying pistols under their Barbour jackets. Liam Callaghan looked every bit the international banker with his smart pin stripe suit and pale blue shirt with a white collar accompanied with a dark-blue spotted tie. Slim built, his greying hair was slicked back, and his tanned complexion oozed the wealth of a man who spent a lot of time in sunnier climes.

'Good day, now which one of you gentlemen is Mr. McLagan?'

Maniac responded with a nod of the head.

'Well, I see you have unloaded the cash for me already so you have.' Liam observed looking at the ten sacks spread out across a table, 'how much is in each one?'

'Two hundred thousand pounds.' replied McLagan.

' I'm not going to count them all. I believe in honour even amongst thieves like ourselves!', Liam laughed then continued, 'I will take a random sample by opening up one of the sacks and my assistants will count the contents to verify what you have just told us.'

Liam's henchmen moved in, opened one of the sacks then began to count the contents with the efficiency of two experienced bank tellers. After a couple of minutes, the older employee confirmed Maniac's balance.

'Everything seems to be in order. I'll give you a receipt which you can take back to Mr. McNab and I'll await instructions from Veronica Benson where she wants it transferred to next.'

Maniac looked a little bewildered by the casual manner of Liam Callaghan's approach and spoke out, 'All this moving money about is way over my head. I am used to guarding any cash with my life, but if this is what my boss has chosen to do, I have to give way to your expertise.'

Liam Callaghan signalled to his accomplices to gather up the sacks and load them into their car. Without any further conversation, he shook hands with Maniac and Willie then left O'Hara's yard at speed, with two million pounds in the boot of his Range Rover!

Maniac took out his mobile and phoned Geordie McNab. 'Hi Boss. I've handed over the cash and have a receipt to prove it. Willie and I are getting a return load arranged by Aiden O'Hara and we'll be back in Edinburgh tomorrow.'

'Thanks Maniac, I hope it all goes well for Veronica Benson's sake or I will be taking a contract out on her and her companion.'

Beverley Thomson also phoned Geordie McNab confirming that Liam Callaghan was now holding the two million pounds which would soon be transferred to a bank in the Cayman Islands. To put Geordie's mind at rest she fictitiously made up that Veronica Benson was attending to the next movement of the funds personally while she was in the Caribbean.

The success of today's delivery prompted McNab to make hasty plans for more of the same which would result in Willie Bristow making several journeys to Dublin in the future.

Chapter 30

Hugh McFaul wasted no time in contacting Grant about Mhairi and Beverley's progress in setting up Geordie McNab.

'Morning Grant, everything has gone to plan at this end so now we have to decide when we will put into action your strategy to arrest McNab. Simultaneously this could enable us to go to Estonia and remove any future threats from Igor Shertsov, Boris Andropov or Kurt Jansen.'

'How will you do that Hugh?' asked the DCI.

'That's for us to decide, and you will probably never hear the answer to your question from the Department.'

McKirdy understood the underlying innuendo, 'As you wish Hugh.'

Changing the subject, Grant asked, 'Any further word on Mohammed al-Basiri's movements?'

'No Grant, the trail's gone cold but GCHQ at Cheltenham are on the case and they usually turn up something which will lead to his whereabouts.'

'I'll keep our eyes open. Edinburgh does not have a huge Asian population so he may be easier to spot here.' McKirdy suggested.

'Both Mhairi and Beverley Thomson, who is working with her, will monitor McNab closely and if we hear anything about his movements, you'll be the first to hear.'

'Thanks Hugh. Good to catch up. I'll brief my team about what you have said.'

McKirdy buzzed through to the main office for Lomax and Luxton to join him but only Lomax appeared, 'Where's Avril?'

'She's taken the morning off to pick up her new car.'

'All right for some' muttered McKirdy before filling in Lomax about the latest MI6 report, 'If her priorities are personal rather than operational, I will have a word. Ian, keep what I have just told you between ourselves at present.'

McFaul put down the phone and began to think how he could handle carrying out the assassination of serious criminals. The police tended only to carry out such actions reactively using Armed Response Units, but the security services assaults were more of a personal nature done by individuals or smaller teams of hitmen.

Three weeks had passed before Veronica Benson received an unexpected call from the unsuspecting Geordie McNab.

'Hello Veronica, glad to hear you got back safely from the Cayman Islands. Was it a successful trip?'

His question almost caught Veronica out, 'Eh yes… it was. We were able to tie up some loose ends for our clients and of course it was convenient to be there when your first transaction of funds came through.'

McNab continued, 'I'm impressed with your services and the reason for my call is to let you know I'm going off for a week's holiday to Marbella with the wife and Kids. Maniac will be with me with his brood.'

'Well have a good time. I take it I can still get you on this number if there are any problems?' Veronica asked for the purpose of keeping tracks on Geordie.

McNab hesitated before replying, 'Yes, I think so, but Maniac and I are going to disappear from Marbella for a couple of days to fly up to Tallinn and meet Igor Shertsov and his mate Kurt Jansen. I have been giving them a lot more business lately and I want to discuss our pricing structure as I think I'm due a discount.'

Veronica backed up Geordie's discount claims, 'Yes you should get some bulk discount allowance for increased business. So, you will be away week commencing March eighteenth, have a good time and we will talk again when you get back.'

Geordie corrected Veronica, 'We fly out on twenty-fourth March and will be back here on the thirty -first.'

'Remember to use plenty of sun-tan lotion if you and Maniac ever get out the pub!' Veronica joked, 'Bye for now.'

Richard Hartley shared the good news Mhairi had passed to Hugh by setting up an ad hoc meeting in his office with Hugh and Cam in attendance.

He began, 'This is the breakthrough we have been looking for. I can't believe that McNab is going to lead us to two of the three men responsible for Elke Kohl's death, the chances are Boris Andropov will be there, so that could give us a clean sweep to eliminate or detain all the guilty parties.

To achieve our objective, we'll need some help from our embassy in Tallinn. I will have a word with our man in Tallinn and arrange cover. The weapons required for a successful operation will be despatched in a diplomatic bag to the British Embassy in Tallinn and returned the same way to avoid any problems at the airport when you leave for home. Any questions?'

'I assume our mission is to terminate the three Estonians only. McNab and McLagan will be apprehended and returned to the U.K. direct without returning to Marbella on the way.'

Hartley took a customary swing in his armchair before answering, 'Correct Hugh, but any resistance in that quarter should be dealt with in the same manner as the unfortunate Estonians.   McFaul stared back at his Controller, 'Understood Sir.'

Chapter 31

The door of the mosque opened, and a dozen pairs of eyes were drawn to the entry of the athletic figure of Mohammed ai-Basiri who had arrived in Nelson once more to pick his final team for 'The Edinburgh Engagement' as he referred to the impending attack on the Scottish capital.

His offensive would consist of seven main players and five others whose duties would be more logistical (drivers and equipment bearers). The prominent seven were those who would be responsible for creating havoc directly and would probably pay for their involvement with their lives. Not all the volunteers were from the north-west of England, two had travelled down from Scotland, one from London and a couple from Yorkshire which left two local young men Bahram Yousef and Moussa Kaffir.

Mohammed had purposely recruited the team from different regions to discourage cronyism, which he had seen in the past could lead to doubts in some young minds. Now it was time for his motivational speech.

'Sit own pleas. For those of you who have not met me, my name is Mohammed al-Basiri. You have come here with high reputations for serving the Muslim cause in your local communities and have been identified as true soldiers of Allah. You all, by your own admission, are prepared to die in the name of Allah in the fight against the infidels who have controlled us for so long. I have chosen targets for an assault on the enemy but the details of such an attack will remain with me until hours before it is launched. What I want to find out today is what military skills are here in this room? For instance, does anyone have any experience in using rocket launchers?'

The assembled company mumbled amongst themselves until a hand went up in the second row.

'My name is Ali Gosham from London. I was in the Army Cadet Core at school and in the summer holidays we went on training course to Salisbury Plain where we were allowed to fire all types of small arms, the largest of which was a rocket launcher.'

Al-Basiri could not believe his luck and intervened, 'Did your training also involve assembling your weapons?'

'Yes Sir.'

'Ali Gosham, You're my man! The rest of you give him a round of applause. He will lead a section of our attack.'

The assembled company clapped their hands and chanted a prayer to Ali Gosham.

Mohammed brought the meeting to order and took notes of the other skills his young team possessed before approaching the most important question of all.

His face grew serious as he asked, 'Who amongst you is prepared to die and go to heaven? There your every desire will be thrust upon you by seven beautiful virgins. Our attack may require the services of a martyr who will have an explosive vest attached to his body which he will detonate it when given the command by me.'

Reality had hit the group and a stony silence entered the room as the bowed heads decided on their future. Slowly a small hand went up. It was Bahram Yousef.

'al- Basiri I have been brought into this world to serve Allah and I can think of nothing more honourable than to die in the fight against the infidels. Please can I become a martyr?'

Having secured the two principal players for his impending plan Mohammed summed up the future for his team, 'Please be ready to move at short notice. Do not discuss this gathering with anyone. Any leakages from today's meeting will be punishable by death. Go now and say thanks in your prayers to Allah for selecting you to carry out his Word.'

After the boys left for home Mohammed spoke urgently with Ismail, 'I have a provisional date for the attack which I will release to you one week in advance so like I told the boys you must have everything in place to move seven days before execution day.'

'Mohammed does our offensive have a name?' asked Ismail.

'E. A. P. after the write Edgar Allan Poe.'

Ismail gave Mohammed a puzzled look, 'That tells me nothing which means nobody else will guess what you are up to.'

Mohammed just smiled and walked away.

Two weeks later al-Basiri conducted a further meeting with his offensive troops to finalise the detailed procedures of his plan. The group were all ears as they sat at desks in a side room of the local sports centre. The notice on the door of the room read 'Cricket strategy meeting in progress.'

Ismail and Mohammed greeted all the boys individually as they arrived, who were chatting amongst themselves until Ali Gosham, the last to come into the room, sat down. Al-Basiri took centre stage like a schoolteacher giving a science lecture with a pointer in his hand before removing a cloth draped over a blackboard to reveal a map of Edinburgh. A murmur went through the room as the excited young men saw their potential target for the first time. Mohammed allowed them ten seconds to talk amongst themselves before opening his address:

'Friends, Edinburgh is my choice for our offensive and I want to explain my plan in detail so you all know the part you will play in the fight against the infidels who for too long have ruled over you and your Muslim brothers.' Turning to the map he continued using his pointer, 'The centre of the city is very concise with many of the main buildings covering a small area. This area here', pointing to a large green expanse is the Queen's Park or Arthur's Seat as the locals refer to it. It overlooks two of the most important buildings in Scotland – Holyrood Palace which is Queen Elizabeth's main residence when she is on official duties in Scotland and the other is the Scottish Parliament, the home of the devolved Scottish Government.

Both these buildings, I was assured, could be reached by firing a rocket launcher from a position on the hill but having measured the distance by theodolite I think any rocket fired may fall short of the targets. What I am now proposing is we utilise the use of drones which can be fitted with explosive devices. This attack would be carried out under the cover of darkness although our preparations will commence during the day. There are several entrances into the Park - from Duddingston Village, Pollock Halls or Meadowbank.' Mohammed pointed to the entrances on the map as he spoke then continued addressing his audience 'Three teams of two will each make their way up the hill carrying rucksacks which will contain various parts of the drones. Ali Gosham and his team will be responsible for assembling them when the group meet up under the cover of St. Margaret's Chapel.

Kazan lifted a finger, 'Shall we be armed Mohammed?'

Mohammed had expected this enquiry, 'Yes you will all carry semi-automatic pistols which you can use anytime, provided you have come under attack. I do not want to draw attention to ourselves prior to the launch of our offensive.'

'Anything else?'

'When do we go to Edinburgh?'

Mohammed looked around the faces of his followers as he answered, 'Not for discussion at present but you will be given forty-eight hours warning. If there are no further questions, I wish you a safe journey home.'

The group exited the lecture room leaving Ismail and Mohammed to reflect on the proceedings.

Ismail congratulated his friend, 'I thought that went rather well Mohammed. There did not appear to be any doubters amongst them, and I thought it was an excellent idea of yours to use drones instead of a rocket launcher. Most of these kids are familiar with computers so they should have no problems in guiding the drones in on your targets.'

'I would agree with that so all I will have to do is take delivery of them and store them here if I can.'

'That would be an honour Mohammed.'

The drones were smuggled into the U.K. from Turkey who specialised in producing military drones which were used in attacks on their enemies. The shipment arrived at Newcastle disguised and hidden in a consignment of cotton shirts. By importing the drones from Turkey, they were unregistered and would not attract the attention of the British authorities. From Newcastle they were taken to a warehouse in Leeds before finally ending up in Nelson. Ismail contacted the ter-rorist's Weapons Division based in Manchester and they arranged to instruct Ali Gosham how to assemble the weap-ons from components into finished products. Once they completed their task a seminar was held for the attack force to familiarise themselves with the drones at a nearby coun-tryside location. As expected, all the young men expressed a talent for controlling drones.

Everything was now in place and all Mohammed had to do was name the date and he chose Friday 20th March.

Chapter 32

March 15th.

Campbell Anderson put down the phone and couldn't wait to tell his colleague what he had just heard, 'Hugh, GCHQ have just sent an urgent message warning of an imminent threat of a terrorist attack in the U.K., the location of which they have not yet been able to pinpoint. What drew my attention to the communique was it mentioned that Mohammed al-Basiri might be involved.'

'The last time he came on our radar was when you thought you saw him in Edinburgh during your City Tour of the Capital.'

'Did MI5 say anything else about the threat?

'The only other clue they got from their informant was the code name being given to the attack 'E.A.P.' No doubt the boffins at Cheltenham will be running this through their de-coding systems. You'd better let Grant McKirdy know about the alert, as it could be his patch that's about to be the potential target of a major terrorist incident.'

When Hugh called, Grant Mckirdy was trying to solve the domestic murder of a man whose long-suffering wife had electrocuted him before leaving town with a younger man, who was the bingo-caller at a local establishment in Pilton on the North side of Edinburgh.

'How are you Grant?' said the jovial McFaul.

'Pissed Off' - if you will excuse the language. I hate domestic crimes as at the end of the day the crime has come about by love having gone by its sell-buy date. If people would just admit to each other sooner that the party was over it would save Police Scotland a lot of bother and leave funds to solve real crimes. That is my Grump for the Day over. Hugh what can I do for you?'

'Grant, sorry if I've caught you at a bad moment but we thought you should know that there is word on the wires of an imminent terror attack which could feature our mutual friend Mohammed al-Basiri. The only further piece of information available to us, now is the code name for the attack which is 'E.A.P.'

'We have not had any sightings of al-Basiri for some considerable time, but I'll put out a reminder to my force to watch out for him. We are more concerned currently in watching the activities of Geordie McNab as it is next week he's meant to be going on holiday to Malaga. As you told us, he is going to break his holiday up and fly to Tallinn. Do you know what day during the week he is supposed to be flying to Tallinn?'

'No. not yet Grant, but I've got our team checking the passenger lists of all aircraft flying from Malaga' Hugh confirmed. 'In fact, our systems will extend to any airport should he choose to change his departure arrangements.'

'Thorough as usual Mr. McFaul. We will give some thought to Mohammed al-Basiri and see if anyone here has any information that could help us break the 'E.A.P.' code.

'I'll look forward to seeing you soon Grant, when you are standing at the bottom of the aircraft steps waiting for Geordie McNab to be delivered into your custody on his way to Her Majesty's pleasure.'

'Yes, he'll probably be home before the wife and kids which'll be a far greater headache for him than being in Saughton Prison as I believe she is a real tyrant.' informed the D.C.I.

'Oh well, at least she will have Mrs Maniac for company -the two of them deserve each other after years of living the high life! On that joyful note I will say goodbye for now Grant.', concluded Hugh and put down the phone.

The thought of an imminent terrorist incident around Edinburgh worried the D.C.I. who immediately informed Superintendent Law and requested he asked the de-coding section if they could decipher anything from the letters E.A.P. Later that afternoon Jim Kinghorn, Head of Intelligence at Police Scotland came into McKirdy's office to give Grant a report on his department's search.

Kinghorn was not your usual police officer. Having studied maths at Edinburgh University, he decided he did not want to be bogged down in some boring admin role in a bank or insurance company in Edinburgh, of which there are many. Instead, he joined the police as a graduate entry and after initial training was seconded to Intelligence. He took the concession of wearing casual dress to the extreme turning up for work in jeans, t-shirt and trainers over his skinny frame topped by a head of thick black curly hair and a patchy beard.

'Grant, we have run 'EAP' through our algorithms doing our usual scans of place names, celebrities, sports stars etc and we have only come up with a possible but unlikely name Edgar Allan Poe, the eighteenth-century writer. When we are looking for suspects, who may be out to cause civil unrest, we check out events which link in one way or another. This weekend, on Friday evening, there is a performance of classical music being held in the Usher Hall. It's being sponsored by the Scottish Government who are entertaining trade delegation representatives attending a big conference starting on Saturday. The connection we linked to Edgar Allan Poe was one of the novels he wrote - 'The Fall of the House of Usher.'

Kinghorn looked across the desk at a rather bemused McKirdy, 'I see you smiling Grant, but it is co-incidences like this which go undetected. They have a bad habit of demonstrating a lack of professionalism in our service which the media like to latch on to.'

McKirdy took on board what the scruffy Kinghorn was saying and replied, 'It is a long shot, but I agree we can't leave anything to chance. I'll inform my criminal investigation teams and ask uniform to step up their presence in the Lothian Road area starting today. There is a known terrorist who could be at large in Edinburgh so better to be safe than sorry. Thanks for your help Jim, I will keep you informed if I hear anything further. In the meantime, I will speak to Hugh McFaul at MI6 to share your thoughts to him and see if he agrees with your thinking.'

For the second time that day McKirdy called Hugh McFaul.

'Hello McFaul speaking.'

'Hugh, it's Grant again. Following on from our chat this morning I've ran a check through our intelligence department to see if they could de-code the terrorist threat you called 'E.A.P.'. Jim Kinghorn, the Head of Intelligence at Police Scotland has just been in my office and he has come up with a loose interpretation for the code. This Friday there is a Musical concert being held in Edinburgh to launch British Trade Week with senior representatives from all the G20 countries. This is the biggest political event to be held in Scotland for years and as you can imagine our biggest security headache. Kinghorn ran the code through his systems, to find a vertically integrated relationship with events in Edinburgh. It sounds crazy but for the initials 'EAP' he has come up with the author Edgar Allan Poe. Poe is a famous writer of several books including, 'The Pit and the Pendulum'. How Kinghorn has related him to events in Edinburgh is he also wrote 'The Fall of the House of Usher' and where do think the venue is for Fridays performance? - **THE USHER HALL!'**

'Grant, Kinghorn's thesis is a bit thin but experience has told us not to ignore any possible theories when dealing with espionage.'

'I also have a new communique from a MI5 agent based in the North of England who has alerted them of an imminent attack. All we know at this stage is it involves placing explosives on two major state buildings. It depends what you class as state buildings, it could be anything from The

Tate Gallery in London to Stormont in Northern Ireland! London is the obvious target but based on what your intelligence has come up with you'd be wise to keep everything on high alert.'

McKirdy protested at McFaul's last remark, 'Oh we are always wise Hugh, and we're taking this alert extremely seriously. I'm about to go and brief my staff. Thanks for the additional warning and hopefully we'll be able to divert disaster from these horrible fanatics. Bye for now Hugh.'

After Kinghorn left Grant McKirdy's office he summoned his team and briefed them about the possible terrorist threat. D.C.I. Andrew Langlands, who was responsible for patrolling the streets of Edinburgh stepped up the police presence around the Usher Hall area three days before the scheduled concert was due to begin.

Chapter 33

The changes in police activity did not go un-noticed by Mohammed al-Basiri who had posted observers in the city, posing as tourists. When he received the news of the increased police patrols it led him to have second thoughts about releasing Bahram Yousef as a human bomb. He decided to leave a disappointed Bahram in Nelson but not admit to the team a change in his plans which might be interpreted as a sign of weakness. Mohammed now had to put all his faith in the technical skills of Ali Gosham to organise the drone attacks on Holyrood Palace and the Scottish Parliament.

Bahram Yousef was furious at what he considered to be a personal rejection by Mohammed al-Basiri. The Afghan had not explained to him why he wasn't going to Edinburgh and Bahram interpreted his honourable place had been given to someone else. al-Basiri had not revealed to his team anything about the intelligence report he had received regarding the increased police presence for fear of a security leak by one of them.

When he returned home Bahram was in such a bad temper that his parents sat him down and questioned their son what was the reason for his mood change? His father Anwar had long suspected changes to his son's character coinciding with his recent frequent visits to the local mosque. Being a successful businessman Anwar was constantly attending business network seminars, where he listened to the fears of his business colleagues. Many were worried that that local youths were in danger of being radicalised and carrying out atrocities which would reverberate back on them leading to a downturn in business.

'Braham, explain yourself. You have not behaved in a rational manner since you returned from meeting Mr Goulan. What's your problem?'

The sixteen-year-old bowed his head in silence expecting his action to end the conversation but his father was an expert in communication and tackled the problem head-on.

'I'm hearing on my travels that many people are suspicious of Ismail Goulan. He is not a nice man. He has connections to revolutionary Islamic forces he encourages the services of innocent young men to carry out their dreadful deeds.

Answer me! Have you been radicalised by him Bahram?' Anwar asked in a demanding rage.

Despite his new-found beliefs Braham was still a boy who had been reared to respect his elders. He loved his father, and his body language gave Anwar the answer to his question.

'Your mother mentioned you are going on a trip to Scotland organised by Mr Goulan. What is the purpose of the visit? I do not recall you having any previous desire to go on holiday with boys from the mosque.'

'You'll be glad to hear I'm not going now!!' screamed Bahram at his parents.

Anwar retorted angrily, 'Do not use that tone with us! Why the change of mind? Has the trip been cancelled?'

Braham was not enjoying being put under the spotlight and replied defiantly, 'I'm no longer needed! Satisfied! I'm going to my room.'

Braham's mother Usha spoke for the first time, 'Braham, what do you mean by 'not needed'. Not needed for what? I hope you have not got yourself involved in any illegal activities that would bring shame to the Yousef family in the eyes of the local community. Our family has worked hard for over fifty years building a business to give you and your brothers the comfortable lifestyle you have always enjoyed. Bahram, open up and tell us what is going on!'

The Yousef traditionally kept family discussions private, the parents choosing always to protect their offspring from

225

outside influences. Bahram had never seen his parents become so animated as they were today, and it frightened him that they might disown him and expel him from the family home. Suspension of any son or daughter from the house was looked down upon in Asian families. It would also exclude them from their circle of friends.

Anwar Yousef broke the silence, 'Well Braham, you are not leaving this room until we get an explanation!'

The boy understood the seriousness of the situation and the mental pressure being exerted upon him by both his parents staring down at him. His eyes began to well up and his body shook with guilt as he finally succumbed to their parental pressure.

Braham sobbed, 'I wanted to serve Allah but in doing so I would have brought shame upon the Yousef name. I was chosen to be a martyr carrying an explosive vest which I was to activate during a concert being held for G20 trade delegates in Edinburgh. My teachings told me this was an honour and I would be rewarded in Heaven with the company of seven beautiful Virgins. Today I have been told that I am no longer required to undertake these duties.'

Usha let out a scream as she couldn't contemplate that her little boy had offered his life for something which she doubted he fully understood, 'Bahram, please don't believe all what you hear from Imams. They are giving you their interpretation of the Koran which is an antagonist version based on hating infidels. That is a belief which we in this household have no intention to contribute to.'

It was Anwar's turn to probe further, 'So is one of the other boys taking your place?'

'I don't know.'

'But they are all still going to Edinburgh – to do what?'

'Dad, I cannot say another word.'

'I suggest you do because if there is a serious or violent incident in Edinburgh in which even some of your friends die, you can be assured the security services will be on our door-step within hours. You will be named as an accomplice and will probably spend the rest of your life in jail. What is it going to be Bahram? Freedom or imprisonment. Whatever you decide to answer I am phoning Ali Haroughi our local Member of Parliament whom I know very well. As I see it we can tell him we have information of national importance, or if you do not want to co-operate I hand you over to the security services, who will make your life hell in the days ahead.'

Bahram continued sobbing for a few minutes, wrestling with his loyalties to the Muslim cause or the loss of his entire family.

'Phone Mr. Haroughi.'

'Hugh, more info coming through from MI5. Ali Haroughi, the MP for Pendle and Colne has phoned in to say that a local businessman has information on a possible terrorist attack in Edinburgh.'

'Cam get on to '5' and tell them what we know about Mohammed al-Basiri and ask for a full copy of Ali Haroughi's interview with the local businessman.'

It was after six o'clock when Anwar Youssef received a call from Ali Haroughi, 'Anwar, security services want to meet you and Bahram as soon as possible but away from Nelson. Take your car up the M6 to Junction 38, Tebay Service Station, where a blue BMW 6 registration number DU 17 RTS, will meet you and take you both to a secret location.

Ninety minutes later Anwar drove into the darkened Tebay Service Station which was still busy with lorry drivers and businessmen who had stopped for their evening meal. The BMW had positioned itself to see all new arrivals and flashed its lights at Anwar's Jaguar estate. Anwar parked alongside the BMW before getting out the car to be met by a tall man in a dark suit who did not shake hands.

'Mr Anwar Youssef, and you must be Bahram.', he said turning to the boy, 'Come with us please. Could you please use the blindfolds provided on the back seat until we reach our destination in about twenty-minutes.'

Twenty minutes later, the BMW drove into an underground garage. The 'Nelson Two' removed their blindfolds and rubbed their eyes as they were exposed to bright lights. The drivers led them through several passageways before opening a large polished oak door, which led into a windowless room illuminated by fluorescent lighting which lit up the pale blue walls. Behind a metal desk sat three security officers, two male and one female. The stout man in the middle looked up as he adjusted the papers in front of him and asked Anwar and Braham to be seated.

'Mr Youssef thank you for being so prompt in responding to our request to meet up. During this meeting refer to me only as Mr A, the lady on my left is Ms B and the gentleman on my right Mr C.'

Anwar nodded then replied, 'We are here to report on some suspicious movements my son observed at a mosque in Nelson.'

For the next two hours, with only a short coffee break, the three MI5 officers cross examined Bahram in detail, trying their best to find holes in his evidence. Bahram stuck to his story that he was approached by Ismail Goulan to meet Mohammed al-Basiri for the purpose of becoming a martyr. He confessed to only wanting to find out what Ismail and Mohammed were planning as he had no intention to agree to becoming a martyr. His family had always been opposed to radical clerics so when he discovered what they were about to undertake he sought advice from his father.

A. asked, 'You say that Mohammed al-Basiri is planning a drone attack on Holyrood Palace and the Scottish Parliament - while simultaneously carrying out a suicide bomb attack at the Usher Hall. Where is he getting the drones from as all drone owners in the U.K. have to be registered?'

'I am not sure Sir, but I overheard Ismail and Mohammed mention Turkey.'

'Seems unlikely and I hope not, as they are members of NATO.'

'Do you have a date for the assault on Edinburgh?'

'No Sir, Mohammed would only say we would all have to be prepared to move at short notice. I expected all three to happen at the same time.'

Ms B addressed Bahram next, 'We are grateful to the Youssef family for displaying such considerable courage in contacting the security services. We in turn will have to reciprocate, by creating a false trail to deflect any suspicion away from yourselves. We are used to putting out 'false news' so expect to see the media channels carrying a story about an amber warning for the U.K. In it they will communicate fears for the London area which should make Mohammed al-Basiri think he is safe to continue with his plans to attack Edinburgh.'

'We'll put a tracer out to detect al-Basiri's whereabouts and make plans to have the threat aborted.' added the slim bespectacled Mr C.

It was now time for Mr A to summarise the proceedings, 'If I can bring matters to a close as it is getting late. Mr. Youssef as far as you and your son are concerned this meeting never took place and I stress for your own safety you keep it that way.' Addressing Braham solely he continued, 'Braham, continue to meet your friends in Nelson. This will help to giving the impression that you are still part of the group. If your life is put in danger at all, contact us via Ali Haroughi, your local MP and we shall take whatever steps are necessary to secure your future.

It is unlikely we shall ever meet again so on behalf of Her Majesty's Government I thank you once again for your help.'

Mr A leaned across the table and shook hands with Anwar and Bahram who also exchanged handshakes with Ms B and Mr C .

As Mr A predicted the Yousefs never did clap eyes on any of the security staff attendees again.

After being blindfolded again and kept in silence for twenty minutes the Youseffs were back at their car, ready to return home to Marston. 'Thank Allah that's over my son. Anwar sighed. 'you did well to stick to your story which reduced your chances of a long prison sentence. Bahram, remember what Mr A said and act as though nothing has changed since you were rejected from the role of suicide bomber.'

'Thanks Dad, for you and mum being so understanding. The last few hours have made me realise how lucky I am to have you as parents and how close I was to ruining my life physically whilst bringing mental agony to our family.'

'Gentlemen, I am just back from a meeting of COBRA (Cabinet Office Briefing Rooms) where the politicians have their say before we get the task of implicating a successful outcome.'

Sir Graeme Gaunt, MI5's respected Controller looked round the conference room with its large windows over-looking the Thames. At short notice he'd gathered represen-tatives from the armed forces, police, and emergency ser-vices. The respective leaders of these divisions sat in a semi-circle facing Sir Graeme together with their respective personal assistants.

Gaunt continued, 'You will all be aware that we issued an amber warning yesterday for the public to be on their guard to prevent a probable terrorist attack on one of our major cities. We purposely made this vague to make the terrorists think we have not a clue what they are up to. Within these four walls we can be more specific. Following a tip-off from the north of England, it is almost certain Ed-inburgh is the target. It is the host city for the British Trade Fair next week. We don't know the actual date of the attack, but it is most likely to be Friday March 20th.

We believe they have three possible targets in mind Holyrood Palace, The Scottish Parliament and the Usher Hall. All venues will be secured and heavily protected against possible attacks but the problem we have with this assault is they are likely to deploy the use of drones and a possible suicide bomber. How many drones is unclear, or what level of expertise they have in their ranks for operat-ing these weapons which presumably will have explosives attached to them. Originally, we believe they were looking to hit the targets using rocket launchers but decided against them as being less accurate than drones. Our task, gentlemen, is to set up defences to deflect them from accomplishing their plans.'

'Over to you for suggestions on how we go about it.'

Brigadier Roderick McWalter was first to re-act, 'Sir Graeme we have the advantage of knowing the targets. Most of us in this room are familiar with the city having spent some time at The Military Tattoo during the Edinburgh Festival.

Edinburgh is a compact city, and my immediate thoughts are any attack using drones will be launched from the Queen's Park, most probably under the cover of darkness. The terrorists will be able to camouflage themselves on the slopes of Arthur Seat. Another area they might consider operating drones from are the streets around Abbeyhill which is closest to the Palace. Remember, drones for this operation will be small by military standards and can be launched in small locations and very frequently so we should be prepared to put in electronic diversion systems.'

'Excellent initial analysis McWalter, you have set the scene for anyone here who has not been to Edinburgh. However, have you a plan to stop the attack?'

'Timing is our enemy, as not knowing when my troops will be required, will mean we shall have to be prepared to use several teams of plain-clothed SAS over say, a seventy-two -hour period. Some will be disguised as street cleaners or maintenance staff during the day, while others will be camouflaged and hiding on the hillside.!'

Superintendent Stephen Law was next to speak. He had flown down to London that morning from Edinburgh, 'The area in question has in normal circumstances twenty-four hours cover by my force, some of whom are armed. During the British Trade Week, we have implemented plans to increase our capability by bringing in officers from other parts of Scotland. This in our opinion should be sufficient to stave off any manual breaches should the opposition decide to change their tactics.'

'Can I ask you two and your staff to put your heads to-gether and devise both an offensive and defensive strategy for our purposes? Next I would like to hear from the emergency services.'

Albert Stringfellow, head of the Scottish Fire Brigade and Professor Craig Kinleith of NHS Scotland, had accompanied Superintendent Law on the flight from Edinburgh where they had discussed their strategies towards any possible emergencies.

Stringfellow explained how confident he was in responding to any emergency should it arise as his men had been in all manner of disaster situations. Professor Kinleith also gave a confident account of being able to contend with any atrocities should developments take a turn for the worse. He added that all the targets were situated only a maximum of ten minutes away from Royal Infirmary of Edinburgh, the biggest hospital in Edinburgh.

Sir Graeme issued his final instructions, 'Brigadier McWalter will oversee field operations, reporting to me here regularly during the operation. We shall pull our resources together to finalise clearance of this mess created by our Muslim enemies against our democracy.'

Good luck gentlemen.'

Chapter 35

Mohammed al-Basiri had arrived in Glasgow in the early hours of the morning courtesy of an HGV lorry bringing a delivery of fresh fruit to the market. To keep out of sight he hid in the driver's sleeping compartment above the driver where he was able to go over his plan of attack several times. The rest of his squad would transport themselves individually by different modes of transport to Glasgow before doing the fifty-mile journey to Edinburgh the following day in a large fresh fruit delivery van. During the journey al-Basiri issued his team with automatic pistols and ammunition which they were instructed only to use in an emergency or to defend themselves.

Before they left the van al-Basiri finalised his instructions to his men who were all wearing dark green combat trousers and jackets. In their rucksacks they had black balaclavas which they would wear as darkness fell. 'We shall be arriving in Edinburgh around three-thirty and you will be dropped off in twos. Stretch your legs and at four o'clock start your ascent of Arthur Seat and as per the plans I handed out this morning meet up with your colleagues at St. Margaret's Chapel. I will be conducting operations on the ground near the target area and will be in constant contact with you through my mobile. Report to me immediately anything you see as suspicious.'

The van arrived in Edinburgh late in the afternoon as the March sunshine was creating long shadows over the city. As planned the van made three stops on opposite sides of the Queens Park at Duddingston Village, Meadowbank and Pollock Halls and each time two terrorists jumped down from the van each one carrying a rucksacks which contained individual parts for the drones to be assembled later.

Mohammed had a final word with Ali Gosham who was last out of the van at Pollock Halls, the Edinburgh University campus next to the Royal Commonwealth Swimming Pool, 'Ali, the success of our attack this evening is down to your expertise in assembling the drones. Your rucksack contains the same explosives you have been using during your training, which will detonate as they land on their target. How long will it take you to assemble the drones?'

A serious Gosham replied, 'We conducted assembly time trials during training. My best time was seven minutes and the worse eleven minutes to have the drone ready for take-off. The problem with this type of equipment is ensuring that the electronic navigation system is engaged. When I have each one ready for flying, I will do a short trial run before putting the next one together.'

Mohammed congratulated him on his organised thinking, 'Excellent Ali, you seem to have everything under control. Be ready to fire the first drone at Holyrood Palace on my command at seven-thirty. The second explosive should be directed at the Scottish Parliament building seconds later then the action repeated twice using the remaining drones. Once all six have been fired, split the team up and get off the hill the same way you entered. I will give you directions by phone where you can pick up our vehicle to get you home.'

An hour later the three teams had arrived at St. Margaret's Chapel, the last to arrive were the Duddingston contingent who had a longer journey which started with almost two hundred steps up Jacob's Ladder before passing Dunsapie Loch. All six huddled together using miner's torches as Ali shouted out instructions as he put together the drones using the same precision that he had demonstrated in the training rooms at Nelson. As he had predicted it took the best part of an hour to complete the assembly of the drones for action. On completion, Ali texted al-Basiri, 'Everything in place for the attack.'

Mohammed responded, 'Well done Ali!'

Captain Trevor Hardcastle, the SAS officer appointed to stop the threat from al Qaeda by Brigadier McWalter had plotted every movement of al-Basiri's men from the minute they arrived at Arthur's Seat. From his base two hundred feet above the terrorist's stronghold he watched, using night-vision binoculars, and waited for them to emerge with their weapons. The terrorist made their way a short distance west to get the best vantage point to launch their missiles. They laid the six drones and the electronic navigation devices out in front of them and waited for Mohammed's command. Trevor Hardcastle smiled to himself, 'I have seldom had such an easy target in all my military career, it will be like shooting fish in a barrel.'

The time was 7.10 P. M.

Hardcastle described the scene below him to Brigadier McWalter based in a conference room at Edinburgh Castle only two miles away. The Brigadier wasted no time in launching the defence offensive, 'Captain, they're ready to pounce by the looks of things, Close in now and instruct your men to remove the threat by aiming at the equipment. This will cause explosions and probably result in casualties, but they are negligible compared to the damage that will be created if these damnable things are enacted!

The dozen SAS troopers immediately reacted to their commander's instructions and fired their silenced automatic rifles. Ali Goshan was talking to his friend Isil, 'Does it make you feel proud to be serving tonight in the fight against the infidels Isil?', he asked.

Isil did not answer. Neither did Ali hear his response as they both perished under the gunfire which set off a series of explosions and blew them into the here-after!

Only two of the terrorists survived the bomb blast and drew out their automatic pistols and fired off aimlessly into the darkness up the hill for the ten seconds it took the soldiers to end their lives.

Mohammed al-Basiri was hiding in a nearby cemetery which was shrouded in darkness but beautifully positioned to see both his chosen targets. It was colder than he had expected but his heart was beating fast as the minute hand on his watch started its descent to 7.30. Ten minutes before the scheduled plan all hell broke loose as large explosions lit up the sky from the darkness of the hill. Mohammed could not understand what had gone wrong and rang Ali for an explanation, only to hear the sound of a dead dialling tone.

al;Basiri quickly texted the van driver who brought his team to Edinburgh and told him to get out of Edinburgh and back to Glasgow as quick as possible avoiding the M8 motorway as the police would most certainly be stopping all traffic

The Afghan cursed his failed plans and thought of fleeing the cemetery immediately before reconsidering his next move. Staying in touch with the deceased may be the answer to his survival, as the police hopefully wouldn't bother to check burial grounds until the morning. He brought up Google Maps on his phone, put in his destination as 'Leith' and when the route appeared, he extended his search to 'Places of interest' and inserted 'cemeteries.' a number of resting places were listed, and Mohammed studied how he could get from his present location just off Regent Road to arrive at the offices of the only man he knew in Edinburgh, albeit vaguely, drug landlord Geordie McNab.

Almost twelve hours later al-Basiri arrived at his destination in Leith. It had been a long night involving climbing over graveyard gates and fences in the back gardens of modern housing developments. His meandering route kept him away from main roads as he carefully avoided being spotted by any nocturnal dog walkers or homeless vagrants who could blow his cover. His first stop was the Eastern Cemetery off Easter Road where he hid behind a mausoleum for several hours. He exited the holy resting place by standing on a tombstone leaning against the perimeter wall nearest Leith. Soon he was crossing Leith Links, famous for the early development of golf, only a short journey to McNab's yard in Salamander Street.

He was relieved when he saw a light on in McNab's office and even more so when he spotted the burly figure of Geordie sorting out his plans for the day. Geordie McNab had the Scottish work ethic and was always at his desk by 6.30 every morning preferring to be ready to get his staff working on their arrival.

Al-Basiri burst into McNab's office without knocking giving Geordie a huge fright making him instinctively reach for the baseball bat under his desk, 'Mohammed!! What a fright you gave me! What are you doing barging in here like that!

Mohammed took a deep breath before answering, 'Sorry Mr McNab. I need your help; the police are looking for me. I have to get out of the country quickly.'

McNab leaned back in his chair as he suddenly realised why Mohammed was here, 'I take it you had something to do with these explosions up Arthur Seat last night which I heard about on the radio this morning.'

Al-Basiri did not conceal his guilt, 'Yes, the failure is down to me.'

'I should turn you over to the police.'

'You and I know you won't. You have too much to lose and I know too much about your business. I have told my lawyers that in the event of my premature death they can reveal all my business contacts to Interpol.' Sensing that McNab was not convinced Mohammed reached into his coat jacket and brought out his automatic pistol. 'Don't think about reaching for the phone Geordie. Instead, let us plan my escape.'

Chapter 36

Brigadier McWalter held a de-brief the following morning in the Conference Hall at Edinburgh Castle attended by the army and all the Intelligence services. D.C.I. McKirdy attended with his boss Superintendent Law.

The Brigadier began, 'Morning ladies and gentlemen, last night's prevention exercise was extremely successful, and I would like to thank you for the joint effort you put in to make this possible. So far, we have accounted for nine enemy fighters and although some were unrecognisable, due to their proximity to the exploding bombs when they went off.

Their leader Mohammed al-Basiri is still at large and as I speak Police Scotland are carrying out a massive sweeping search of the city. The usual security checks are being undertaken at all airports and seaports throughout the U.K. To date al-Basiri has proved to be a slippery customer but this time I feel confident we will apprehend our man. Have you any questions regarding last night's operation?'

Lieutenant Hunter was first to raise his hand to attract his leader's attention, 'Sir have forensics been able to identify the weaponry from last night and any clue as to how they got hold of it?'

'Yes.' replied the Brigadier, 'Early indications are that the terrorists used material manufactured in Turkey. Closer examination pointed towards it being smuggled into this country hidden in a consignment of fruit. The Foreign Secretary has reported our findings to his equivalent in the Turkish Government and we await his response.

'Next Question.'

McKirdy raised his hand, 'Did all nine deceased come from the same area?'

'No, we don't think so. When forensics inspected what was left of their underwear, forensics confirmed they had been purchased from different outlets spread throughout the land.' confirmed McWalter. 'However, MI5 had been given a tip-off which centred around an Islamic cell based in the town of Nelson in Lancashire. They will be receiving a visit from the security services later today.'

'Has there been any re-action from the local media to last nights' explosions?' enquired a member of the Fire service.

'Only the usual conspiracy theories that residents were phoning in to see if the Capital was under attack from Russian bombers. I instructed the MOD to send out a brief to say we had been carrying out night exercises to protect Edinburgh and its citizens in the unlikely situation of a possible terrorist attack. on two of our most important state buildings, namely Holyrood Palace and the Scottish Parliament. I added we thought it better to carry this out with the element of surprise to avoid having our vital exercises being upset by members of the public.'

The assembled company chuckled at the Brigadier's answer which brought the de-brief to a close.

Chapter 37

Half an hour after Mohammed al-Basiri had barged into Geordie McNab's office they were joined by 'Maniac' McLagan who could tell from his boss' body language he was not a happy man this morning. The reason for his discomfort was the man sitting behind the office door Mohammed al-Basiri.

'Morning Mohammed what are you doing here?', he asked trying to appear friendly until he could identify Geordie's reason for the glum look.

'I have a little problem which I'm hoping Mr McNab is going to resolve for me.'

Turning to face McNab, Maniac asked his boss 'What sort of problem?'

'Mohammed is on the run from the police following the explosions you probably heard about last night.'

Maniac turned nasty 'We don't want to get involved in any of that shit, before you know it, you'll have MI5 visiting you and their remit outranks the police by some way. I think you would be daft to help him, better to remove him right now.'

The bodyguard made a lunge towards Mohammed but was not quick enough as the Afghan had anticipated his move and produced an automatic pistol which he smashed into Maniac's face splattering his nose into a fountain of blood.

'Sit down Mr McLagan, Geordie and I were having a sensible conversation before you reacted to the only way you know how – by resorting to violence.'

Geordie McNab smiled at Mohammed being able to outsmart Maniac, 'Mohammed's right, you resorted to your natural way of solving problems without thinking first. It is not a practical solution to remove Mohammed from the scene. He knows too much about our business and has left instructions with his lawyers to expose anyone who attempts it.

I have spoken to David Holton, skipper of the Northern Star who is about to leave on a fishing trip and will be picking up gear for us from Igor Shertsov somewhere in the North Sea. If we can get Mohammed up to Peterhead tonight, he will take him to Igor Shertsov then presumably from there a safe passage through Estonia back to Afghanistan.'

McLagan asked, 'Geordie, how are we going to avoid the police checks on the M90 up to Peterhead?'

'With difficulty Maniac, I'll ask Holton if there are any lorries carrying return loads back to Peterhead which has suitable hiding places. Leave this with me. Mohammed you must be starving. Tell me what you want for breakfast and I will get one of the boys to go round to the local café.

Dave Holton was relaxing in his lounge when Geordie phoned and explained his predicament. Holton had only recently taken to smuggling and he was keen to help his new business acquaintance.

'Geordie there is a great deal of traffic leaves Peterhead every morning to deliver the proceeds from the market. All the haggling amongst the fish salesmen commences at five in the morning, and then the catch is divided and sent to the fish wholesalers round Britain. On the way back the hauliers bring back the fish boxes from the day before in the refrigerated vans with the cooler systems turned off usually, unless they are carrying fresh food back to the Aberdeen area. Some of the vehicles have false compartments where the captains store what they don't want the Customs guys to see. If you can get al-Basiri to the Kinross Service Station for four o'clock tomorrow afternoon. I'll have him picked up and brought here. Once he'is in Peterhead, we'll smuggle him on board the Northern Star where he will remain until we set sail tomorrow night.'

A delighted Geordie McNab replied, 'Don't worry I'll deliver Mohammed to Kinross in the afternoon,'

Next morning McNab's favourite driver, Willie Bristow, left Leith with a truckload of animal waste carrying Mohammed al-Basiri. The Afghan, wearing protective clothing, was hidden from view in the middle of the slurry, safe in the knowledge that the consignment was unlikely to be stopped by the police. At Kinross Servce Station Willie parked a good distance from other vehicles allowing Mohammed time to get some new clothes on until the friendly refrigerated lorry arrived and transported him to Peterhead and safety on board the Northern Star.

Chapter 38

Three days later.

'Come on Geordie, we have to be at the airport two hours before departure and you are still on that bloody computer.', snarled a frustrated Ella McNab, 'the bairns are getting restless and becoming a pain in the arse.'

'Okay Ella, that's me finished my work. Have you got the boarding passes and passports?'

'No, you're in charge of the travel arrangements. I've had enough to do packing all the cases but remember to bring the travel documents for the McLagans as well!'

Geordie collected everything from his bureau, loaded the cases and his two kids Harry and Mia into his four by four and set off for the airport. Maniac and his wife Carol along with their brood, Jimmy and John, were waiting for them in the departure hall. Edinburgh airport was busy, and the two gangsters were conscious of a larger than usual police presence. The last seventy-two hours had failed to flush out any sightings of Mohammed al-Basiri. He was currently on board the Northern Star one hundred and fifty miles out in the North Sea coughing his guts out as the trawler swelled over the waves.

Four hours later the two families were in their two-bedroom suites in the five-star Real Excelsior in Puerto Banus. The women unpacked the cases, throwing swimming apparel in the direction of their excited offspring to get them out of earshot while Geordie and Maniac headed for the nearest bar.

Geordie took the opportunity to remind Maniac of the real purpose for their visit.

'Alistair, two days from now we leave for Tallinn to see Igor Shertsov to discuss better terms for the increased business he is receiving from Scotland. The situation has improved in our favour now that Dave Holton will be delivering Mohammed al- Basiri into Shertsov's care. He will be in Tallinn when we arrive and I have asked Shertsov to keep him there so we can hopefully get him to reduce his prices, especially now that we've just saved him from a long prison stretch.'

Does Shertsov agree with your thinking Geordie?'

'Yes, Igor is a mean, hard, East European who'll also be looking for a bigger slice of the action now that the level of business is expanding. We are meeting him in a hotel in Tallinn with Boris Andropov.

Your role Maniac is always to watch my back There'll be a package waiting for us at our hotel in Tallinn consisting of two hand pistols and ammunition. These weapons won't give us the upper hand, as I expect everyone attending the meeting to be suitably attired. If you see any signs of aggression towards me swing into action fast. Here's the girls coming so I'll change the subject.'

'Well ladies you look all set to take the poolside by storm. What can I get you to drink?'

'Oh, I think we'll kick off with a bottle of prosecco with a few nuts and crisps served on the terrace overlooking the pool besides these two empty sunbeds are positioned.'

Putting on a posh English accent Geordie responded, 'What the Madam wants, the Madam gets.'

The waiter delivered the wives' drinks to the table between the sunbeds. They had both removed their white towelling dressing gowns to reveal their swimming apparel. Ella had on a small black bikini which emphasised all her hard work in the gym and the tanning parlour. Carol clearly did not work out and had squeezed her overweight mass, with some difficulty, into a blue floral-patterned one-piece swimming costume. Geordie and Maniac remained at the bar hoovering up more drink, by using the excuse they could monitor the children easier from there, as they played in the swimming pool.

For the next few days both families enjoyed all the superb facilities the Real Excelsior had to offer especially the all-inclusive food and drink. Wednesday morning Geordie and Maniac bid farewell to their wives.

'Now Ella when we're gone you look after the kids and don't get too drunk.'

Ella glanced up Geordie, then pointed to some husky young men at the bar, 'I think Carol and I will be able to entertain ourselves in your absence.'

'You wish.' grunted Maniac who moved off with Geordie in the direction of a taxi waiting to take them to the airport.

The cab had just moved off when Ella unclipped her bikini top and lay back topless on her sunbed exposing her silicone-filled breasts, 'Well Carol, I might as well show the boys over there what's on offer!' she laughed.

Chapter 39

Richard Hartley called Hugh McFaul and Campbell Anderson to his office after receiving a notification from Puerto Banus that McNab and McLagan were on their way to Malaga Airport.

'Morning gentlemen, I have just received word that two of our targets are on the move. McNab and his colleague McLagan have left their hotel on their way, we believe, to meet up with Igor Shertsov and Boris Andropov. McNab and McLagan are co-stars in this operation. Our main target remains the Estonians. Our thanks must go to Mhairi McClure for getting into Geordie McNab's confidence and alerting us to this link-up in Tallinn.

I shall speak to our embassy in Tallinn and arrange with our ambassador to make his security staff available to you, to give you back-up to confront the Estonians. Police Scotland will also send a deputation to Tallinn to apprehend the Edinburgh drug dealers who they believe may have been responsible for the sinking of the 'Caledonian Princess'. Some debris from the boat has since surfaced and forensics have indicated that they are certain the cause of sinking was the result of an explosion. Be ready to leave for Tallinn immediately. When the two Scotsmen arrive in Tallinn, we shall have them followed to their hotel where they will be continued to be monitored until you arrive. Any questions?'

'Yes Sir', answered McFaul, 'Can you clarify our remit when we confront the Estonians?'

'Hugh, I don't have to tell you my attitude towards enemies of this Service who have murdered one of my agents. I'm giving you both my permission to rid the world of these ruthless gangsters who killed Elke Kohl. All I ask that you carry out this assignment discreetly and only after Police Scotland have left with McNab and McLagan. There is a private jet waiting for you at City Airport which will get you into Tallinn not long after the flight from Malaga touches down. Go now and remember this Department's reputation is at stake and I want you to send a message to Eastern Europe not to mess with our agents!'

'Grant, the 'Super' wants to see you.' D.C. Lomas informed his boss Grant McKirdy when he popped his head into the D.C.I.'s office and found McKirdy on the phone. McKirdy raised his hand to acknowledge receipt of the instruction.

Ten minutes later Grant settled down in the polished wooden chair opposite Superintendent Stephen Law. 'Morning Grant, it's all happening this week starting with the terrorist attack four days ago, which unfortunately did not lead to the arrest of Mohammed al-Basiri. I've just received word from MI6 that your friend Geordie McNab is on his way to Tallinn to meet up with the Estonians who ship all the drugs to Scotland. MI6 are sending Hugh McFaul and Campbell Anderson plus assistance from British security staff based at the embassy in Tallinn. I'd like you to link up with them and the Estonian police. They will assist you in arresting our local gangsters who will be brought back for trial. Arrangements will be made for you and your team to fly to Estonia this afternoon.'

'Thank you, Sir. I'll go and organise our departure. I'll be glad when we put McNab behind bars for a long time.'

McKirdy called in D.S. Lomax and D.C. Luxton into his office, 'Great News! Geordie McNab and his minder Maniac have left their hotel in Puerto Banus and are at Malaga Airport waiting to board a flight to Tallinn. The good news is we will be joining them in Tallinn. Hugh McFaul and Cam Anderson are also going to Tallinn to apprehend the three Estonians they hold responsible for Elke Kohl's murder.'

'How are we going to get there at such short notice?',
enquired Lomax.

'I want you go home immediately after this meeting and
pack a bag for two nights stay in Tallinn. Take a taxi
straight to Edinburgh Airport. I have arranged for MI6 to
fly up from London and pick us up in their private Jet.'

'Well Done Sir! That's a first for all of us.'

'We shall be met at Tallinn Airport by Commander Rudi
Lerindowski who will assist us with the arrest of McNab
and Maniac. Off you go and I will see you both at the airport.'

Three hours later Grant McCall's wife dropped him off
at the airport and he made his way to the VIP lounge. Ian
Lomax was already there but no sign of Avril Luxton - instead another CID officer Ken Harrower stood beside Lomax.'

'Hello Ian, where's Avril?'

'Grant, she called me at home to say she was not feeling
well and feels she has a migraine coming on. She has suffered with them in the past from time to time. Ken was
available to step in and I will be able to brief him on the
flight, the only problem I see is he does not have a firearm
but I am sure the Estonian Police will be able to supply
one.'

'That is a pity about Avril, Ian. I hope she is all right.
I'll get Diane Falconer to pop in and check on her condition.'

The three Edinburgh detectives were escorted by one of the
airport ground-staff, who accompanied them downstairs and
out on to the runway to meet the private plane.MI6 had obtained special clearance to land and take-off immediately.
The Cessna jet pulled up only fifty yards from where the
boarding party were standing. One of the pilots opened the
door, rolled out steps, and signalled it was ready for board-

ing. The jet engines continued to engage as everyone climbed up the gangway and into the comfort of the plane.

'Welcome Grant and Ian, who's your replacement? I was expecting to see Avril with you.' shouted Hugh above the din coming from the jet's engines.

'She's not well, so Ken Harrower who I've known for years has stepped into the breach.'

The sandy-haired athletic Harrower introduced himself and they all settled into the plush armchairs which faced each other. The seating arrangements allowed them all to discuss their 'plan of attack' down to the smallest detail. All that was left was to do was brief the Embassy security staff supplied by the British Embassy in Tallinn and the local Estonian armed response team.

Just under three hours later the jet touched down at Tallinn airport and the visitors were taken to waiting cars without going through customs. The cavalcade made their way to the town centre where they entered the British Embassy by the rear door. The Ambassador Sir Harold Sutherland was waiting for them with three of his security guards Geoffrey Pinkerton, Alex Innes, and Gordon Weir. Hugh McFaul and Cam Anderson had met all three gentlemen during MI6 seminars and rated them all as first class operators.

The occupants of the Cessna jet were not the only people heading towards Estonia. The Northern Star under the command of Dave Holton set sail from Peterhead with Mohammed ai-Basiri on board and three days later met up at sea with The Koidutaht. Captain Shertsov gave a warm welcome to Mohammed, who he expected would return his generosity for arranging a safe passage out of the U.K.

'Good to see you again Mohammed, did you enjoy your sail in the Northern Star?'

'No, I certainly did not! I have been suffering from sea sickness from the moment we came out of Peterhead harbour. I don't know how you guys manage to do this for a living.'

The five-star Hotel Telgraaf was the first stop for Geordie McNab and his bodyguard. The hotel was a classic building in the centre of Tallinn close to all the amenities for tourists who wanted to enjoy a city break. City breaks were far from the minds of McNab and McLaren who wasted no time in contacting Igor Shertsov.

'Igor, McLagan and I have booked into the Telgraaf. I'm going to book a conference room for eight o'clock tonight when we can all get together and discuss our business procedures. I'll arrange for us to eat and drink in the room during our talks then we can go out later to a nightclub.'

'Sounds good Geordie. There will be four attending from my side - Boris Andropov, Kurt Jansen who arranges all the crossings for illegal Immigrants, Mohammed al-Basiri and myself. See you later!'

Downstairs in the lobby Sandra Mitchell and Graham Aston sat drinking coffee. They had followed the Edinburgh duo from the airport to the Telgraaf Hotel and once they had seen them safely booked in and been allocated rooms, they phoned the British Embassy.

Shortly afterwards a short plump man wearing a three-piece navy suit under his cream raincoat approached the hotel reception. He produced identification from inside his jacket pocket whilst announcing to the gentlemen behind the desk, 'Inspector Kaliosky, Tallinn police. Can I speak to the Manager please?'

Josef Landowska, the manager of the Hotel Telgraaf rushed to the reception foyer as soon as he received the police inspector's request. Experience told him in Estonia you never get on the wrong side of the police.

'Inspector, I am Josef Landowska, how can I be of service to you?'

Inspector ran his eyes quickly over Landowska, a late forties tall, slim figure with thick waxed black hair and a goatee beard, before answering, ' Can we go somewhere more private, I have an urgent matter I want to discuss.'

'Certainly, Inspector, there is a meeting room available across the hall.'

Once they were settled down in comfortable chairs Inspector Kaliosky looked across the polished wooden table and opened the conversation.

'Mr. Landowska, this afternoon two British gentlemen booked into your hotel using their own names George McNab and Alistair McLagan. We have strong reason to believe they are here to meet up with Estonian residents who transfer drugs from Parnu to the U.K. by sea. We are co-operating with the British security services who want to arrest your two residents whilst we in turn will detain any Estonian citizens involved. Can you tell me if they have booked their evening meal, or made any arrangements for going out on the town to taste the delights of Tallinn?'

Landowska was bewildered by what he had just heard and picking up the telephone on the table called the front desk, 'Antoni, can you tell me if Messrs McNab and McLagan, who booked into the hotel today, are eating here tonight?'

'Just a minute Sir while I look at the Diner List for this evening.' seconds later Antoni replied, 'Mr. Landowska, they have requested a private room for six diners at eight o'clock but have not given me the names of the other four invitees.'

'Thank you, Antoni.' Josef said putting down the phone and looking the policeman in the eye, 'You heard that. They have booked a private room for what looks like a working dinner.'

'Mr. Landowska, we appreciate your co-operation. I shall reveal to my superiors what you have told me, and it will be up to them as to what action they take next. Everything we have discussed is highly confidential, please do not tell anyone about our conversation unless you want to spend some time in prison. '

Upstairs Geordie McNab's mobile received a text from an unlikely source, it read:

'British security, including Police Scotland are in Tallinn. The Ferret.'

The only problem for Geordie McNab was he had turned his phone off after calling Igor Shertsov.

Chapter 40

Sir Harold Sutherland sat at the head of the oval table in the Conference Room of the British Embassy in Tallinn. In front of him to his right sat the representatives from MI6 and on his left his own security men.

The ambassador read out a message from the Tallinn Police, 'We visited Hotel Telgraaf this afternoon and can confirm that George McNab and Alistair McLaren have booked in. Mr Landowska, the manager confirmed that they are dining in the hotel tonight at 8.00 p.m.in a private room where they will be joined by four guests.'

Hugh McFaul interrupted, 'Four guests? I wonder who the fourth one is? We only reckoned on Igor Shertsov, Boris Andropov and possibly Kurt Jansen. Maybe Jansen does not feel safe either, without a minder in that company. Sorry Sir Harold please continue.'

Sir Harold responded, 'All I was going to add was this espionage business is a bit out of my remit so I will leave you gentlemen to work out your strategy. My wife and I have been invited to the opera this evening by the Estonian Foreign Minister.'

The ambassador stood up and left the room.

Hugh McFaul continued the proceedings, 'Grant, since we are on foreign soil, which traditionally is the remit of MI6, I hope you have no objections to me taking control of the situation.'

Grant smiled, 'Okay by me Hugh, all police Scotland want out of this is to see these two villains put behind bars.'

'Good, now let us work out how we can make this a successful evening   .'

At 6.30 p.m. a delivery vehicle reversed into the goods entrance behind the Telgraaf Hotel and eight figures, seven wearing combat gear and one in a tuxedo, emerged and entered the hotel. Josef Landowska was waiting for them and escorted them up the stairs, avoiding the kitchen area, to a room two doors along from the proposed meeting room.

One of the embassy staff unzipped his rucksack to produce two mini cameras which he took next door and planted them at opposite ends of the room. The others were glued to a monitor familiarising themselves with the room and making sure the sound systems would pick up everything which would be under discussion later.

Everything was in place by seven o'clock all they were waiting for now was the enemy to arrive!

Geordie McNab and Maniac arrived at the foyer ten minutes early and were informed that the manager would like to meet them. Josef Landowska joined them a couple of minutes later accompanied by Alex Innes from the British Embassy wearing a tuxedo whom he introduced as Gary Mackie, 'Gary is one of my most senior waiters and as he is British, I thought it would be good if he supervised the dining staff this evening. He speaks both English and Estonian which may be helpful when you are ordering your meal or anything else you require.'

Gary shook hands and escorted the two Scotsmen to the private room where a temporary bar had been set up with a waiter in attendance.

Maniac ordered first, 'A large McAllan whisky with ice, Geordie you'll want your usual. Waiter, add a large gin and tonic to my order.'

The two had only just settled into their seats at the table when the doors burst open and the Estonians marched in with Mohammed al-Basiri in tow.

Hugh McFaul and the rest of the British contingent were watching proceedings from a room two doors along the corridor. McFaul exclaimed on seeing al-Basiri, 'Jesus Christ!!

I do not believe it! How the hell did Mohammed al-Basiri get here? This is going to be a memorable night if this all comes off.'

Gary Mackie seated everyone round the table and organised the pre-dinner drinks and passed out the menus for the assembled company to place their orders. Maniac McLagan was watching Gary closely and little doubts about his professional ability were starting to bother him and he whispered in Geordie's ear, 'I'm not sure about that head waiter. We should check and see if he is armed.'

Geordie focused on Gary before announcing to the others, 'My colleague is concerned that we have not searched the head waiter for weapons.'

Igor Shertsov came to the hotel's defence, 'The Telgraaf is one of the oldest hotels in Tallinn and I would imagine carries out strict investigations as to whom they employ. However, if it will relax you, we can carry out a body search when he returns.'

Everyone's attention was drawn to the door when Gary appeared with two waitresses carrying the six starters on trays. Gary removed each first course in turn and placed it in front of the guests. He was about to leave the room when Maniac stood in his way and in a blunt Scottish accent uttered, 'Excuse me pal, do you mind if I carry oot a body search. You see none of us know you.'

Gary looked Maniac firmly in the eye and smiled, 'Of course Mr McLagan. I am surprised it has taken you so long to ask. When we had the G20 summit here two years ago we were all searched before the guests came into the room.'

Gary lifted his hands in the air and Maniac ran his hands over his body, found nothing of interest and sat back in his seat, visibly disappointed.

The diners devoured their first course and made idle chat until the dishes were cleared and the main courses were laid in front of them in the form of three fillet steaks, two lobster thermidor and a chicken vindaloo for the home-sick Mohammed. For the next five to ten minutes silence reigned over the dining room as they all enjoyed the excellent cuisine.

Hugh watched every move as did the rest of the party who all had their separate roles to play. The seven of them were dressed in full black combat gear including bullet-proof tunics, their faces hidden under balaclavas with only slits for their eyes and mouths. Picking up their silenced semi-automatic Glock 7s, they all followed Hugh quietly along the corridor until he was outside the double doors of the dining room. He signalled to the others before kicking the doors hard making a spectacular entrance on the startled diners. The rest of the security team charged in behind him and surrounded the table as Hugh shouted instructions, 'Don't move! Put your hands in the air! I would not advise any of you to make a false move if you value your life! One at a time stand up, move away from the table, get down on your knees and slowly empty your pockets on to the floor!'

Kurt Jansen was first to follow Hugh's order followed by Igor Shertsov and Boris Andropov. Surprisingly only Boris was the only Estonian who had a gun. Next it was the turn of Mohammed al-Basiri who had both a gun and a dagger. Geordie McNab bowed in front of his captors leaving Maniac to ponder whether to chance his luck when Cam Anderson intervened, 'I would not advise you to try anything stupid Maniac, we've been at target practice all week.'

Maniac kicked his weapon under the table and Ian Lomax bent down to retrieve it. Cam appeared to lose his concentration and went to help Lomax back on his feet. As he did so he laid his pistol on the table. Boris Andropov saw his chance, he leapt up and grabbed the pistol, in the hope of firing it off indiscriminately in the direction of Hugh and the others. Andropov's action set off a retaliatory response from the MI6 officers killing Boris along with Igor Shertsov and Kurt Jansen, who had also sprung to their feet in an attempt to escape the hail of bullets which spat out silently from the Glock7s. Those who remained kneeling were in a state of shock.

The Police Scotland officers had all been on armed response manoeuvres but had never seen anyone killed in action before. Mohammed al-Basiri cursed under his breath as he would rather have died with the others than face years in prison. Geordie Mc Nab wept as the reality of the situation sunk in while Maniac screamed profanities at his attackers until Geordie told him, 'Maniac, shut your mouth.'

Grant McKirdy approached McNab and announced after taking off his balaclava, 'George McNab, I am arresting you for dealing in drugs and for masterminding the sinking of the Caledonian Princess with all hands on-board.' Turning to McLagan he repeated his words, with the exception of changing 'Mastermind' to 'Planting explosives which led to the sinking of the Caledonian Princess.'

'Maniac don't say another word. McKirdy here is having a good day. It has taken him a long time to catch up with us as we have managed to ferret his every move. I'll let our lawyers protest our innocence in court.'

Josef Landowska came into the room and was immediately sick into a napkin at the discovery of the three corpses on the floor with blood streaming from them in every direction. Boris had been hit on the chest and neck, Igor had taken several bullets to his chest and lower back, while blood cascaded from two holes in Kurt Jansen's head and body.

'Apologies Josef, one of the captives made a move for a gun so we had no choice but to prevent him and his colleagues firing at us. Now we shall get this mess sorted out and pay for the damage we have caused to your carpet. I'll talk to inspector Kaliosky and have the bodies taken to the morgue. Can you phone them and ask them to come to the rear entrance of the hotel?'

'Certainly, Mr McFaul. I will attend to it.' replied the ashen-faced hotel manager as he continued to stare at the carnage surrounding him.

Grant McKirdy let out a deep breath after Lomax and Harrower had hand-cuffed the remaining three prisoners, 'Christ that was close, when Andropov grabbed the gun, I thought some of us were goners.'

Hugh sought to give the detective some assurance by replying, 'We are taught never to relax in these situations and when Andropov launched himself towards Cam's pistol there was only going to be one winner. The fact the other two jumped to their feet near where they had dropped their own guns was the catalyst for us to show no mercy.' Looking at an embarrassed Cam Anderson he added, 'Cam, what the hell were you thinking about putting down your weapon? I'm not pleased at your completely thoughtless unprofessional action. You and I will discuss this later!'

Turning to D.C.I. McKirdy he continued, 'I will leave you to escort your two Edinburgh prisoners to the local jail, where you can make arrangements to fly them home. We will return to London with Mohammed al-Basiri and hand him over for interrogation to MI5. It has been a successful day, but not one to celebrate when we have three dead men at our feet. Have a good flight home everyone.'

Hugh concluded by shaking hands with the Scots before accompanying them to the rear of the hotel where transport was waiting for everyone to go to their various destinations.

Fifteen minutes later the MI6 contingent plus Mohammed al-Basiri entered through the British Embassy gates in their blacked-out mini-bus. Al-Basiri was taken down and locked in a cell in the basement ready to be transported to London in the morning. Alex Innes was still in his dinner suit, but it was the other four who were getting hot under the collars and were delighted to be able to discard their balaclavas.

Hugh McFaul made a typical Irish remark, 'I don't know about you boys, but I need a bloody good drink !!'

'Follow us gentlemen, we shall raid the bar upstairs and remember there's no rush as Ambassador Sutherland is at the opera.' responded Alex Innes.

Chapter 41

Two days later Hugh and Cam sat facing the smiling figure of Assistant Controller Richard Hartley.

'Welcome back gentlemen and congratulations for accomplishing a successful outcome for the Service. Those bastards who murdered Elke Kohl deserved all they got. Did you stick to my suggested plan Hugh?'

'Yes Sir, we did. After Maniac had helped us by kicking his gun under the table Lomax crawled down to get it. Cam put his own automatic on the table within reach of the Estonians, one of them picked it up with the intention of firing it in our direction. What he failed to know was Cam's Glock was only capable of discharging blank cartridges, allowing me and the other Tallinn based MI6 officers to assassinate them without witnesses realising it.'

'Good!' said the spy catcher, 'I have used that strategy before when I was operating in the field. When any member of this Service is killed doing their duty I have absolutely no qualms about not having to follow the rule book to avenge their death. If anyone asks me for an explanation, I will claim you acted in self-defence. Take a few days off and when you come back, I will get you to tie up a few loose ends.'

The 'Loose ends' consisted of Hugh and Cam visiting Elke Kohl's parents in Saxony to give them a bravery medal on behalf of the British Secret Service. They also confirmed that Elke's death had not been in vain. She had made a significant contribution to the fight against international drug dealers, the Afghani terrorists who supplied them, plus removing the practice of supplying young women for the illegal sex trade from the port of Parnu.

The last piece of the jigsaw was to visit Mhairi McClure at her Buckinghamshire safe house. Richard Hartley and Hugh

McFaul found Mhairi in relaxed mood chatting to Beverley Thomson whom she had befriended. The visitors had not come bearing glad tidings.

Mhairi had enjoyed her 'freedom' and it showed in her dress sense. She had returned to wearing smart business suits, visiting the hairdresser regularly and applied make-up to a face which looked much younger than when she'd come out of prison.

Hartley and McFaul called Mhairi to the meeting room they had booked the previous day. Hartley put some papers on the desk as Mhairi came in.

'Hello Mhairi' he began in a cold voice, 'I think you know why we are here. The task we set you to gain the confidence of Geordie McNab has now ended successfully with the said McNab now awaiting trial for drug dealing and possibly the sinking of a fishing trawler with five men on board. The Service owes you a debt of gratitude for your assistance in this matter. Through you supplying us with information on McNab's movements, we were able to apprehend four villains who were enemies of the State.

You may well be called as a witness at McNab and McLagan's trial, but you would not be seen by the public and would only be referred to as 'Miss A'.

'I have spoken to the Home Office and they have recognised your valuable contribution to what I have just said by reducing your current prison sentence by three years. To have this ratified I require you to sign this paper confirming your agreement.'

Mhairi was slow to respond and with a tear in her eye she said, 'Mr Hartley I've enjoyed working here with Beverly and if I can ever be of assistance again in the future you know where to find me.'

'You never know what lies ahead Miss McClure.'

Mhairi signed the letter, stood up and surprised the MI6 officers by shaking hands. She left the room in the company

of two guards to pack her bags and start on her return journey back to HMP Askham Hall Ladies Prison.

Chapter 42

Two weeks after the arrest of McNab, Grant McKirdy sat looking out his office window towards Fettes College, one of the most expensive public schools in Scotland. It was a fine Spring morning filled with sunshine and crisp fresh air which was the opposite of the dour mood the D.C.I. found himself in. Usually after such a successful result he would be on a high. Was his cynical, suspicious mind playing tricks on him.?

He picked up the phone and placed an internal call to Ian Lomax. Ian was still enjoying his successful trip to Estonia and bounced into his boss' office.

'Morning Ian, there is something serious I want to discuss with you. I have just been going over the McNab case and trying to find out how he operated and managed to keep ahead of us. Forensica have given me a list of all his phone calls and texts he made or received especially the final one – the one he did not have the chance to open reads:

'British Security, including Police Scotland in Tallinn.' (signed), The Ferret.'

'Good God, Grant! Do we have a mole in the department? If McNab had got that message our whole operation would have been scuppered.'

'Exactly Ian, I know it was not you as you were close to getting your head blown off. When we cautioned McNab do you remember him remarking 'It has taken you a long time to 'Ferret' us out as he put it.'

'Grant, he did say that.'

'A play on words now I have read this text.'

'I spoke to Diane Falconer earlier and asked if she called on Avril after we left for Tallinn. She said she went round to her flat in Bruntsfield but nobody was in and a neighbour told her Avril had just left carrying an overnight bag.'

'Oh Christ, I can't believe this.' retorted Ian.

McKirdy followed his thought process, 'Ian if you think about it, Admiral Arbuthnott committed suicide shortly after we visited him, and 'Maniac' had been verbally threatening him. You were due a visit down to Eyemouth to interview Peter Fraser, the skipper of the 'Caledonian Princess' which was mysteriously sunk at sea before you had the chance to see him. Some relics from the boat have surfaced and it is looking like the 'Caledonian Princess' was indeed sabotaged.'

'Ian, I do not have to spell out how serious this is for Police Scotland and for our department. I want you to go through all your cases since Avril Luxton joined us and see if there have been any other instances where she may have leaked information to the enemy.'

A despondent Lomax put his head in his hands pulling down the skin on his thin face before mumbling, 'I'll see what I can find Grant.'

Unfortunately, Ian Lomax did not find any further evidence of Avril's malpractice, leaving Grant no choice but to take his suspicions to Superintendent Law. Law was furious with his D.C.I.'s accusations at the thought of a mole in one of Police Scotland's regional centres. He cautioned McKirdy to be certain of his facts or Miss Luxton could end up suing for compensation which, in her case, could be a considerable sum.

Grant decided to take the bull by the horns by calling a team briefing attended by D.S. Lomax. D.C. Harrower. D.C. Luxton and himself. Once everyone was seated round the table Grant launched the meeting and laid out the agenda and switched on the tape recorder positioned to his right.

'I have called this meeting following a discussion I had with Superintendent Law who is investigating the possibility that there could be a mole operating in Fettes HQ. We are not the only section being investigated' McKirdy lied 'but what I want to establish this morning is that it is not within this team.

I asked Ken Harrower to join us this morning because he was party to everything which went on in Tallinn leading to the arrest of Geordie McNab and Alistair 'Maniac' McLagan. Before leaving Tallinn, you will recall we loaded all the luggage belonging to our prisoners for further examination.'

Lomax and Harrower nodded in agreement.

'Among the articles was McNab's mobile and forensics have printed a list of all the texts he had received. The final one listed before Geordie's arrest reads, 'British Security, including Police Scotland, in Tallinn. – (signed) The Ferret.' The Ferret is the sender and as only four of us knew at short notice we were going to Tallinn - the culprit is in this room!'

McKirdy's last remark cast the interview room into silence as each officer studied their companion's body language

'I have had my suspicions recently during the McNab case, whenever we thought we were penetrating his empire something seemed to go wrong. The mysterious sinking of the 'Caledonian Princess', before we had a chance to interview the skipper, is a case in point.'

'Can I Return to our journey to Tallinn. Avril, why did you call off at short notice?'

Avril was not used to being cross-examined but kept her cool and decided to tough it out, 'When I was driving home to get my overnight bag, I felt unwell. My head felt like it was going to explode, and my sight was blurred. It got worse when I reached home so I had to lie down, and that's when I phoned Ian.'

Grant asked innocently, 'So did that keep you in the house for the next few days until you recovered?'

'Yes', Luxton replied quietly.

The D.C.I.'s tone changed dramatically, 'That is a bloody lie! I sent P.C. Diane Falconer to enquire after your welfare and you were nowhere to be seen! A neighbour told Diane she had just missed you leaving your flat with an overnight bag. The real reason for you calling off going to Tallinn was that you knew you would have come face to face with Geordie McNab who might expose your other identity as **THE FERRET!**'

A normally quiet natured Ian Lomax could not contain himself, 'I can't believe this is happening. Avril, has D.C I. McKirdy summed up the situation correctly? How could you stoop to warning a couple of thugs of our presence in Tallinn? If it had not been for the quick actions of our MI6 colleagues, we could have been killed and our wives would be widows! When did you start working for McNab?'

Everyone looked at Avril for a response as her face reddened, revealing her guilt, prior to tears running down her face and her body descending into an uncontrollable tremble as she tried to reply.

'I...I met McNab when I was on a girl's night out. I had too much to drink and had run up a huge bar bill, which I could not afford to pay. McNab settled it for me then I went back to his office where still drunk out my mind, I repaid him by having sex with him. Afterwards we talked. McNab said I could do better for myself by making some extra money in exchange for information about our movements which could affect his drug empire.

I have always been materialistic,and I soon received access to more money than I ever would even if I had been promoted to a D.C.I. in the police. '

McKirdy continued angrily to voice his disappointment 'Your complete lack of moral fibre has brought disgrace to the good name of the police! I had doubts about how you managed your private life on a constable's salary as I heard about your trips abroad, your new car and the flat you shared in one of the smarter areas in Edinburgh. I thought you had wealthy parents but recently I drove you home and your description of your home life was not one of opulence.

I need you to hand over your Police Warrant Card now! I am formally charging you with perverting the course of justice by supplying enemies of the State with information which could allow them to avoid being held at Her Majesty's pleasure. Anything you say will be taken down and used in evidence against you.'

'Ian! Ken! Remove her down to the cells and out of my sight.'

Grant was left alone to reflect upon how everything In Tallinn could have gone completely wrong if McNab had read the last text sent to his mobile. The situation could have reversed itself and he would have been amongst the corpses decorating the floor in that private room at the Telgraaf Hotel.

These unbearable thoughts weighed heavily on D.C.I. McKirdy who went home early. Driving the few miles to his home in Corstorphine his mind continued to analyse the events of the last month. He opened the front door of his house and was greeted by his wife Anne and two young sons David and Brian. He embraced all of them tightly in a huddle as the grim reality sunk in, of how close he had come to being killed.

Maybe one day MI6 will reveal to him that he was never in any danger!!

ACKNOWLEDGEMENTS

Once more I have enjoyed writing and publishing my third novel 'Joppa Rocks' which would not have been possible without the support of friends and family.

I would like to thank my proof-readers Eddie Bracken and my sister Alison Anderson who also had the additional task of reading my book out loud to me.

The cover is the work of Keith Anderson who also produced the design for my second novel 'She's Not A Lovely Girl.'

My profile photo is the work of my lovely daughter in-law Ambar D'Andrea.

My thanks also go to Nancy Sturgeon for allowing me to call my novel 'Joppa Rocks' which is the name her late husband David gave to a Scottish Country Dance tune.

All the above would not have come to fruition if it had not been for my wife Joyce supporting me all the way through.

Bill Flockhart
10th December 2020

PREVIOUS NOVELS BY BILL FLOCKHART

'OPERATION LARGE SCOTCH'

One reviewer described Operation Large Scotch as 'A real page turner, I could not put it down.'

'SHE'S NOT A LOVELY GIRL'

The sequel to O.L.S. was described by Mark in the United States as 'Even better than the author's debut novel creating a good two book story.'

Printed in Great Britain
by Amazon

65734950R00161